PENGUIN BOOKS

Loving Ways

Maurice Gee is one of New Zealand's best-known writers. He has won a number of literary awards, including the Wattie Award (twice), the New Zealand Fiction Award (four times) and the Aim New Zealand Children's Book of the Year Award.

Maurice Gee's novels include the three books in the *Plumb* trilogy and *Prowlers*, *The Burning Boy*, *Going West* (winner of the Wattie Award in 1993) and *Crime Story*. He is also an award-winning children's author, his most recent being *The Fat Man*, which won the Aim Children's Book of the Year Award and the Esther Glen Award in 1995.

The author lives in Wellington with his wife Margareta and has two daughters and a son.

ALSO BY MAURICE GEE

Novels

The Big Season
A Special Flower
In My Father's Den
Games of Choice
Plumb
Meg
Sole Survivor
Prowlers
The Burning Boy
Going West
Crime Story

Stories

A Glorious Morning, Comrade
Collected Stories

For children

Under the Mountain
The World Around the Corner
The Halfmen of O
The Priests of Ferris
Motherstone
The Fire-Raiser
The Champion
The Fat Man

MAURICE GEE

Loving Ways

PENGUIN BOOKS

PENGUIN BOOKS
Penguin Books (NZ) Ltd, cnr Airborne and Rosedale Roads, Albany, Auckland 1310, New Zealand
Penguin Books Ltd, 27 Wrights Lane, London W8 5TZ, England
Penguin USA, 375 Hudson Street, New York, NY 10014, United States
Penguin Books Australia Ltd, 487 Maroondah Highway, Ringwood, Australia 3134
Penguin Books Canada Ltd, 10 Alcorn Avenue, Toronto, Ontario, Canada M4V 3B2

Penguin Books Ltd, Registered Offices: Harmondsworth, Middlesex, England

First published by Penguin Books (NZ) Ltd, 1996
This edition 1996

1 3 5 7 9 10 8 6 4 2

Designed by Richard King
Typeset by Egan-Reid Ltd

Front cover photographs by Jocelyn Carlin
Author photograph by Grant Sheehan
Cover design by Nik Andrew
Printed in Australia

For Margareta

I would like to thank Chris Pugsley for sketching in Alan Macpherson's army career; also Rosie Little and Bruce Hamlin for elementary lessons in pottery and allowing me to use Estuary Arts, Parapara, as a model for Inlet Arts. Chris, Rosie and Bruce are not, of course, responsible for mistakes I may have made.

Ben Alder Orchard usurps the place of Zagros Orchard on the Tasman Bluffs but no other likeness is intended. The characters in this novel are, as always, fictional.

I am grateful to Creative New Zealand (the Arts Council of New Zealand, Toi Aotearoa) for financial help.

Siblings

May	11
David	25
May	42
Alan	60
Alan again	78
May	95

Interlude

Robert Macpherson	119

A death

David	133
Alan	151
May	174
David	186

Epilogue

May and Alan at Wharariki beach	207

Siblings

MAY

MAY MACPHERSON made one of her escapes. Eight people, sightseers all, performed their ambling dance in the showroom, while Evan, driving the slab-roller like a car, kept his eye on the ninth, who might turn out to be a customer. Sometimes she could not bear this part of the business – the selling season, when on days Evan would call 'boom days' more than eight hundred people (nine hundred once) passed through the showroom. She found his pleasure in making a sale, that muted pleasure only she could identify, questionable, even unpleasant, and his explanations unnecessary – that he threw the pots while his partner May created the designs, except for the fish, the fish were his. He became ingratiating. She wished that he would not say created; and wished, especially, that he would not name her. It gave part of their privacy away.

She should not feel like this for she was no shy flower, in spite of her name, but loud and hearty, effervescent and, she would admit, common too, and she loved to know there was money in the bank, money, like foundations, under her, and loved the things that money would buy – for she had discovered foreign flavours and tastes.

She slipped by Evan with a brushing of her fingers on his forearm, against the grain of the black hairs there, whispered, 'Ten minutes,' went out past the big kiln and climbed the gravel path above the pond. It was just, she thought as she went up, that she had not expected love to come along at her age, and work, an occupation – she was occupied by both; and the surprise of it remained alive in her, and the delight. Her sensitivity began there. Evan could not be blamed. Pleasure and surprise were in him too and found an outlet different from her own. Selling was his reassurance that it would last – and naming her a reassurance too.

'So pull yourself together, May,' she told herself out loud. 'And get back there and pull your weight as well.' The customers liked to see her stroking away with her brushes and stains; it made them feel part of a process owning and using would complete. She climbed on all the same, wanting to have her sight drawn out to a far horizon which would empty trouble from her mind. Then, going down, it would fill again with the fresh pleasures of her day.

Before her eye went out, though, it had to cross the settlement down there, and it was always a question whether the fibrolite shacks and the weedy gardens would depress her or bring a sense of community. Depression made her guilty, it seemed like a failure in sympathy, but the us-and-them cosiness and aggression of the other would seem bogus in the end, and depress her too. She had tried communities too often and had come to know that she was better off alone – or in a pair.

The sea was white today, like zinc, and the sky so pale one had to concentrate to bring out the blue, but the town, hamlet, settlement – what name? rural slum? – declared itself, and she took pleasure in its unsealed roads and sandy paths. Lean-tos sheltered woodpiles left over from the winter. Upturned dinghies lay in back yards. Here and there flower gardens shone, borders stood out in yellow and red, and vegetable patches made geometrical shapes. Little bits of suburbia in the rural slum. Men were digging, and a painting man crouched on a roof; and two women were carrying an aluminium dinghy through the sand dunes to the beach. She could name them, both sexes. No strangers there. And fill you in on their histories. The women, for example, were lovers – which put it too simply if the word meant only sexual partners, as it seemed to do in people's minds – and the man on the roof a retired accountant, with a partner too (a woman), kneeling on the lawn, digging out dandelions that trespassed there. Lesbians settled in Woods Inlet, half a dozen, but what was keeping the gay men away?

She could see George Otway's forearm shine and red creep

on the silver, and see the yellow gloriole of Daphne's lacquered hair, but was too far away for the implements they used. Knowledge though she had. Daphne's eyes were murderous as she attacked the weeds. George had taken his paint pot up a ladder to be safe. It was possible that one day Daphne would kill him; but impossible that he would sell the house and take her back to Wellington, where she longed to be, and so, perhaps, prolong his life. 'I love Woods Inlet, May, and I'm never leaving it. Why doesn't she just pack up and go?' 'A wife's place is beside her husband,' Daphne said.

May turned her shoulder to them and let her gaze go out to sea, thirty kilometres, to the punctuation, stops and dashes, of Farewell Spit. Some days you could not see it, others it drew a pencil line, but today was an intermediate day and it made itself mysterious. She had never taken the drive up the beach to the lighthouse and never meant to, although Evan had been twice and had come back fresh and shining-eyed, talking of the seabirds and the quicksand and dunes like in the desert with wind curling sand off their tops. Another sensitivity in her: she meant to keep the spit unspoiled – no, delicate, a place she could make into a shape with her stains. When she wanted empty sea and coast and untamed birds to screech at her, she would go, out of season, to Wharariki beach and walk to the south end, opening the archway rocks and, like Evan, find her way home with shining eyes. The archways too had found a place in her designs. When you looked in at those sea-carved doors your eye passed over to no real world. How hungry you might then become, driving home, how full of longing for pleasures that were familiar.

A breeze was blowing round her and she enjoyed her sense of parting it, of blood reddening her cheeks, and enjoyed the contents of her head – homely, domestic, practical; but not limited, her thoughts, to kitchen, workshop, glazepot, kiln or Evan – capable of wide concerns, and flights, and fears. Her eyes went to the road where it dropped out of the cutting. She was fearful of trouble from there, all the way from Nelson and Ruby Bay, along that thread no act of will, only act of weather, could break; through the apple lands and hops and tobacco, over the hill set with marble teeth, up through the farms to Takaka and along the coast. The road delivered father, brother, daughter. Or, more easily, the telephone might bring them. If she listened she might hear it. A black car, a grey car, came out of the cutting. Her father drove a black car – though Heather drove him now, at ninety-one – and David a grey one; but neither was a modest man; their cars were more powerful than these.

They crossed the causeway at a steady pace, disappeared into the bush and passed with a pleasant thrumming the sign reading *Inlet Arts*; faded into silence along the Collingwood road. She raised her arms and let the breeze blow into her shirt and cool her armpits. She was tough with them both now, father and brother, and would not let them bully and demand – although anticipation could make her sweat. It was only when she faced them that she became sure; faced them here, on her own ground, behind her moat of trees. Then how definite she would become, and happy with it. Evan was at her side, ready to lend a hand, but even without him she would stand secure. I really have grown up, she thought, I'm free. It's only from Heather that trouble can reach me now – Heather, coming up behind.

She lowered her arms, then hugged herself, not out of fear but a quick desire for love from her daughter – not a desire that lasted, for there was no hope, and part of her new happiness came from no longer wishing. It was like turning a coin; it could be done by a simple flick of the mind. She saw gleams of red and white through the trees – car roofs in the sun, in the parking yard by the showroom – and heard doors slamming as people left – without buying probably; and felt a spit of anger that they'd not made Evan happy, and not read the message she had painted on the pots. Lousy skinflints in their fancy cars; they don't deserve to know, she thought. Deep pockets and short arms, Evan would say. They had honking voices, phoney English. She would bar such people if she could – set up a voice test at the gate and try them for an honest kiwi twang.

May laughed, and thought of Evan's voice with its lovely, ugly glottal stop. It had got in the way of a sale or two. She had seen fastidious withdrawal, mental shrinking, and had wanted those people off the property fast. Evan must not be hurt. He was so homely and so chaste.

See how he had built things here, unadorned: the house and the pottery. See how he had moulded the pond into the fall of the hill. She could almost believe its surface had been made by the smoothing of his palm; and the rushes there, the swans and their reflection, the amiable ducks, might be things he had created with a thought. I could make it as a pendant or a brooch, with silver and lapis lazuli, May decided; but it would be too far out of nature, too adorned, like this tank she stood beside, that had been white when he had left it but now was painted with fantails and bellbirds and flax and ferns and, low down, creeping things, centipedes and wetas and skinks. That was her contribution, and quite unnecessary although nice. And it was fun. 'Do I frighten you?' the weta said in a speech balloon. 'Your time's up,' a fantail grinned at a fly. If Evan lacked anything it was a sense of fun.

She drew two or three deep breaths and went down the path and down the steps and past the kiln and found him wrapping a vase, one of their most expensive, and saying to the customer, 'My partner, May, does the fruit designs. She's got a marvellous sense of colour.'

'You can almost taste the juice in that peach,' the woman replied.

'It's a nectarine,' May said, but smiled at her. 'They're more mysterious, I think. More female too.' She touched Evan's arm, smoothing it, and went to her bench, where she was decorating tiles, and put her head down and worked for half an hour, while three more cars drove up and nine people passed through and Evan made another sale. Then, for a moment, the showroom was empty.

'All right?' he said.

'Yes. There's a new pair of ducks.'

'I saw them this morning.'

'And George is painting his roof. I don't think Daphne knows how to climb a ladder.'

As usual he took her seriously. 'She can wait for him to come down though.'

'I think she's happy killing weeds for a while.'

'It's no joke, May.' He went to the storeroom and brought back a new nectarine vase. 'Sixteen stitches in your shoulder is no joke.'

'No.'

'Or dioxan mixed up in your porridge.'

'Being dragged to a place you hate is no joke either.'

'She can leave. She'll get her half. There's no shortage of money.'

'But she can't arrive back in Khandallah with no husband. She can't do it, Evan.'

'She'll kill him.'

'Or cripple him. And then take him back. An invalid husband is okay. But I don't think she's that smart any more.'

A car chewed its way up the drive, doors slammed shut, expensive voices approached the showroom.

'BMW,' Evan said. 'Here goes.'

'Sell them a fish.'

'A family of fishes for this lot.'

She smiled at him, pleased with his lightness. He had been like that on the night they'd met in the Collingwood pub. She went there when her loneliness stopped aching and really bit – she had felt it sometimes like a weasel's mouth stitched in her side and knew the short journey for those teeth to reach her heart. Then she would die. Dead of loneliness. Would people understand, in a woman who repeatedly declared that she was happy with her own company thank you? Evan had put an end to that. She had ridden her bike along the Collingwood road from her little shack or shed or hovel by the inlet, come into the warm public bar, drunk three beers, and was easy enough to talk to the barman – who said, 'A tank, you want? See that joker over there, he'll build you one. Hey, Evan.' Evan walked across. 'Ma'am?'

And with that greeting they began to move in harmony, lightly either one, but with a growing wonder and excitement in her – not, I like him, but, here's someone who likes me.

The shack was gone now. It had been chopped up for firewood. The tank he had installed on the hill was out of use, supplanted by the big one with flax and bellbirds on it. A sign by the road said *Inlet Arts* and a metalled drive led up to the parking yard and down again in a loop, and house and pottery and showroom sat unadorned on a plateau fringed with bush, and nectarine vases and fish plates and floral tiles stood on islands or hung on the walls, where her paintings hung too, bright and bold (selling perhaps four a year); and there was a new kiln, controlled by a computer; and there were advertisements in glossy magazines. The top end of the market: eight years ago the phrase would have been double Dutch to her. And happiness double Dutch too. Now – she watched Evan make a sale – the mortgage was paid off, there was money in the bank; the roof didn't leak, she drove a car instead of pedalling a bike; she had a job, work that she was good at; and she had no stitch in her side. She had Evan. There was love.

And there was privacy. The customers left – but here were two more cars, arriving as though pulled by a cable dropping the BMW to the gate. And here was Sally pushing her bike.

'The help's arrived.'

'Go easy on her, May. She's not a bad person.'

'Oh, I like her.' I just don't like her here, she almost added – which Evan knew well enough. He seemed to think that employing someone to help with the sales increased their financial stability. Sally was one of the Inlet lesbians. He had expected May would be kind to her for that.

'I've finished these. I want to go across and see the Otways. Just in time, Sally, I'm just off.'

'Take the car,' Evan said.

'No, I'll walk.'

'Not on the road. Not in this traffic.'

She smiled at his care for her, and was irritated by it.

'You can use my bike,' Sally said.

'I'll take the dinghy.'

'Tell Junior . . .' Evan said.

'Yes, I will.'

'And be careful with Daphne.'

'Don't turn your back on her,' Sally said – which May thought ungenerous in someone who herself had not been judged. All the same she hesitated crossing the yard – perhaps she should have taken Sally's bike to make the girl feel more accepted in her job. She almost laughed. Life was too complicated for her. Guilt. Susceptibilities. Desire. She could not have what she would most like – Evan and May left alone in all the world.

Another car passed her, gritting up, and full of carsick children from the look of them. They would yahoo on the paths and scrape their initials on the tank and throw clods of clay at the ducks. She half-turned to go back, then went on. Evan would not allow it. Evan could be stern. He would lose any number of sales to protect what he and she had made.

She went out the entrance, waited while a too-fast car and a bus went by, crossed the road and walked fifty metres on the edge of the seal, then climbed down the bank where the causeway began. A path, invisible to strangers, led through tufted rushes and islands of low scrub to her dinghy tied to a waratah hammered in the mud. It was aluminium, riveted, two metres long – a tin-can boat that skated on the surface like a toy. Inlet people could use it if they wanted. Twice now the oars had been stolen, and once the dinghy had been unroped and left to drift out on the tide. There was also the matter of the turd on the seat. Someone was jealous that May and Evan had done so well.

She dragged it to the tide-line, rowed along the shallows, then coasted with dripping oars, listening to the crackle and hiss of water taking the swamp. It was heaven, she supposed, for the crabs down in their crab-holes. What beautifully punctuated lives they must lead. And the little fish darting in tepid water over the sandflats, a new world opening with each tide. Nonsense, she told herself, they don't have consciousness. I can enjoy it but they can't – then laughed at her need to be superior to a fish. She swept with an oar and turned the dinghy, headed across the shallows and felt the channel tug like wind on a car. The hull turned cold under her feet. She kept clear of the causeway bridge where the tide sliced through and soon was in shallow water again. She shipped the oars and let the dinghy glide. Jumped out as the keel touched; grabbed her sandals. One-handed, she heaved the dinghy to where it would lie safe.

Up the bank, across the road, along a sandy alley to the one proper gate in all the row. 'Gidday, Daphne. How's it going?'

The woman on the lawn looked up from her weeding. 'You should have said you were coming. I'd have put the kettle on.'

'I've had a cup already,' May lied. 'Great day for weeding. You've got it looking like a bowling green.'

Daphne was frowning at May's bare feet. She wiped her knife on the grass, one side then the other, then stood up and dusted her knees. 'I'll call George. He's on the roof.'

It's just as well I'm not after him, she'd have me with that knife, May thought. 'I saw him from my place. Okay if I go up and have a look?' She laid her sandals on the grass. George peered down from the roof.

'May, I thought I heard your voice.'

'Saw you painting. Thought I'd take a look.'

'Come on up.'

'Don't be silly, George, she can't climb ladders.'

'You watch me,' May said. She was sorry for the woman but was prepared to humour her only so far. George offered his hand. She ignored it and walked beside the gutter. 'Good colour.'

'Red's best for roofs.'

'Blood red.' Which was careless of her. Daphne watched with her face upturned. Her hair made yellow petals but her face was pinched and birdy, unflowerlike. In a moment she pushed her knife into the lawn and went inside.

'How is she?'

'Better now. She's got some tranquillisers. I've promised her . . .'

'Yes?'

'I'll sort it out.'

'Can you?'

'I'll think of something. I've got to think of something.'

They whispered but their voices seemed to curl down through the windows like smoke. May climbed beside the new paint to the chimney and looked across the inlet at her own house set in the bush, with its windows shining. The showroom stood at the other end of the plateau, and there was Evan in the door, seeing people off. His bald head made a point of light.

She waved but he did not see her. Why should I care about anyone but Evan and me?, she thought.

'She should have stayed in Khandallah. I told her I'd keep the house for her.'

'Your voice will go down the chimney.'

George moved away and squatted with his brush between his knees. Paint, fat and slow, dripped on the iron. She saw the scar of Daphne's scissor-stab inside his shirt.

'I would have gone to visit her. It would have worked with me here and her there.'

'She'd have been an abandoned wife.'

'Yeah, I know. I lived like in a prison there, May.'

'She's in one here. She should get proper treatment, George. She can't be left like this for too much longer.'

'I'm not putting my wife in a loony bin.'

'This is a loony bin. For her.'

It was a pity that she liked this man. There was so much about him not to like. She wanted to go home to Evan and her work and pull them closed behind her like a door. And yet she would feel, after a time, thinned by that rather than completed. It would only be homecoming for a while. And there was her superstition, too, that if she stayed too happy, too enclosed, she would endanger what she had.

'We weren't meant to be happy, her and me,' George said. 'All my life I've never been able to relax. And she's wanted what she couldn't have. I don't think she ever knew what it was. So she settled for – God knows. A husband with his shirts properly ironed. All I want to do is walk on the beach and go out fishing. And she wants croquet and church. And me in the garden with my cuffs buttoned up. That's happiness. How do you and Evan manage it?'

Oh don't put us in danger, May wanted to cry. 'We have our ups and downs,' she said. But would not give an example, although he waited, looking up at her. Paint slid like blood down a gully in the iron and dripped into the gutter.

'Did you get rid of the poison?'

'Yeah, threw it out. But she's all right now. Tranquillised. Shit, after forty years, a tranquillised wife.'

May climbed down the ladder. When she looked back from the road he was painting again; and Daphne was kneeling on a cushion, slicing off dandelions at the root. Tranquillised, yes, but still committing little acts of murder. George must know that it could not last.

She followed the road towards the beach. On her left the inlet water kept up its increase. She let herself be governed by the tide, which gave her ten minutes for George and Daphne and ten for Junior Mott, then an easy row before the water rushed out. Why was it that once she and Evan had got together other people, all those she had not connected with, all those who had turned their backs or looked darkly on her, should step forward and make demands? Had Evan somehow made her available to them? And had she locked him away – for he kept himself more private than he once had? No pub now, confessional, women weeping on him. Women, he had told her, had often come to cry – and, though he did not say it, take what they could get of him after that. She had not cried, she had laughed. Was that the reason she had him now? Laughter was good for starting, and to go on with, and things could be rounded later on, and darkened a little, which was natural. She and Evan looked at each other nakedly. And so Junior Mott could be spared a glance, out of charity, even though he answered with looks from under his brow, especially for Evan, with whom he had been close.

She turned in at his gate, stepped around a torn clay bag and a maggoty dog bone. Oh Junior, she thought, why do you work so hard at being squalid? An ashpile in the yard showed where he did his raku firings. Cracked mugs, cracked plates poked out of the mound. It was like an archeological site, except that no scrap of beauty or interest lay there. The dog, a labrador white in its snout with age, slumped half out of the shed doorway. It raised its head, gave a woof, collapsed. May put her hand on the doorpost and leaned in. Junior was at his wheel, turning something ugly. Oh no, don't judge, give him a chance, she thought. But it would be ugly, although he would say 'useful'. May doubted even that. It would come out bent, lopsided, and he would coat it with a muddy glaze and take it to the market in Nelson or Takaka and it would sit on his stall – some mug or jug or bowl – and never sell until it was marked down; and who would use it after getting it home and taking a closer look at it? He dipped his hands, worked away, pedalling evenly. Old ways were best, he said, otherwise a piece of work had no integrity. He knew she was in the door but would not look until he had 'found the shape'. Found it, lost it, spoiled it – although she did not doubt an ideal shape existed in his head; glimpsed once, perhaps, but not to be recovered. And why would he not know that care and thought and technique were a part of it? And good materials? And equipment? And why couldn't he see colour? Face it, May, why couldn't he see shape?

He stopped pedalling and the wheel came to a halt – and there it was, a drinking mug that, with its handle on, would look like a goblin chamber pot. He wiped his hands.

'Yeah, May? What is it?'

Did you drop a turd in my dinghy?, she wanted to say. He was the only one in Woods Inlet with sufficient hatred for that. Enough muddy brown in his perceptions. She wondered if he was colour blind. With those eyes he could be. They seemed to curve on the surface and follow the bones of his face. Eyes like wrap-around glasses. God, he's spooky, she thought. And a widow's peak that wanted to grow down the ridge of his nose. It's like a pick-axe. He's got a pick-axe in his brain.

'Evan asked me to call.'

'Yeah?'

'We're doing a first firing and there's a bit of space if you've got anything you'd like to put in.'

'I wouldn't put my stuff in with yours.'

'Is that what you want me to tell him?'

'Tell him what you like.'

'All right.'

'This is to drink out of.' He indicated the mug on the wheel. 'Your stuff is for money.'

'No integrity, Junior, is that what you mean?'

'Sure, May, you can laugh, but I got hands' – he showed them – 'and I got an eye and I can see. All you got is a bank account.'

She almost laughed at the arrogance of it, but sadness held her quiet. Hands, an eye, were what he did not have.

'I can make things,' Junior said. 'You can only count up your money.'

It got past her pity and stung her. She enjoyed reading Inlet Arts' statements from the bank – but it all, every dollar, came from work; and the plates and jugs and tiles that she and Evan turned out were beautiful and useful, they were pleasing, and they had messages, the nectarine, the spiny fish, and Farewell Spit, if people cared to read – and her paintings too, if they could see; yet this ugly man . . . She hung on to the doorpost until the anger that would make her fly at him had passed; until she could say, evenly, 'Tell me, Junior. Tell me how you see.'

'You wouldn't understand, May.'

'Because I've been wondering, are you colour-blind?'

He kicked his bucket aside, splashing water on the dirt floor, and half rose and came crouching at her, pick-axe man with ropy muscles in his arms and fingers like chicken bones. The labrador had risen too and was snarling at her.

'Out, bitch, out. Get off my section,' Junior said.

'Yes, I'll go.' She was more frightened of the dog than him. He was bits of dry stick wired together and could not be dangerous when the sun was shining. Darkness was needed for him to act. She backed away and turned and walked, quick but in no panic, and stopped at his gate and said, 'Are you the one who shat in my dinghy?'

'I'll do worse than that, bitch. I'll shit all over you and your wanker boyfriend.'

'Oh Junior, poor Junior,' she said, and went away. But his hatred had splashed on her like dirty water. It was in her mouth, she tasted it. She walked fast on the road and reached the dinghy, where she cleared her throat and spat him out. She rowed across the inlet and became cold and ruthless: thought of ways Junior might be hunted out of their lives. In the shallows he came down to size, which was a pity because it allowed him a place: the sad man, the crippled man, Evan's lost friend. She would not tell Evan about today's encounter. She would say that Junior had no pots and he could stack that corner of the kiln. And Evan – she could hear him: 'So he's still like that, eh? I wish he'd let me give him some glaze with a bit of colour.'

They had been 'best mates'. Junior had let Evan use his wheel, and Evan had loved it – had felt shapes pumping down his arms like arterial blood. Nothing would do for him then but making pots. So it had begun: Inlet Arts. And here they were, eight years later. And down there, back there, with his lumpy clay and lopsided mugs, was Junior Mott.

May pulled the dinghy into the rushes. She took a handful of muddy sand and scrubbed the seat a sixth or seventh time. She splashed it with water, then tied the boat to its waratah. Cars sped by on the causeway but up the hill she sensed the easy busyness of the workshop, and beyond it the humming, silent humming, of the bush. My place, she thought, he can't get in. And nor can George and Daphne. No one can.

She climbed up to the road. A big boxy four-wheel drive went by. It pulled up and reversed. A man let down the window and looked out.

'May,' he said.

She stopped and tried to understand his unnatural smile. Oh damn him. Oh bugger him, she complained.

DAVID

HIS FIRST THOUGHT when he woke was, She can't do that to me. The course of his day was set by it. He would wash and shave and eat and walk about the flat – bedroom, bathroom, kitchen, sitting room – and drive out and park on Rocks Road, where he would smoke, looking at the sea; then drink at the pub all afternoon, and come home and heat up a dinner and look at the box and go to bed; and all the time he would be thinking, She can't do that. So everything was set by her, whatever he did. All day her voice was the only one he would hear: 'We're finished, Dave. Don't you ever come near me again.'

He pulled on his dressing gown and tied the cord with a knot. He walked to the kitchen and put the kettle on. 'She can't,' he said, hearing the water tremble into life. He stood on the mat in front of the sink and drank his tea. It was too pale, he hadn't let it draw. That too she had caused. She stood in the way and put his timing off. Parts no longer fitted into place. So there had to be a pulling round to make things mesh. There had to be a levering and a correction.

Force, he thought. Force must be applied.

He saw himself turning her inside through a door. Get in there and stay in there and don't come out till I say. That was the proper way to do it. Take hold of her and feel her bones. Look at me when I'm talking to you, he would say. He hooked his thumbs to fit her collar bones and saw her pupils grow large and her blue reduce. You're my wife. Do what I say or by Jesus, Freda, I promise you . . .

She was small. She was half his size. At the beach he sat her on his shoulders like a child, and in bed he fitted down around her like a box and she was enclosed. He felt her sharp bones digging into him and understood how easily she would break. But the sharpness of her, in laughter and in words. The quickness that left him a quarter turn too slow, and she was moving into a new place and would be gone if he did not wrench himself round. She thought that she was smarter than him, and higher up some social bloody scale, but all it was, she knew a few more words and could get them out, and if he could just hook his fingers in and hold her still . . .

His tea had gone lukewarm and he poured it down the sink. He shaved and showered and breakfasted and backed out his car, a Chev Silverado he'd liked to call his 'wagon', a name that did not seem to fit any more. He drove about evenly in the morning traffic, with logging trucks, school buses, back and front, and felt that he was going somewhere. But then came the country and he had to turn back. Hills climbed up and went down and dirt roads branched off and there was no destination.

She can't do this.

He filled his tank at the petrol station before the saddle, then headed back to town. He drove by the sewage ponds and through Atawhai, where the telegraph poles grew out of the sea. They seemed unnatural and made him pity himself. He was as much out of place as that. How did he get back to his proper place? He took the by-pass and drove along Rocks Road but turned off when he realised where he was heading. Stopped at Tahuna and bought a packet of smokes, then doubled back up the hill and parked at the lookout, where he smoked half the pack as the morning passed. He was smoking too much, and would drink too much in the afternoon – but too much in relation to what? There seemed to be nothing left to measure against. Nothing of himself in the past, nothing in the future.

He got out of the car and stood in the lookout, where the telescope pointed at the weeds. The half-million-dollar houses stood on the cliff edge, angled away from each other, and Tasman Bay stretched uncoloured to the park, and the Arthur Range stood in the sky. He saw the bluffs beyond Ruby Bay, and the plateau where his father's orchard grew, and Takaka Hill, with

May in behind it making pots, making money; and at his feet half of Tahuna beach, waves thick with swimmers; and Tahuna on the flat: golf course, airport, camping ground – and none of it had any connection with him. He was cut off. The people on the beach down there were as small as insects yet he was the one who felt small.

I have to make something happen. I have to get back in.

He could only start his life up by getting Freda again. It came down to a move as simple as that. He was not molesting her the way that fucking order said, he was just getting back what was his. He would take her by the shoulders and walk her to his car. Or he would go inside and sit in the kitchen and wait for her. Hi Freddie, I've come back, I live here now, get me a drink. And then they would climb in the wagon and drive over the hill to see old May. He needed to score off May and show her that Freda was his wife before it would start to move properly again.

He left the lookout and walked a short way into the weeds, trying to open up Stoke, but her house was out of sight around the hill. It seemed to him that she was hiding from him and he said, 'No chance, Freddie. You can't hide.' He flicked his cigarette away and went back to the car. They'd tear that bit of paper up, that non-molestation order. Or she'd tear, he'd make her, while he watched. They'd take the bits over the hill and drop them like confetti on May's floor. Stay out of our lives.

He drove down the hill and went left and then right through Tahuna. He drove past the high school in the seaward half of Stoke and up a street by the packhouse. The smell of apples wrapped him round as he got out of the car. He breathed it in deeply, a winey smell. Freda wasn't bossing him any more. All it had needed was a decision. You couldn't break a marriage up with a bit of paper.

Inside the gate he stopped and frowned at a child's wooden truck filled with gravel on the lawn. She must have taken boarders. A teething-ring lay in the dirt. He flicked it away with his toe. You didn't take boarders who had kids, they knocked a place around and took the value off. I'll get rid of them, he thought, we're not a fucking charity, Freda.

He opened the front door and walked in. At once he heard laughter from the kitchen. He thought it was the radio, but a woman's voice said, 'Wally, Wally, Wally, who's my boy?' He went into the kitchen and saw a fat woman, breasts half bare, kissing a baby on its stomach. A skinny bloke with a red bandanna round his hair put his cup of tea down and said, 'Who are you?'

'Who are you, that's the bloody question,' David said.

'You can't come in here, mate –'

'It's him, Sonny. It's her husband,' the fat woman cried.

'Macpherson's my name. Where's my wife?'

'There's an order out against you. Sonny, ring the police.'

'Freda,' David shouted, 'get in here.'

'She's gone, so it's no use. You clear out.'

'She doesn't live here,' the man said. 'I live here. I pay the rent and that makes it my house. So fucking piss off mister else I'll do you.'

'She rented it to us,' the woman cried.

'Go next door,' the man said. 'Call the cops.'

The woman put her baby under one arm. She scooped up another child, who had appeared in the door, and ran from the house.

'Freda,' David yelled.

'You don't listen, do you? She's gone. And her name's not Macpherson now, it's Prentiss. She's taken her old name. And looking at you, mate, I see why.'

'Jesus,' David said, and moved at him.

The man turned, barefooted, wiry-armed. He snatched an iron frying pan from the dishes on the bench. Water slopped out as he lifted it. 'I'll knock your fuckin' head off, you come near me.' He grinned with crooked teeth, which made his straggly beard jut like a tail. 'Want to try me?'

'Okay. Okay,' David said. 'So where's she gone?'

'How would I know?'

'You must pay the rent.'

'To her lawyer. That's where her mail goes too. Ms Prentiss. Now get out.'

'When did she go?'

'Last week. We got this place on a six-month lease. You're trespassing, mister.'

'Did she say –'

'She didn't say nothing. We didn't ask. She told us if you showed up we should call the cops. That's what my partner's doing now.'

'Listen –'

'And I can knock your head off with this thing if I want. Comin' into my house. Shit, it's self-defence.'

'Okay, I'm going. Tell her – no forget it. I'll find her.'

'The poor fuckin' bitch.'

'What?'

The man lifted the frying pan. 'Have a go. You're pretty good handing out black eyes, I hear.'

David went out. He walked down the path, then turned and looked back. Sonny appeared on the porch, with the frying pan in his hand. On either side of him windows shone. David knew that Freda wasn't in the house, yet if he pressed his hand against the walls they would clatter down and expose her. He went out the gate and saw the letter box on its post, with a letter poking out its mouth. He snatched it and read the name, Freda Prentiss. It drove into him like a nail.

'Hey,' Sonny cried, starting down the path.

David put his foot on the letter box and heaved. The sides skewed and the roof unhinged. He seized the box in two hands and wrenched it off its post.

'Come near me I'll tear your fuckin' head off,' he said to Sonny. He threw the broken box into a flower bed. 'You tell her I'm her husband and she's coming back to me.'

He got in his car and drove away. His finger had torn on a screw. Blood, he thought, I'll give her blood.

He drove out to Richmond, where he stopped at a chemist and bought a packet of bandaids.

'Accident, Dave? Living life too fast?' the woman behind the counter said.

'What?'

'You'd better let me help you put one on.'

Mary Noyes, the chemist's wife. He'd met her at a party,

where he'd thought she fancied him. Freda had said sure but not to get big-headed, or big anywhere else; you qualified as long as you were married, and all Mary ever did was tease. 'So calm down, old Randypole. Come on home.' He shivered as he remembered it. He let the woman wrap a bandaid on his finger.

'Have you come out to look at your old place?' she asked.

'No.'

'He's expanding. You should have hung on there, Dave. How's Freda?'

She knew. Everyone knew. He pulled his hand away from her and walked out of the shop, leaving the packet of bandaids on the counter. He walked in the main street and came to the yard, and read the new name painted everywhere: *Barlow Motors, LMVD.* His name was gone, wiped out, under this new fat red one. The empty section next door was newly paved and cars were being lined up on it now, with Barlow there, hands on hips, sticking out his belly. David stepped back. He did not want anyone seeing him. He felt as if he was starved and naked. Freda had done this to him.

He walked close to walls, back to his car. Too many people knew him in this town. He felt eyes pricking at him and turning away. There were women here Freda had gone to school with, and old boyfriends, and friends of Prentiss, whose name she had taken back. The bastard couldn't be got at, he was dead. He'd been standing at the back of her all the time they'd been married, and David had wanted to tear him like a picture off the wall, but every time nothing was there, until she put him up in the same place again.

'Prentiss.'

'Pardon me?' a woman passing said.

He got into his car and drove out of town, turning into back streets to avoid the car yard. He went along the Brightwater road past berry farms and cornfields and vegetable stalls. No destination again. He felt empty spaces ahead of him and was almost surprised at Brightwater to find roads going left and right. He turned left and drove into the hills, then chose the Lee River instead of the Wairoa because seal went that way and gravel the other. Pools showed, with glossy surfaces, and others with people swimming in them, and cars came at him, grinning boys at the wheel and girls drying swimsuits out the window. It was a work day yet all these people were here. He was out near the edges and no meaning was left.

A gate, a rutted track, a paddock opening out: he drove in and saw a pool shining through the trees. Rapids ran out by an undercut bank. A man and a woman sunbathed on yellow towels on a shingle fan. David got out of his car and walked on the bank. He strode out, half running. Her hair, black hair, bottle hair. He came to an oil drum spilling rubbish from its top and started down a clay path to the shingle. The woman raised her head and looked at him – flat nose, chinky eyes that stopped him dead. He felt for a moment that Freda had changed her face; and he started again, another step, then took a handhold on a tuft of grass, anchored himself, turned around. He went back to his car and leaned on it as if he had fallen over and climbed to his feet again. In a moment he opened the rear door and found some cans of beer and took a mouthful, fizzy, warm; spat it out. He hurled the can over the trees into the river.

'Hey, you dumb bastard,' someone cried.

He got in the car and swung it round. He drove back to Brightwater, where the potter's showroom on the corner instructed him where to go. He bought a pie and ate it driving west over the long bridge across the Wairoa. He went north to the coast road and turned towards Golden Bay. May was the one who would know. Sisters, they called themselves. Talking dirty in their female language – hormones and bleeding. Sending him out of the room as though he was too young to hear. He turned the memory round and sent it back. He drove through the apple lands to Mapua and Ruby Bay and up the road cut in the bluffs above the camping ground. His father's orchard opened out, with pickers in the trees. David drove past. He had not seen his father since before Freda had left, and would not again until they visited together and he held her by the waist and said, See, she's come home. No, not that: something more punchy. Old Tugboat Charlie would stand there as though he still had a strap in his hand.

Find her first and hook your fingers in and don't let go, and then go to him and say, There, you old bastard, you don't know shit about anything. And if that meant he lost his share of the property, well, he had lost it already, hadn't he? May's daughter, turning up from nowhere, worming in, would get the lot.

I'll contest it, David thought. Alan will contest it. We're the sons.

Alan Breck Macpherson. David Cluny Macpherson. Sons of Robert, who did not bother with a second name. There was also May. Each of the children had a different mother. Alan and David were legitimate. They were named from Robert Louis Stevenson's *Kidnapped* – but Alan got the best character, Alan Breck, while David got a mixture: David Balfour, who was a little wowser prick, and some fleabitten clan chief, Cluny Macpherson. 'We descend from him,' Robert Macpherson claimed, but the boys recognised it as more of their father's bullshit – although Alan didn't use words like that. Alan was nine years older and he took little notice of his brother. May was David's companion. She mothered him as well as she was able after his own mother grew sick and died. David does not thank her for it now. It had moved him further from his father's notice. He believes there was a place he might have filled, and failing to move in had cost him his inheritance. It was not his father's love he wanted, or his approval, just a recognition that the line passed down from Robert Macpherson to his sons. He wanted his half share of the money. But May had shifted him across to the illegitimate side. And now her daughter had overturned everything, every rule, and even Alan, lieutenant-colonel retired, was elbowed out. There was nothing fixed any more, or to be certain of – even things David had once thought he was denied.

They grew up on the orchard, the brother who had seemed even less than the half he was and more than nine years older, the tubby freckled sister from the wrong side of the blanket, and David who even now cannot describe himself. One mother was long dead, in Auckland, far away; one had been only short term, a housekeeper, sacked; and the third lay wasting, with no life outside her room, and very little in it, while the father laid about him with his presence and filled the house.

They had to know his quarrels and know that he had always been right. He was offhand about dangers – fogs and storms and reefs and snapping cables. No one had ever doubted his courage. But his judgement – no harbour pilot, no liner captain in gold braid ever told Robert Macpherson what to do. And when he was passed over for the harbour master's job and they chose an Englishman instead: 'Packed my bags, walked out of there.' He bought an orchard in Nelson and stayed a landsman for the rest of his life.

David was confused by that. Had the tugs meant nothing? Hauling the beached trawler off the sand, with an easterly punching hard to roll it on its side, or towing the loaded barge through the breakwater on a shortened cable, with a blizzard pushing behind? All given up because he didn't get a desk job? David felt thinned out every time he heard the story. Who wanted a father who grew apples when he might have been a tugboat captain? He had come to see Robert Macpherson as swollen in his presented part but with a hollowness behind. And he too, David, was diminished, with a hollow in the back of his head.

When Alan left to go to Duntroon – left in a smiling way that meant he was never coming back – and David was alone with his father, except for May, who did not count, then he was thinned even more and his meagreness was underlined. Robert Macpherson demanded and harangued just as before but was unable to lower his eyes to the smaller boy. David learned that he could edge his way out of the room. The voice in there would fall silent only when it finished everything it had to say.

The seasons passed. The boy (and the girl too) learned how to thin and prune and pick and grade. He stood by an open window watching hail strip blossom from the trees, saw his father stride into it and raise his fists at the sky. Hail beat on his forehead and sent him running for the lean-to shed. David wrapped himself in a window curtain. Warm in there, Arab-like, with only a slit for his eyes, he saw his father punch the wall and throw himself in a circle, then run hunched-up for the house, where he bled across the room and slammed into the bathroom. He thrust his hand under the tap and bellowed with pain. David made another turn inside the curtain, which strained in the pelmet, almost breaking free. He was in a cabin riding out the storm while his father had run his boat on the reef. The hail stopped. Robert Macpherson came out, fist wrapped in a towel, and found the boy and beat him, left-handed. Out in the orchard the ground was white. The trees that had been massed with blossom were turned to grey. Hail lay on the boughs as though children had piled it there in a game. Robert Macpherson dropped his strap and went out again. He walked into his trees, left and right, with no aim; and David, in the window, wiping his face, knew that he hurt less than his father, and was glad.

He and May took the school bus to Mapua. Later they went to Nelson, to the colleges, and David, tall now, almost as tall as his father, and strong and bullocky, although slow on his feet, played lock in the first fifteen. He put the shot and bowled fast, although with no control. He got on well, but could not please his father, and said to himself, I'm leaving soon, stuff the old bugger.

Housekeepers came and went. Robert Macpherson got one or two into his bed but there were no babies and no new marriage. He pestered others until they had to leave. May grew up unnoticed and ran away at seventeen with a picker twice her age, a man with bad teeth and beads in his hair. Like Alan she did not come back. My turn, David said when he finished school. He found work in a bank and stayed for a year, but knew that behind a counter was no place for him and the house he shared in Nelson with school friends no freedom hall, as the others called it, but a set of walls enclosing him. Every place, every event, was an extension of the orchard. He kept his eyes open, kept alert for the better thing that would happen soon. And would have made it happen, would have broken out, gone to Sydney or London or even the States, if one Sunday afternoon, drinking with his mates and their girlfriends in a house above the Maitai River, he had not witnessed an arrest. One of the girls ran in. 'There's a crash, they're chasing him,' she cried.

He reached the sundeck above the river in time to see the

man start his run from the smoking car that lay on its side with its wheels still spinning, half across the footpath, half on someone's lawn: a skinny man, long-haired, limping through a back yard, holding out an arm that ran with blood, and crossing the river thigh deep. He fought his way through barberry and gorse up the hill to the higher road, and passed the sundeck twenty metres away. David heard him sobbing. Standing by the rail with a beer in his hand, he met the man's eyes and raised his glass, not in encouragement but to show him what he couldn't have. 'Go on, you'll make it,' screamed the girls. The two chasing cops were still in the river. David looked up the hill. He saw another policeman waiting there, hands on hips. Saw him push his hat back on his head and smile and wait. That's me, he thought; and when the torn runner broke on to the road and fell to his knees and rolled on his side, and the policeman reached for him: That's what I am.

He applied for the police college and was accepted on his second try. For twelve years he was a policeman and he never went home in all that time: never heard from his father or Alan or May. That was how he liked it; families were a waste of time. He wanted nothing except maybe some of his father's money at the end.

He was happy in his job, happy for a time. He wanted to do well, wanted promotion, but found there were tests he could not pass; not official ones – he was bright enough for paper tests – but ones he was only half aware of and turned to see but could never find. He started to believe that something was kept from him by the boys up top, some bloody masonic secret that he didn't qualify to know. Why not ? Why not? He was good at his job, he was a good cop, they could see. Then one day he chased a kid through the city streets – still had the leather jacket he'd nicked trailing in his hand, bloody kid -- and trapped him in a stairwell and rammed his arm up his back: heard a bone snap, humerus. Heard the sound again, back at the station, as the sergeant slammed his ruler on the desk; knew that he was done for and he'd never know why. What was wrong with them and wrong with him? He stayed two more years, banging at it, then got out. Said, just like his father, Stuff your job; didn't look back at the bastards as he went. He looked back at the orchard though; saw money there.

His father financed him into the car yard. It was a business deal and David got him paid out as fast as he could. He wasn't going to have that face looking over his shoulder a single day longer than he had to. All the same, he kept his eye on the money there. Someone had to have it in the end. He called on the old man three or four times a year, took him a bottle of whisky now and then, and showed him each new girlfriend to let him know he wasn't deficient in the sex department. Then Heather arrived at the orchard and worked her way in before he saw what was going on. He watched her in a baffled rage at the way his life was pushed off its course again. But tried to stay patient. No one lasted with the old man. She'd do something wrong. He kept his visits up; a bottle of Dimple Haig each time he went out. He could find no other way to state his case.

Except marry Freda. May – he knew May again, it had seemed sensible – brought her across the room and said, 'My friend, Freda. You can look but keep your hands off, eh.' He had her that same night. Knew he would as soon as he grinned and saw her eyes dilate. Married her – which he hadn't seen coming on that night. Took her out to Ruby Bay and let his father see.

She was more than a step in an argument, though. Freda was like coming up for air.

He drove through Motueka and Riwaka and started the long climb up the hill. Every few moments, sweeping round a bend, he saw the fruit and hop and tobacco lands, always more flattened out and toy-like, with the sea brimming at their edge and the flooded estuary spread out like a hand. Pine forests with blocks milled out of them blackened the low hills beyond the Tasman orchards and cut Rabbit Island into strips. This was a view David approved of – land portioned out and put to use. The road stopped climbing and crossed the tops, where bracken was coming back and limestone outcrops ruined the properties for farming. Away to the left mountains pushed south, with hidden valleys in them: more land put to use. He came to the first of them, the Takaka Valley, and felt a lurch in his stomach as it opened out. It was as if a finger had come down on the hills and made this indentation that seemed, always, too sunken and low. You felt the sea should rush in and drown it. The paddocks down there, the roads and houses, were pasted on. He needed to drive fast down the looping road, back and forth, squealing on the corners, to restore himself. Once down it was all right, everything was solid, and he was impressed by the taming of the place, by the engineering.

He drove fast up the valley – it was like climbing up to the sea instead of going down – and went through Takaka without stopping. The town was busy with tourists and he wanted none of that – rug shops, pottery shops, none of that crap. He made his way out and saw the white sea glittering ahead; and it came to him, now that he was half an hour away, that this of course was the place Freda had run to. She had holed up with May. The two of them would be there, talking their female stuff. He should have worked it out earlier. Freda was always buying pots and saying that she'd love to try making them one day. She'd asked May once, joking, to take her on as an apprentice.

He passed Patons Rock and Onekaka. From the top of each rise he glimpsed the Spit. It was all that brought people here – that and the beaches and the Heaphy Track. There was no real reason for Golden Bay, which was why it had so many dropouts, he supposed. May had been a dropout, living in a shack, until she'd had the luck to get her hooks in Evan Yates – and look at her now: bloody rich, and all from the con trick, all from pots you were just supposed to look at and say ooh and aah.

At Parapara he slowed down and thought how he would do this. No good just grabbing her, although he wanted that – put her under his arm, walk out, lock her in the boot if he had to. But it wouldn't work; there'd be a fight. Freda would kick and scream, and May too probably. Evan Yates would get into it, and Evan was big enough to do some harm.

David pulled into a layby. He smoked a cigarette and watched cars go by. More cars than he liked. And too much of the day left. It would have been better done at night; but once he got her home in Stoke, and those hippies arseholed out, he would make her see where she belonged. He meant not to hit her again, but talk to her and lay it down: marriage was for life. He would get her stripped and into bed. First though he had to go up there and smile at her. Sorry, sorry, he had to say, and put his John Wayne look on. Act sheepish. Freda, we'll give it another chance. My fault, lovey. Please come home.

He ground out his cigarette. If she's there, he thought. She mightn't be there. If she's not, by God I'll tear that fucking place apart.

He pulled out of the layby, went up a rise, and there was Woods Inlet, Parapara's twin – same houses, same causeway, same hills. The water lapped into the trees – high tide, turning tide. The place looked okay with its mudflats hidden. You could see why people might come for a holiday, but he couldn't understand coming to live – unless you were picking the tourists off, like May. He shook his head, trying to shake her out. The turning round in her life seemed unnatural. He'd had her marked as a loser and could not get her placed any more. The pottery and the house up in the bush looked like someone's country estate. May belonged in mouldy kitchens or in beat-up shacks.

He coughed and rolled his window down and spat, and saw her appear from the bushes at the end of the causeway. She slipped her sandals on as he went by, twisting like a girl. Her bum pointed this way and that, and he thought, She's getting thin, she's supposed to be fat, and he shivered with anger that she wouldn't stay still; then braked the car, reversed, rolled the window down the rest of the way. He remembered to grin.

'May,' he said.

'What are you doing here, David?'

'Visiting.' He kept the smile. Hard work. 'Just thought I'd see how you're getting on.'

'I told you to ring. Evan and I can't stop work for visitors.'

'I'll stand and watch. Hey come on, give us a bit of a welcome. It's not like I'm over here all the time.'

She stepped close to the car as a bus went by. Its wind made her hair stand up then slant into her mouth.

'Jump in. I'll drive you home,' he said.

She went around the car and opened the door. 'You can't

stay long, David. It's our busy season.'

'Still packing them in, eh? I thought they'd have woken up.'

'What to?' She looked at him sharply, meaning perhaps to be dangerous, but he grinned at her and got the car moving.

'You can't eat off that stuff. You could brain someone with the plate you gave me.'

'If you don't like it give it back. Anyway, David, I gave it to Freda.'

'Freda, eh? How is she?'

She took a moment to reply. 'Very well, I imagine, these days.'

He shrugged off the jab. Her pause meant she was thinking, she was hiding something.

'I've been hoping you could tell me,' he said. 'I've been worried about her.' He began to enjoy himself. Playing like this moved him on, it got something going. He felt the strain go out of his face. 'Hey, May, relax. I'm not here to cause any trouble. I've done a lot of stuff wrong, I know, but it's okay now. I've got my brain straight.'

'Oh?'

'Freda doesn't need to be scared of me. We love each other, you know that.'

'Do I?'

'Come on, May.' He had turned into the drive that climbed to the pottery, and he stopped the wagon and smiled again. 'Give me a chance. People don't stay the same. Look how you've changed.'

'You leave me out of it.'

'Special case, eh?'

'No –'

'All I'm saying is, if you can get yourself sorted out why can't I?'

She opened the door and put her leg out. 'I'll walk up, David. Why don't you go home?'

'Hey, just answer my question.' He found that he could say things and move himself around while standing off to one side, listening and watching. 'Come on, May.'

She lifted the leg back in but did not close the door. 'Hitting is what you do. It's your way of life.'

'That's pretty unfair.'

'You hit her once and promised that you'd never do it again. Then you hit her again, and promised not to, and so it went on –'

'Hey –'

'How many chances do you want? And then there's all the other ways you found out how to hit her. Keep her just the way you wanted, which was – no, listen – someone who turned you back into David Macpherson when you couldn't find out who you were. Hit her, eh? That's my fist. Look at her cry. I did that, I'm David Macpherson and if they don't know out there at least she knows it here. Jesus, David, she wasn't yours to do things to like that. You came home and sat in her as though she was a chair, and when she wanted anything – ah, what's the use. Go home, why don't you? I don't know where she is and I wouldn't tell you if I did.'

'Freda's my wife.'

'That's one of the things she was, but not any more.'

Where was he now? He struggled but could not find himself.

'Don't you hit me,' May said. 'I'll put you in court.'

'Bitch. You bitch. Fucking bitch.'

'Ah, David.' She stepped out and narrowed the door. 'Look, get some help. Go and see someone. I'm not against you but I won't have you here. There's nothing I can do to help.'

'Where's my wife? You tell me or by Christ –'

She slammed the door, half raised her hand and walked up the drive, then turned into the bush before he could move to run her down. A horn blared at his back. Another car had turned in and moved up close behind. He could see the driver's hand tapping the wheel. He shouted out the window and saw her face draw back. He let out his clutch hard, spraying her with gravel. No bloody woman honked at him. He drove up the hill and swung into the parking yard; saw May come out of the bush and half-run to the showroom door. She called out something. Evan Yates came out.

David opened his door and walked towards them. He did

not know yet if he would hit May. The other car, the woman in it, turned into the yard. She wanted him to stand aside while she found a place but he thumped his fist on the bonnet hood, stopping her. He did not need to hit May after that. He felt in control again.

'Gidday, Evan. I just thought I'd come and get my wife.'

'Stop right where you are,' Evan Yates said.

'I know she's here.'

'You're on my place, David. Freda's not here. Even if she was you couldn't have her.'

David lost his focus. Foreground and background ran together and he could not tell a small thing from a large. A door slammed behind him. A voice said, 'How dare you hit my car?' He swung backhanded, and his fingertips sent something looping away – a pair of glasses. Evan Yates jumped in close and tried to spin him round but David broke out of his clutch and ran to the showroom door. He had seen a face in there, swimming among the mugs and plates. 'Freda.' May tried to hold his shirt but he ripped free and went shoulder first into the room, where Freda, in jeans and shirt, backed away from him. He gave a cry. He spun in a circle. Not Freda. Not her.

'Stay away from me,' the woman said.

Then Evan Yates had him, an arm around his throat, and was wrestling him outside. He felt gravel cut his back and water splash his skin as though it were scalding. May had a hose playing on his face. He heard Evan say, 'Take that away, May. We don't need that,' and then he lay still. He felt as if he had no bones inside and that he was packed into a tiny space, into a box.

Before Freda had left him he had been spread wide and she had been small, at the centre, where he had come to at the end of the day. Now he was shrunken, and wrinkled, and dry, and she was out there filling all that space and he could not put his hand on her.

MAY

IN THE MORNING Evan finished stacking the kiln. He walked down to the gate and turned the sign from 'Closed' to 'Open'. May saw him come out of the path and cross the parking yard and she called from the window, 'Heather's getting her.'

'I'll bet she didn't like that.'

'No –' and then she turned away, for Freda had come on the phone: 'May? What's wrong?'

'Ah, Freda,' she said, and tried to be careful. 'I'm afraid we had a visitor yesterday.'

'Him? David?'

'Yes. It's all right, nothing happened. Nothing too bad.' (Except that he called me a fucking bitch. Two men in one day called me a bitch.)

Freda's voice made an ugly screech, nail on tin, and May held the phone away. She did not want to be involved, even for Freda, whose place had never been questioned – best friend. Only friend. She must not allow this invasion along the edges of what she and Evan had made – this penetration, by David yesterday and Freda now – or let her concern grow into guilt.

'Wait a minute, before you fly off. Let me say what happened.'

'You didn't tell him where I am?'

'I'm not silly, Freda. Before we go any further, he stayed the night. We had to let him. He left about twenty minutes ago so he should be passing through Tasman in about an hour. You'd better not be picking by the road.'

'Jesus, May, what am I supposed to do –'

'Don't screech at me. I'm doing my best. I don't enjoy lying, even for you.'

'Yes, yes, I'm sorry. But you're sure you didn't tell him.'

'Of course I didn't. Look, Freda, David's in a bad way. If he doesn't get some help soon he'll do something silly.'

'What did he do?'

'Threw his weight around. But this time he went right over the top. It used to be just noise and, God, I don't know, punches, but now . . .'

'Did he hit someone?'

'Just about.'

'Who?'

'Sally's friend. Christine. Remember the lesbians across the inlet? She was here. David knocked her glasses off.'

'What for?'

'They were squabbling about parking. Then he thought he saw you in the showroom and he went in there.'

'What happened?'

'We calmed him down. Evan and me.' She did not say that Evan had wrestled David to the ground or that she had squirted the hose on him. Or that Christine Smith, half blind without her glasses, had rushed in and aimed a kick that skidded off David's ribs and took Evan in the pit of his stomach. She'd had to bear-hug Christine out of the way.

'Did she go to the police?'

'No, we stopped her. Evan stopped her. You know him, he's good with women.' Doubled up, holding himself, but reasonable still, with David behind him, cataleptic on the ground.

'I don't want trouble for him,' Freda said. 'I just want him to go his way and let me go mine.'

'But that's why I'm ringing. That won't work. He's not like other people.'

'Did he do his John Wayne act? Aw, shucks?'

'Oh yes, after a while. He's clever, Freda, although he's so transparent. Evan told him he couldn't drive back to Nelson, so he stayed. God knows, I didn't want him here.'

'You don't want anyone.'

May ignored that, put it aside for later on. 'He seemed to

sleep all right. Even if I didn't. But you can see things going on underneath, even when he's grinning. I think he needs treatment. Lithium or something, don't they give them that?'

'Lithium's for manic depression. David's just – he's a bloody loony. And I've got him tied around my neck. Look, I've got to go, your little girl is looking daggers at me. Just let me know, eh, if he comes back.'

'Will you put the police on him?'

'The police are useless. Here's Heather.'

At once a voice said, 'Mum?' and May thought, No, I don't want this, why can't people leave me alone? She said, 'Just a minute, Evan's calling.' She put the phone down and walked to the window. Over there, behind glass, she saw him punching a firing program into the computer. He moved as though under water but there was nothing about him floating or fish-like, just Evan four square and sensible. She felt as if he had put his hands on her and stopped her from spinning. The tenseness went out of her jaw. I'm not dependent, she thought, I'm just happy with him. And I don't want to think about it; all this consciousness is dangerous. She saw that he had coiled the hose and raked the gravel smooth where David had scuffed it. Good, she thought, and went back to the phone: 'What is it, Heather?'

'Robert's not well. I think you should come over.'

'What's wrong with him?'

'Lots of things. Old age. He's gone to bed and he won't get up. I can't look after him, I've got to manage the orchard.'

'And I've got to manage my pottery. So don't think you can get me nursing him. I'm not falling for that one. He's got plenty of money. Hire a nurse.'

'He won't have a nurse. I'm not asking you to come and stay. Just have a look. Try and make him be sensible. You're his daughter.'

And you're mine, May thought, but how often do you come here? 'Technically, yes,' she said, 'but not in any other way. He wouldn't listen to me. Get Freda to look at him, she was a nurse.'

'He doesn't like Freda. Anyway, I've hired her to pick apples. I should be across there in the shed, not talking to you. Are you coming?'

'My season's just as busy as yours.'

'Okay, so you're not.' Heather hung up.

May held the dead phone for a moment. 'Goodbye, dear,' she said. 'Happy families,' she said, working in the kitchen. She was not going to let hers reassemble and make demands. Twenty-five years she had been gone and no one had noticed her absence. She was not going to let them pull her back when it suited them.

When she had tidied the house she drove into Collingwood. She preferred this town to Takaka. A pub, a tearooms, a grocery store, a garage, not much more. The sea on one side, lapping across the sandflats, the inlet on the other, full of swampy islands and dead trees. Population 290. It suited her; met something in her perhaps unfinished, perhaps maimed, but so much a working part that it was essential. On the hill above the peninsula someone had mapped out a city in the early days and declared it the future capital of New Zealand. It never failed to please her, that patch of scrub up there.

She filled two cartons with groceries and was putting them in the boot when Christine Smith drove into the street. May gave a small wave, not encouraging. She got into her car. There was no need for yesterday to keep on – Christine's part in it, anyway. She was a person who put herself at the centre of events, but David's unlucky swipe at her was no big thing; he had done it like a man spitting over his shoulder as he ran.

'Wait on, May,' Christine called, striding from her car.

'Sorry. It's just, we've got a first firing. It's a big day.'

'I suppose that means you'll be wanting Sal.'

'Oh yes. We told her yesterday. I might have to go to Nelson too.' This woman always made her say more than she meant to by an aggressive watchfulness. But May had used her now to force her own attention where she'd meant it not to go – to her father, and Heather's summons. These things increased like a growth. 'So I really have to be going. You can tell her to come early if you like.'

'I suppose he's not still there? That guy?'

'My brother? No, he's gone.'

'Good riddance.' Christine was almost always sharp behind

her placid face, but was easy this morning, and self-admiring. She wanted to be thanked again, and maybe congratulated. Her kick must give her pleasure still, no matter where it had landed.

'It's just as well you hauled me off. I'd have done some damage.'

'Yes. You were impressive.'

Christine took her glasses off. 'Look, I didn't notice till last night. There's a chip in the lens. Down in the corner.'

'Oh, Christine. Get it fixed. Send the bill to me.'

'I might.' She put the glasses on. 'It doesn't bother me. As long as I got a good one in. Has he got a bruise?'

'I don't know. Evan has.'

'He shouldn't have got in the way. Your brother's the guy who's married to that woman Freda, eh?'

'Yes.'

'The one who came across here with a black eye?'

'Yes, that's him.'

'I should have kicked him harder. I should prosecute him.'

'Don't, Christine, please.' Was this what the woman wanted? Little servings of humility? But I'm not asking for David, I'm asking for Evan and me.

She drove back to Inlet Arts, put the groceries in the house and went across to the pottery.

'I've done the shopping.'

'Good,' he said, not looking up from his work.

'I met Christine in there. She's full of herself. She wanted me to say how great she'd been.'

'Did you?'

'A bit. Is it still sore?'

'A bruise, that's all. A bit lower down and I'd have been wrecked.' He smiled at her and she relaxed.

'I'm sorry about last night. I just couldn't, with him in the next room.'

'Hey, hey.' He stood up and put his arms around her. 'You and me don't have to say we're sorry for things like that.'

They were the same height, eyes on a level – no lifting up or bending down. Their shapes though did not match. She was round and he was square. Through his shirt she felt the quilted hair on his shoulders. An hairy man. She had always liked that better than smooth. And liked square in a torso better than those long deltoids and backs shaped like a cobra's hood – magazine men. Evan was a one-off.

'We can lock the gate if you like and spend the morning in bed.'

'So it's like that?' he said.

'Yes.'

'Winter sports. No can do. Not in the season.'

She reached down and felt him, but took her hand away when he began to thicken. She pressed with her fingers on the place where Christine had kicked him.

'Ow,' he said. 'What did Freda have to say?'

'Nothing much. I told her not to work down by the road.'

'That's some brother you've got. You know he's dangerous?'

'I know.'

'If I was Freda I'd take off for Sydney.'

'Why should the woman run away?'

'Yeah. Still . . .'

'It's like saying we shouldn't go out at night.'

'I know. But what do you do? Lock him up?'

'Yes, if he won't leave her alone.'

'He's mates with the police, they won't touch him. Is he still living on his capital?'

'As far as I know.'

'It won't last for ever. He's like a bee in a bottle, May. He's got nowhere to go. Ah, customers.'

'Sightseers, I'll bet.'

'They nearly caught me with a lump in me trous.' He patted himself down. 'Okay?'

'Mister Smooth.'

May sat down to work but let her hands lie for a moment on the bench. Her agitation did not come from Evan, she was aware of calmness there. But why hadn't she told him that her father was sick and that Heather wanted her to visit him? Evan would accept it, no trouble. The trouble came from herself.

*

Her name was not taken from the book. She read it to find out what made it so special, and enjoyed the running around and the narrow escapes, but liked the walking in the hills and the heather even more. She was pleased that Alan Breck had a pockmarked face. She admired him more for that than for sword-fighting. But women had no place in the story – even David Balfour's mother had no place – except for the innkeeper's daughter who ferried Alan and David across the Firth from Limekilns to the Lothian shore. She landed them and rowed away into the night, and Alan said at last, 'It is a very fine lass.' May, helping David, had seen herself as unthanked like that, and without a name, and she whispered Alan Breck's words to herself as she mothered him, and sometimes repeats them today as she rows on the inlet.

She grew up afraid of her father (and is afraid of him still). He seldom noticed her, but when he did he had a way of taking her jaw and slanting up her face. He lifted so hard that she mounted on her toes. 'A real mother wouldn't have left her daughter in a bus stop.' May wondered what was meant by 'real mother'. She had no idea how one of those was meant to behave. David's had been no help to him. She also wondered what a real father would be like.

She has few memories up to the age of five. Piecing things together, she knows that her mother was Robert Macpherson's housekeeper. She must have fallen pregnant after just a month or two ('fallen' seems the proper word to May), and her time on the orchard lasted only half a year. Robert Macpherson found a wife and paid his housekeeper off. 'She wasn't hard done by. She left here with a packet of money.' May was born in Wellington. She remembers a roof torn off by the wind and tiles crashing down outside her window. There are women who gave her cake and women who smacked her. They have no faces, only teeth and hair. Her mother has no face but is a belted raincoat and shoes that clack on concrete steps as she carries May up and down. She smells of facepowder and drycleaner and BO.

Then May sits in the waiting room at Newmans in Nelson. She is wearing new shoes that make an echo of her mother's. A suitcase with a strap around it leans against her knees. 'Wait there like a good girl. Your father will pick you up.' Her mother goes out the door but turns and hurries back. 'If you have to do wees, ask the lady at the desk.' She goes out and gets on a bus. May seems to remember that she made a little goodbye kiss on her fingertips as it pulled out.

Robert Macpherson leans over her. That is something May will not forget. He puts his hand under her chin and lifts her face. He breathes on her, a zoo smell that she later learns is pipe. His fingers are as rough as a nutmeg grater. May cries and he lets her go and runs into the street. He believes her mother is watching from a doorway somewhere and he comes back and asks where she is hiding. May is able to say that she went on the bus. She remembers her instructions and takes a letter from her pocket. He tears it – reads, and whispers a word that May, trying years later to recall (trying now), believes was 'Bitch'. Years later too she reads the letter. 'I've tried to look after her but I can't. Her birthday is February the 9th. Her name is Clare.' There is no signature. May does not know her mother's name, although she remembers a man in a shop picking up something white and squishy that she thought was a towel: 'Tripe, fresh in, Mrs Taylor.' Until she read the letter, taking it from a drawer in her father's desk a few days before running away, she had forgotten that she used to be Clare. Sometimes she considers changing back but has not been able to care sufficiently.

She does not think by choice of her time on the orchard but finds this or that part often in her mind. Those thirteen years have moulded into her things she will never get rid of. A habit of distrust. A habit of withdrawal. Sullenness. Submissiveness. Ferocity. Self-loathing. She thinks of them as impedimenta, although they no longer get in her way. Self-loathing? She likes herself pretty well these days and she thinks with wonder of the time when, twelve years old, she painted her face and arms with duck shit at the pond: goblin smears, and mouths and eyes. No one thing had led to it, as far as she remembers, just little bits of loathing pressed into her by her father's thumb. She felt natural once it was laid on, and happy to recognise herself. Many years later, swimming with Evan in the Aorere, in a pool that curved like glass, magnifying pebbles on its floor, she took clean water in her palms and washed the last of that filth away.

May crosses self-loathing out. She crosses out submissiveness, and won't allow sullenness to be written large. She is gruff more than sullen, a different thing. As for ferocity, it's no impediment, except when her aim is bad, which happens now and then. She mostly hits with words, but has punched or slapped several times: punched Heather's father, Artie with the smelly mouth, breaking two of his teeth off at the gum. She left the commune next day on the boat and never went back or saw him again. And she slapped Heather so hard on the face that it stung her hand, the day Heather told her she was leaving for Sydney. That was bad aim. She did not see Heather for three years; and the slap has not gone away. Heather never speaks of it but touches her cheek unconsciously when she is with May.

I saved her from the magpies, May remembers. How sensible she had been and how simple the remedy; yet she thinks of it as daring and inventive. They were living with Freda in a house in Ngaio. Freda had ferried them across town in a taxi after tracking them down in Newtown in a room with rotting floorboards and a ceiling furred with mould. They were coughing, sneezing, weeping, mother and child. 'Come on,' Freda said, 'you're not staying here.' She shared the house in Ngaio with another nurse. May and Heather moved into the spare room. May cooked and house-cleaned instead of paying rent, and Heather, six years old, started at the local school. She played in a park at the back of house, where there were slides and swings and a seesaw.

The magpies, a pair of them, came home regularly to a giant macrocarpa tree on the edge of the park. It was too dark and spiky to see into, but perhaps they had a nest in there and were raising young. They dived and swooped, complaining, at the children in the playground. 'Ugly things,' Freda said, but May liked them. She threw out crusts of bread when the park was empty and watched them chase the sparrows away. The sparrows were cosy and fluffed-up – greedy too. The magpies ruled. Strong, beady, flashing black and white, they asked for nothing, they simply took. May did not try to make friends but thought they might recognise her at some call – not the chortling they used to wake her in the morning, but a scream outside the range of normal hearing. She wanted one as a familiar.

Heather came in crying. 'Those nasty birds are chasing me.'

'They don't like you near their tree,' May said.

'But why are they only chasing me?'

'Nonsense, dear. They won't hurt. Just wave your arms, they'll fly away.'

Next afternoon she watched from the window. Eight or nine children and several mothers were in the playground. Heather used the seesaw with a girl she'd met at school. The magpies posed high in their tree, on a branch pointing like a finger. She thought afterwards that she saw them take their aim. They dived like German aeroplanes, in an ugly curve, and May screamed as Heather rose to meet them on the seesaw. The lower one struck at her and Heather fell on the grass. May ran out. All she could think was that the bird had taken Heather's eyes.

'She's all right, it's just a scratch,' one of the mothers said.

There was blood in Heather's hair. May carried her inside and sponged the shallow wound with disinfectant. 'It's only me. They only chase me,' Heather wept. May believed her now.

'I'll phone the council,' Freda said that night. 'I'll make them send someone out and shoot those bloody things.'

'No,' May said, touching the luminous hair Heather had inherited from Artie. She had seen how it would attract among the mouse and brown of the other children. For a moment she had seemed to sit high in the tree while the fascinating point of light moved up and down. 'All we have to do is cover her.'

The next afternoon she pulled a grey knitted cap over Heather's hair, tucking in the ends. Then she took her into the park. The child was frightened and did not want to go, but May said, 'Mummy will be there. Would you like a seesaw with me?'

She watched the birds as she and Heather rose and fell. They sat in the tree and took no notice. May wanted to pull off Heather's cap, experiment. She wished her own hair were that white-blonde. Presently the birds flew off on an expedition.

'There,' May said, 'you're safe now. As long as you wear your magic hat.'

But grey, she knew, was no magic colour and it sometimes seemed to her that in making Heather safe she had reduced her.

They stayed only four months in Ngaio. The other nurse complained about May's sulkiness and bad temper. 'She goes or I go,' she said. May and Heather moved to Berhampore; to Newtown; to Mt Cook; back to Newtown – and to Doug, and Gary, and Vince. She saved Heather again – from Vince; bolted to Auckland and shared with Freda there, Freda unmarried still, back from nursing overseas. It had lasted three years, until the slap.

Then she was in Golden Bay, living in her shack. She began to paint – mad, spiky paintings, full of teeth. The magpies were sometimes present, standing in their tree, but she had enough good sense not to distort them. They were birds, black and beady, dangerous. She let them be.

Then came Evan Yates.

When she painted the water tank she left magpies off.

The weight of apples on the trees oppressed her. If they fell simultaneously the hills would tremble. And all the boughs springing up would release so much energy that Robert Macpherson's orchard – Ben Alder Orchard – could be used to light a small town.

May crawled the car in to avoid raising dust. Pickers were in the Royal Gala trees by the cliff, where last season's Dutchman had amused himself by lobbing apples at caravans down in the camping ground. He was, of course, an illegal picker and Heather had had to smuggle him away before the Motueka constable arrived. This year backpackers were banned at Ben Alder, she was using locals even though she had to pay them at the legal rate. May saw them in the trees, on their ladders, with arms flashing in the laden branches. Here and there a face shone, a shock of hair stood higher than the crown of a tree. May looked for Freda as she went by but could not find her. If she was picking by the cliff she would have been able to see David's car underneath her as it wound down to Ruby Bay – and bomb it with apples if she chose. David was not the sole active partner in that marriage, although he was the more dangerous one.

May stopped the car to let a tractor with a bin of Galas go by. She followed it to the packing shed and saw women busy inside – more flashing arms. Heather came out to watch the tractor unload. She was wearing a head scarf – out of contrariness, May believed. People often took her for a Brethren and watched their language until they heard her swear. She saw May and pointed sharp, ordering her to the house. She ran the packing shed like a factory floor and tolerated no outsiders. 'Yes, dear,' May said, but sat in the car a moment, watching this martinet who had been a white weepy child oppressed by birds. Heather had her thick ankles from May, who must have them from her own mother – Taylor ankles. And her crooked teeth, Taylor teeth. There were none among the Macphersons as far as she knew. Heather's crowded mouth was a judgement. A real mother, May always felt, would have scraped up money for orthodontic treatment somehow.

Heather came striding at the car, heavy-legged, and nothing like a Brethren in her shorts. 'You can't park there. Go up to the house.'

'I just thought I'd say hello, Heather. David didn't call in by any chance?'

'Who?'

'David. Your uncle. He was passing.'

'What would he stop here for?'

'To see Dad, perhaps. If he's sick.'

'No one's been.'

'Good. I'll go and look at him. Oh, I'll want a word with Freda before I go. She's down in the Galas I suppose.'

'As long as you don't get in her way.'

'It won't take long. I'll pick a few apples, dear, to keep her numbers up.'

Heather laughed impatiently and went back to the shed. See, I came, just like you wanted, May thought. She would pay for the slap until she died. But she wouldn't let her own little barbs and sarcasms go – must have them to keep the balance right when she travelled to the family side of the hill.

She parked in the yard beside the house, which had the same effect on her as all those tonnes of apples. The old weatherboard building she had grown up in was gone, and this brick and tile fortress had risen in its place. Perhaps it owed something to Robert Macpherson's ancestral memories – castles, keeps, stone cottages, although the colour was wrong. But a heaviness was achieved in the squat walls and rigid corners. May felt that New Zealand houses should be made of wood and in the end should tumble down. Robert Macpherson's was for ever. And surely it was too big for two – the man of ninety-one and the woman in her twenties. What did they do in there, in all those rooms, when their day's work was done? She did not believe in conversations between them.

From the front porch May looked out over apple trees – apples in every direction. The sea stretched beyond them in the north and mountains circled round on the other sides. That was some relief. Robert Macpherson did not have everything in control. She went inside, crossed the barren living room with its dead floral carpet and furniture-shop paintings – he had bought a set of four: beach, mountain, river, lake – and looked into the sunroom. The old man had commandeered it as his bedroom so that he might look across the orchard. May had no doubt that he had watched her arrive and would be ready with a hard word or two.

'Hello, Dad,' she said, 'I'm sorry you're not well,' and then took in his altered face: hollows she had not seen before, bones she had not seen. 'Dad?' Heather had said nothing about this. She had not warned May that Robert Macpherson was dying. 'You really are sick. Heather didn't tell me.' But underneath the shifting, repositioning, in her mind she felt a fierce, long-awaited pleasure. It made a seething in her blood; it carried her across the room to stand by his bed before it sank away, leaving her unsteady.

'Dad, it's May. Can you talk?'

His colour had been red – the red of self-esteem – and his prominences round: cannonball chest, full bulging eye. Now he was faded and his hardness had collapsed.

'Saw you,' he said. 'Saw you come in. You're too late.'

'What for, Dad?'

'Whatever you've come for. Too late.'

A 'real' daughter would kiss him and hold his hand. She knew the distaste it would cause. It would wrench them on to a wrong angle and, almost, be unnatural.

'Have you had the doctor?'

'He comes.'

'What does he say? You've lost all your colour, Dad. You've lost a lot of weight.'

'You know what it's called, don't you? Dying.'

'Is that what he said?'

'It's what I say. I don't need doctors to tell me what I know.'

'All the same, what is it? Has it got a name?'

'Stomach won't digest anything. Whole digestive system's shot to hell. My blood's like water. I can't even lift my hand.'

'It doesn't sound like anything I've heard of.'

'Lung cancer. If you want a name. I didn't get you over here to talk about myself. Did that girl tell you what I want?'

'She didn't say you wanted anything.' Lung cancer. It did not shock her, although it was a name supposed to weaken the knees and bring a blur on consciousness as one apprehended – what? She touched her father's hand and said, 'Do you get any pain?'

'Nothing I can't handle. Get that book. That notebook. Give it here.'

She took a small address book, zebra-patterned, from the bedside table and put it in his hand.

'I want you to make a phone call for me.'

'Who to?'

'I would have got her but she's too busy. That's one good thing you've done: that girl. I don't know how you managed.'

'Her name's Heather, not "that girl". And she should be hiring you a nurse instead of being out there counting apples. Do you want me to get a nurse for you?'

'No. No nurses.'

'You can afford one.'

'No nurses. I don't want any nurses messing me.'

'A male nurse. You can get them.'

'Nancy boys. Stop fussing.'

'So, Dad, you want to die alone?'

'What other way is there? You can come, if you want. As long as you don't start weeping and wailing.'

'No. Not me.'

'What?'

'I'm not coming. I'll visit you but I'm not coming back here to live. I left in 1965 and that was it.'

Another shifting had occurred and she would have to find out what it meant when she had time. Her father wanted her at last. It was like the slipping of a waterlogged bank to block a path she had learned to walk on easily. No, she thought, I don't need this, I won't take any notice. I live with Evan at Inlet Arts.

Robert Macpherson had closed his eyes and brought his lips together, making his face thinner, minimal. She wondered if it was a trick he'd learned; or learned the trembling in his hands. But he would never make himself small, or ask by pretending to be weak, not even when dying.

'Dad, are you all right?' The address book had slipped from his fingers. She put it on the table and leaned close, smelling his desiccated skin. 'What's wrong? What can I do?'

'Get her.'

'Who?'

'That girl.'

May went out of the sunroom, out of the house. She ran through the trees to the packing shed. Heather was directing a new bin of apples into the tank.

'Heather, he wants you.'

'I'm busy. I can't come.'

'He's had some sort of turn. He's asking for you.'

'Jesus,' Heather said, 'he's your father, not mine.'

'So I'll tell him you're too busy then, shall I?'

'Useless. Everyone's useless,' Heather said. She shouted something at the tractor driver – to May it seemed no more than a cry of rage – and set off through the trees to the house, going direct, pushing branches. She tore off her head scarf and crushed it in her palm. Her bare heavy thighs slapped each other as they crossed. There's no softness in this family, not an ounce, May thought. Natural affections turn to stone, we bang against each other and make sparks. She was a part of it, she'd let herself harden and now, faced with Heather or David or her father, could only glance off them and make ugly sounds. She longed for some softness, the touch of someone's hand, but it was like asking for a change in nature now. They were like this, the Macphersons, from choice and then long habit – they had evolved.

She started for the house, taking the road, but had gone only a few steps when she heard her name called. It was an enormous relief – a voice from outside the family.

'Freda,' she said, and put out an arm – could not manage two. Freda came into it and kissed her.

'I saw your car come in. I didn't think you'd show up over here.'

'Dad's sick.'

'Yes, I heard. How bad is he?'

'I don't know yet.' She did not want this sort of talk with Freda, or talk of David, but had to say, 'Did he go past?'

'He must have. I didn't see. I phoned the Pecks. My tenants. He went in there yesterday, throwing his weight around.'

'What did he do?'

'Smashed the letter box. They told him I've gone back to Prentiss.'

'Did they call the police?'

'No, they didn't want trouble. I think they smoke dope. God, can't I pick 'em.' A new hardness in her, Macpherson hardness. May was guilty to see it, for she had brought her friend and her brother together – but oh it was an accident and not by design. And Freda had never been soft; she had pushed people about – pushed May – but had shown no self in it, rather a need to reduce their pain and make them easy. At school May, lonely and sullen, had found herself plucked by the sleeve into Freda's group – to the dismay of most of its members. And in Wellington it had been like that. Now look at Freda – restless, twitchy, reduced in her awareness to things that touched herself. Her face was thinned and somehow adolescent. Changing to

Macpherson had done this and changing back to Prentiss would not set it in reverse.

'What are all those marks?'

'Oh, a rash.' Freda raised her arms. 'Look, it's all over. It's those bloody Galas, the spray on them. It didn't happen in the Coxes. I'll sue Heather.'

'Does it itch?'

'Yes, it does. I was going up to the house to see if she's got anything. Some cream or block or something.'

'You'll have to stop.'

'I don't want to stop. I like picking. And this is one place David won't look.'

'I hope so.'

They walked to the house and went into the living room. From the sunroom Heather's voice murmured, surprising May with its gentleness.

'I suppose I can look in the bathroom? I'm part of the family,' Freda said.

'I'll come with you.' May watched in the mirror as Freda washed her hands, and saw that her prettiness remained; but it was intense and inward-looking and not available to other people any more. She wanted to put her hand out, as Freda had once done, and pull her into safety, out of that absorption with herself.

'Here,' she said, 'this might do. Skin Balm.'

Freda squirted it in her palm and rubbed her arms and hands. 'God, it stings.'

'It's worse than a rash, Freda. It's come up in welts. You can't go back.'

'So what do I do? I've got to earn money.'

'You could nurse Dad.'

'I don't want to nurse him. I've finished with nursing. Anyway, he doesn't like me.'

'He doesn't like anyone,' May said. Looking in the mirror, she saw Heather appear in the door. 'Look at Freda's arms. Look what the spray's doing to her.'

'Who said it's spray? And that's my Skin Balm you're using.'

'Of course it's spray,' Freda said. 'What else could it be?'

'It looks like an allergy. I'm not responsible for allergies.'

May left them arguing and went to the living room. Freda had taught Heather how to wash her hair once and, leaning, had kissed her on the nape of her neck. Then she'd chased her with the blowdrier, blowing warm air in her armpits. The pair had ended up rolling in each other's arms, squealing with laughter. That had been a long time ago. Listen to them now.

She looked into the sunroom. Robert Macpherson was rearranged. It was hard to think of Heather plumping pillows and slicking hair. Did she use spit the way a mother would? Who had taught her that?

'Dad, you look better now.'

'Where is she? Has she gone?'

'Back to the apples,' May lied.

'She looks just like your mother. Same legs.'

May was surprised. He had never mentioned her mother in any but an aggressive or a spiteful way; had punished May with her, when he could be bothered.

'Fay wasn't a patch on that girl though.'

That was more like it. There was much to be said for the settled state of things, it did not disturb.

'Who did you want me to telephone?'

'Here. Give me that book.'

She put it in his hand again and watched him find a page. 'This one. Him. Tell him I want to see him.'

May turned the book to read. Again she felt a sudden lurch of weight away from her centre, and felt a hollow open there. She looked at her father and he showed his yellow teeth – perhaps to grin. He knew how the name would affect her: Alan Macpherson.

The brother she had not seen for thirty-five years.

ALAN

His last job before driving south was to deliver the cat to the cattery. It meant approaching her softly and stroking her a moment, before the betrayal of the box. He would not have thought it unfair if she'd scratched him at that point, but all she did was set up a wailing as he fastened the lid.

'Sorry, cat.'

He kept her for companionship, not affection. A house with only one occupant was not properly filled; and he might never hear his own voice. He put her in the footwell on the passenger side of the car. 'It's a good place you're going to,' he said as he drove. 'And damned expensive. So stop complaining.'

He did not wait to see her released into the pen, but found the motorway and settled in the inside lane, letting fast cars whistle by. He was in no hurry and had nothing to prove. Crossing the bridge he looked downharbour where the Waiheke ferry was sliding on its skates. A school of sailboats stood off Mission Bay. He had meant to be on the water himself today, not heading off into a situation he could get no handle on. There was no way he could plan for it, or even prepare. He simply had to go there, drop down into it and then do some kind of appreciation. This must be, he thought, the way paratroopers feel. But he carried no equipment, unless somehow the years were equipment and all his acquired skills of management a weapon, or at least an instrument he might use. He did not expect to find his feelings engaged, and felt some regret for it as he drove south.

The woman had said, 'He'd like to see you. I don't know why,' and he had said, 'Did you say May? Are you my sister?'

'Half sister,' she said.

'Yes, half. So how is Dad?'

'He thinks he's got lung cancer but the doctor says it's not. He's ninety-one. It's his heart. Can you come? I've got to tell him something.'

'Yes, I'll come.' He would have liked, 'How are you?', and would have liked to say it himself, but she left no opening. He saw that he should not have needed one; should have said what he had wanted to and forced something out from behind her reserve. She must at least feel curiosity. He was, himself, more than curious, he was afraid. He had felt a dogged force in the woman – in May – and recognised it across the years, in the sullen barefoot girl pegging shirts on the line. He had felt his father's force too, without even speaking to him.

At midday, on the Desert Road, with the mountains turning on his right, he came up on a convoy of army trucks and sat behind them happily as far as Waiouru, where they turned into the camp. He was tempted to follow and find people he knew, and look at places, but rejected it as softness. May and his father were the objective and following the convoy a mistake. It blurred his focus. He would look in on the way back.

At Taihape he ate a salad sandwich in his car and drank bottled water; then he made what he thought of as the downward half of the journey, through Bulls and Levin to Wellington. That city moved him to a feeling of loss. He turned out of the gorge on to the harbour and saw the curve of Oriental Bay and the shoebox buildings and back across the water the Orongorongo hills, and names and shapes, space and contour had a familiarity that quickly became bogus. You could not claim your past except through tricks of omission.

On the ferry, moving out, he tried to find the house he had rented in Wadestown but it was hidden in the fold of the hill. Stop looking sideways, he told himself, get ready for Dad and May, and maybe David too. Was David there? She hadn't mentioned him, but had said something about a daughter, Heather. So, she had married and had children; he had no idea what her name was now. Mrs who? His life had been ordered and sensible but that piece of ignorance called it in question.

Where had he been for thirty-five years?

The ferry made a rocking-horse movement in the strait. He stood on deck, holding the rail; controlled his nausea by breathing deep and watching for the channel into the hills. The sunset was bloody with smoke from across the Tasman, and he thought of Australia too, and places he had once seemed to possess – Duntroon, Queenscliff – and knew he could not have them again. It bewildered him, this sense of possessing and not possessing. He had thought of the past as an easy thing and no more to be questioned than breathing. A phone call, he thought, and it's all gone. It was like Phoebe, whom he had loved and wanted to marry – a little conversation, a dozen words, and that was gone. It had been like someone taking him by the shoulders and jerking him round from the window he was looking out to an entirely different view. The configuration of the world was changed. Was he going to find that again, in Nelson, after the call from the child with unwashed hair and crooked teeth?

The channel was a danger, an exhilaration – jagged rocks, bursting waves, seabirds whirling away, and the ferry leaning on its magnetic curve from the broken water into the still. It brought back his confidence and made him feel able and controlled. A week's leave from his job was all he had taken, but it should be enough to hear his father and hear May, and David too, and set himself in position vis-à-vis. He need not worry what that position might be. There had been, in leaving the orchard, an imperative, and then there had been circumstances, over the years, and here he was and there they were, and nothing important was to be expected now. The situation first, he thought, and then I list my tasks, and it shouldn't take too long. I'll be back in Auckland by this time next week. It would take the cat two or three days to settle down. He would give her more attention in that time but not let any new habits form. Their present relationship was the way he liked it.

He booked into a motel in Picton and watched television for an hour – picked up the news – then went to bed, where he cleared his mind of the day and tried, his nightly discipline, for the sense of communion he sometimes reached with God. Even when he failed he believed himself rewarded: movement out of will, out of self, was curative. He failed on that night, with the motion of the car and boat rocking in his mind and the day hanging on, but was not unhappy. He prayed for his father and his sister and his brother, then lay a while enjoying the strange room and distant unfamiliar sounds. It was like being in the jungle. It was like being surrounded, but alone, in the turning world. There was danger and no danger, for that was how He had laid it down.

Sleeping, dreaming, he found himself in a car rushing down a road with broken edges and a huge drop to a foaming creek. There were pools of green water and children swimming and families on tartan rugs eating sausages, and he cried at them, 'When will you know God?' A man and a woman copulated on a shingle bank. The woman had no face and would not be named; the man was him – close, close, on the point of coming, but would not until she had a face.

He woke and was disgusted with himself. He took his water glass from the bedside table and drank until it was empty, then padded to the kitchen for more. These dreams filled him with anger and dismay. He would not be out of control. It was, he thought, the motion of the car and ten hours sitting: they irritated parts and pooled the blood, conjuring up an incubus – or was it succubus, he did not know. An evil spirit. That was why she did not have a face. Many times, years ago, she had worn Phoebe's face.

He lay down and calmed his mind and prayed again: that he might find peace, and that, if it pleased God, he might find a woman to love with his mind and heart, and body too, in the full communion he believed was possible. A bar of light from a car on a nearby hill moved slowly across the room and passed out through a wall. He got up again and used the toilet, then went back to bed and went to sleep, and did not dream again until morning, when images of yesterday and tomorrow appeared, making him mumble and turn. That shallow dreaming angered him, but was easily put aside for shaving and showering and breakfast and the news on the radio. It was only in the car again, driving by the swamp on the Blenheim road, that he thought of what he might be called upon to do. One of those morning images had been of him kissing a strange lank-haired woman on the brow. Her ankles were flea-bitten. There was mud between her toes.

On the by-pass he saw stalls selling vegetables and fruit, and wineries with restaurants attached, and he thought that he should not go empty-handed. A bottle or two after so many years – so much neglect? – would signal goodwill. He could not be certain that wine was appropriate for a deathbed, but it seemed right enough for ninety-one years. The woman – May – had not been certain that their father was dying. He bought Chardonnay because it was recommended, although he preferred red wine himself. When the road began to wind and climb the bottles played a tune on the back seat. He stopped and separated them, and stopped again in Nelson to work out the streets. You used the cathedral as a sighter in this town. The main street ran north from it towards the boulder bank. He was pleased with his mapping and his mind's delivery of information, and he found the inland route with no trouble and drove slowly, looking at his school and the football field where he had scored his try in the quadrangular final against Christ's, and then, on the other side, the hospital where his stepmother had been taken to die in the same week he had left for Duntroon. Did she die? How long had it taken? It shamed him that he did not know. He could not understand how things had been.

Then he was on his route: Stoke, Richmond, Appleby, the river, the hills. The changes brought an unreality – the roads too smooth, the trees too regulated. Corners were rubbed out and hills reduced. New yellow cuttings were sliced like cake. He did not like it but could not feel that outrage was justified. This had ceased to be his place many years ago. Yet the changes put a warp and side-slipping on his approach.

He passed the Mapua school, where because of his size and quickness he had been boss in standard six. The building he had sat in through those years was still there. It seemed like a door he might walk through into a familiar ordered room. He said the headmaster's name and the name of his best friend – who had not stayed his best friend at Nelson College. There cleverness counted: he had stepped up a level. It had been a natural movement, like stepping up to Duntroon after that, and then to his life in the army. It was a long way back to this place, it was going deep down, and no, the room could not be familiar or ordered. The years had turned things on their base and made his orientation wrong.

Past the Ruby Bay store he turned on to the grass and walked for half an hour on the beach, going back towards Mapua and the estuary – reversing, he thought, his approach. But he had the right, didn't he, perhaps he had the duty, if he was to be of any use, to get himself set, to get his stance right? There was no point in going in otherwise.

He walked on sliding pebbles above sundried kelp and mussel shells and plastic bottles labelled in Japanese, until a curve showed him the inlet mouth and the five-mile beach on Rabbit Island running away. Nelson was beyond, across the sea, like a settlement on the edge of a new continent. It made him want the north, his job and house, Devonport village, and the high-rise city just a ferry ride away. The emptiness of land and sea here made him uneasy. Then he saw a naked man and woman lying on striped towels, and for a moment seemed to be back in his dream. But they were sunning, not copulating – and others, naked too, walked on the sand or swam in the sea. It must be a nudist club. Had he missed a warning notice? He turned back, embarrassed. Too many changes; too much dislocation. He walked a hundred metres and glanced back to make sure they were out of sight. Then he sat down with his back against a log stripped by the sea and waited until his mind was calm; and he asked again for clearness of sight and usefulness in the situation he was soon to find himself in, and peace and happiness for his father and his sister and his brother, even though he did not know who they might be.

He was born in Auckland and lived there until he was seven. The 1940s town will not overlap with the city of today but stays off to one side and floats above the ground, not like a cloud or a magic carpet but like a tray on a waiter's hand. Alan might fall off the edge if he steps too far, and come to earth not in the metropolis of the nineties but in the yard of the house set amongst apple trees above Ruby Bay. When he and his father left Auckland and travelled there, they seemed to swerve and tumble down the roads. Twice Alan had to leave the car and be sick, and he remembers better than main streets and rivers and bridges the coarse grass at the roadside and a black beetle drowning in his vomit. He remembers a broken gate at the end, and a leaning porch, and his father cursing a key that will not turn. A black and white cat bolts under the house. 'There's your bed. You'd better go to sleep,' his father said, and Alan pulled used blankets over himself and listened to rain on the iron roof and cried a moment, silently, from loneliness. He was frightened of the dark, and of his father stepping on boards in another room, and the new school he would go to tomorrow. He tried to remember his mother but no face came, although perhaps it floated up when he was going to sleep and no longer trying.

She had been dead only a month. When he was ten or twelve and prone to think of her idealistically, he decided that her death was self-willed, even though his father said TB was the cause. (She lay on a bed and told Alan she was sorry to leave him. That is no memory, although it's hard to tell now, but something manufactured for himself.) He blamed her sometimes, but understood why she had to go, and when he was older and tougher was able to say, 'Good on you, Mum.' By that time he had learned how to hold his father off. He put a shell over himself – sometimes touched his skin and felt it hard – and words and looks and judgements bounced away. Robert Macpherson came at him with a leather belt but the boy let it wrap around his arm and held on. He raised his right hand against his father's left and showed his fist. 'You hit me, Dad, and I'll hit you.' After that there were only words, but words slid off. And there was, strangely, a kind of affection. He ignored it. When he was ready he would do what his mother had done – step out the door and not come back.

May and David troubled him. He suffered bouts of fondness and guilt. They took hidings that were meant for him. He might have protected them, and would have been able when he was in his mid-teens and taller than his father and just as strong, but was frightened of the increase in affection it might bring – his father's for him and his for the children. It was safer to walk away. The hidings did not seem, anyway, as severe as those Robert Macpherson had given him. The orchard was doing well. And his wife, Judith, took an edge off him in the house.

Alan worked in the orchard, pruning, thinning, grafting. He learned to drive the tractor and the car, and watched while his father drained the oil and changed the plugs and soon learned to do those things himself. He never had pay, only pocket money – did not ask for pay. He wanted no stake in the orchard but was seeing out his time; was paying, so he worked it out, for the freedom he would have in a year or two – freedom from these people and this place.

But May – May and David – troubled him. He barely remembered May's mother: she was there and gone. She baked bread, she made stews, and she shouted once, 'Tell him. Go on, tell him about us.' Alan did not need to be told. He knew where she slept, he heard the bed – and he saw her departure as a slinking off, not the exit his mother had made. He did not miss her cooking or her presence because in a few days his stepmother took possession of the kitchen and the bed.

May was the elder by seven months but David was first to arrive. His mother loved him as well as she was able, for Robert Macpherson did not believe in love – in touching, in kissing, in words of endearment. He would not allow the existence of feelings he did not have. She hugged her son when they were alone, and did not mind if Alan came on them embracing, but she pushed the child off and faced away when she heard her husband walk into the house. She ran into the apple trees when Robert Macpherson whipped the boy and later on she bathed the welts raised by the strap on his legs. Robert did not mind that: it gave him, Alan saw, a kind of satisfaction.

No one bathed or hugged May, even on the night when she arrived at the orchard. The stepmother stood her naked in a basin on the lino and washed her down with a soapy cloth. She fed her and instructed her, not unkindly. 'Find a name for her,' Robert Macpherson said, and the woman answered timidly,

'May is nice and short.' 'It'll do,' Robert said. 'You're May now, girl, does everybody hear? That other thing is out the door.' Alan does not know if the new name was made legal. 'That other thing', he remembers, was Clare. It would not have suited the slow dim child with the fat legs. 'May', he sees now, was little better.

When he found the word 'sibling', he was able to put 'sister' and 'brother' aside. Their connection with him was through the father, and sibling, new and ugly, fitted that. It placed them in a hole: May in her dress with the colour washed out, and her runny nose and her teeth black-filled, and David with his stained face and – so it always seemed – his runny nose too. They had nothing to do with him on his steady course. Nor did his stepmother, more and more in her room, and scarcely able to lift her hand from some weakness in her blood. He heard medical names and forgot them; he would not know her disease. His own health depended on his singleness of mind.

He played three years at fullback in the school first fifteen – liked the solitariness and the catching and long kicking and the knowledge that never failed him of the angle for the tackle and for touch. He scored in the final against Christ's, coming up from nowhere outside his wing and rounding the opposition fullback easily. His father drove in for the match and stood on the windy hill with his collar up and his hat pulled low: solitary too. Alan felt no kinship with him. On the drive home he said, 'An army recruiting officer came round last week.'

'Yes?' Robert Macpherson said.

'I'm going to Duntroon. It won't cost you anything.'

'How long?'

'Four years.'

'I suppose I have to sign something, do I?'

Alan saw that he was pleased. By accident he had chosen a course his father approved of. He would have liked to say that he was going into the army so that he need never come home, but that might make it harder getting away – and it was not the only reason. He had risen quickly in the school cadets – again without trying. He enjoyed seeing things done by rule. Lines were laid down and you walked on them. He found an excitement in that, in finding a way that was straight. And he liked the special knowledge of command, and its formality: closeness was there but nothing personal. Adventure, which the recruiting officer had stressed, made little attraction. He saw it as something he would bring in control – enjoy in a military way.

'You can get killed in the army,' his father said.

'You can get killed anywhere. Anyway, I'm going.'

'When?'

'In the new year.'

'If you get in.'

'I'll get in.'

May got ringworm just before he left. He kept even further away from her. He was not taking ringworm to Duntroon.

'It's that cat she's feeding,' Robert Macpherson said. 'You'd better take the gun and shoot it, Alan.'

'Not me.'

'Scared of guns are you, Mister Soldier?'

'You shoot it. It's got nothing to do with me.'

Robert Macpherson took David with him to the pickers' hut. He showed him how to load and aim the .22. Then he made May put mincemeat in the cat's plate. He sent her away and lay down in the grass with David. It was the first time Alan had seen him do anything with the boy. When the cat came out from under the hut David shot it. The bullet smashed its hindquarters and the cat thrashed on the ground, fighting itself. Robert Macpherson ran up and stamped on its neck. He let David shoot another bullet into its head, then made him dig a hole and bury it. Alan saw how pleased the boy was but could not tell whether it came from his father's approval or the killing.

When he left on the bus next day he put them out of his mind – his father shaking hands and giving him a pound note folded to the size of a penny stamp, his stepmother in hospital, David gleaming in his eye from yesterday's murder, and May slinking in the trees to watch him drive away. He felt the miles lengthening behind him. The road ahead unrolled like a tape and he could travel on it but they could not. He crossed the strait and went by train to Auckland and got on a plane at

Whenuapai. It took only a moment to break out over the west coast beaches. In six hours flying they reached Sydney. The Tasman Sea stood behind him like a wall.

He could not make it lie flat until, four years later, as Lieutenant Macpherson, he made the flight in reverse, and the train ride and the ferry, to Burnham Depot, outside Christchurch. He did not need roads unrolling or seas as barriers after that. He had turned in a spiral not a circle, and although he was close again was further away. If he thought of them at all – May and his father and David – they were as flat as paper, they lay like photographs on a page, and he turned them and forgot; or they were like cut grass lying on its side. There was nothing to keep him; and although he knew you did not get rid of the past, he had secured his a long way off. As for the continuity, that would not break, he turned in the spiral, turned again, through the years, and the stretching out of time made far-off things grow thin.

So he went on. In the chronology he sometimes makes, he is on patrol with his platoon in Sarawak, checking for Indonesian infiltration. There is danger but the Ghurkas next door see all the action. Then he is a captain at Narrow Neck, where he learns Auckland and the pleasure of sailing small boats. Then company second-in-command in Vietnam, an Anzac battalion – feels professional, keeps a critical eye on the Aussie talent spread too thin. It is quiet at Nui Dat. He would like more action and feels less in danger than in Sarawak. Waiouru then; and the even staircase of promotion after that: a staff job in Wellington, Major Macpherson in Army Plans; Queenscliff, in Victoria, the Staff College; senior major, brigade major, middle command, but again no action, and no real soldiers here, territorials. He is commandant, Army Schools, Waiouru – lieutenant-colonel. Then desk in Wellington, Defence HQ, where blue fights light blue and green fights both of them. He tires of it. One day he will make full colonel, and maybe brigadier after that. But being single is a disadvantage. And he has never had a battalion, that counts too. So Alan Macpherson retires from the army and takes his pension. He steps out into the world with little knowledge of it; and finds himself poor in all sorts of ways.

There is no chronology for his years from thirty-nine to fifty-four. He finds a job but finds no wife. Phoebe occurs like a storm, and then is gone, leaving ruin in her wake. He rebuilds, but cannot make a safe dwelling without Christ. That incoming is no blinding light; he feels his way, then he thinks it out – and seems to think himself out of it several times, but is drawn back. In the end he has faith, it lies beyond question, although all around it questions never stop. There is so much in religion he can't be sure of and doesn't like, but doubt exists to one side of the Son, the Man of perfect goodness placed by God on Earth. He needs no other knowledge outside that – but has, of course, knowledge of all sorts.

Some of it stands in very close. He has always had women and he cannot let them go. But he cannot accept them, after Phoebe. The next woman in his life must come to him across that ruined ground. Nothing can be easy any more, and nothing is for pleasure. (Nothing is for pleasure alone.) He sees her coming, picking her way, but she will not take a face. She must possess his knowledge and that seems impossible.

He longs to cut through this, to treat it as a military problem. But he has lost certainty in gaining faith. He has lost his old strength: to learn the situation, choose the option, execute. I need to get her out of my head, I need just to bump into her, Alan thinks. He thinks too much. But does not show it. The women who get two or three steps with him, and no more, come to believe he is afraid – of affection, possibly of sex. His life in the army has spoiled him, they believe. They think him, in fact, empty headed, even simple, and do not regret moving on. Some of them stay friends. They are fond of him. He takes them to dinner, in rotation, which they enjoy, although his conversation has no substance and in the end is repetitive. By some trick they can't understand, he continues to give the impression that he might at any moment spring into action. He is a handsome man too. (They are surprised, in the end, how little that counts for.)

Family does not come close, even when a knock sounds on the door and his father steps into the house. The old man turns down tea and asks for a beer, and tells Alan he should have stayed in the army and been a general. 'Haven't you got a wife?' he asks. Alan says, 'No. I'm not a homosexual if that's what you're thinking.' Robert Macpherson makes a sound of disgust and pushes such notions away with a thrust of his hand. He stays only half an hour. Alan drives him to the ferry, and his father passes into a kind of oblivion. He draws away backwards like a spider into its hole and when Alan gets home he is surprised to find a beer can on the table. He crushes it in his hand and drops it in the rubbish.

Then it is early April 1994. The telephone rings. A woman's voice says, 'Am I speaking to Alan Macpherson?'

'Speaking.'

'This is May, from Nelson. I'm ringing for my father.'

The past comes spinning up and holds him hard.

He is more and more possessed by it as he drives south.

Ben Alder Orchard. In his day it had been Macpherson's, but naming was part of marketing now. You had to have something snappy or suggestive, so his father had gone to the book again, and had taken secret pleasure, no doubt, from naming this green lowland place after a bare hill in the Scottish Highlands.

Alan drove in slowly and parked at the side of the house: a new house, brick veneer, with a concrete patio behind a wrought-iron fence. He was not surprised or sorry to find the old weatherboard, iron-roofed one gone, and he went up the steps, put his hand inside the slider doors and tapped on the glass. The unhurried walking, unhurried knocking, settled him down. 'Anyone home?' A breeze was stirring curtains and turning pages of a book left open on the arm of a chair. Whoever was reading it would have lost her place. He stepped inside and stood still, looking for something that might give him bearings. Picture, vase, table, chair? There was nothing. It was not to be expected after so long. Hostile ground, he thought: watch out for the trap. He felt that May might charge at him from a doorway and knock him sideways off his feet. The absurdity of it made him smile. Just take it calm and easy, one thing at a time. He stepped across the room and looked through a door held open by a rubber doorstop.

His father was sleeping in a bed. Sunlight fell across his hands, making the knuckles shine like a row of bald heads. His face was in shade and was turned to one side. What if I'm the one who finds him dead? He went into the room – a sunroom with a polished floor and sliding windows nudged a little open for the air – and stood at the bed, beside a kitchen chair for visitors. He did not want to wake the old man, who might, he thought, be frightened to find a stranger in his room, but wanted to make sure he had the right person. There was nothing in the face he could recognise. The tugmaster features were gone, melted away. Skin lay glazed on bone or was sucked into hollows. Alan should feel pity, he supposed, but could not. He recognised a final state.

He read the name on a bottle of pills on the bedside table: Mr R. Macpherson. It gave him the jolt the old man's face had failed to bring. 'Okay, Dad,' he whispered. He felt that he might pray for him now, although not with any feeling of kinship – but touch his hand, establish contact, and ask forgiveness for them both. Yet words would not come. There was too great a stretch of time to cross. He wanted to see his father's eyes and hear his voice. He returned to the sitting room, where the book still flicked its pages on the chair.

A toilet flushed in another part of the house. His mind switched from the old man to May but he had almost nothing to base expectations on: the memory of a child, a woman's voice. She must be washing her hands. Touching up her lipstick, tidying her hair? He was unsure of what women did. Steps sounded in the hall and someone small in trousers and a shirt came into the room. 'Who are you? Don't you knock?' she said.

'I did. But I didn't want to wake . . .' He indicated his father's room. 'Are you May?'

'No, I'm Freda. I suppose you must be Alan. You've made good time.'

'Where's May?'

'You won't see her unless you go to Golden Bay.'

'Golden Bay?'

'Over the hill. That's where she lives. She doesn't live here.'

'I thought . . .'

'Sit down, why don't you?' She shifted the book from the arm of the chair and smiled at him. 'I'll make you something to drink. Is tea all right? I can make coffee. Or do you want to have a look at your father?'

'I had a look. I thought May would be nursing him.'

'I'm the nurse. For a while. You don't know who I am, do you?'

'No, I'm sorry . . .'

'Your sister-in-law. I'm David's wife. But not Freda Macpherson, I'm Freda Prentiss. David and I are getting a divorce.'

'I'm sorry . . .'

'Don't be. I don't know how long you're staying, Alan. You are Alan, aren't you? I suppose I'm right?'

'Yes.'

'It's just that I hadn't heard of you. Well, I guess I had, David brought you up a couple of times. But not as someone who might come here. Robert asked for you.'

'May said.' He was disconcerted by her quickness; could not take her in. 'Why is she in Golden Bay?'

'She lives there with her partner. Evan Yates. Have you heard of him?'

'No.'

'What a family.' Turning her face like a knife. 'They've got a pottery. You know, make pots.' Her hands shaped one. 'You should go and see. How long since you saw May, anyway?'

'Thirty-five years.'

She laughed, flashing her eyes. 'And the same for your dad?'

'No –'

'Don't you want to know how he is?'

'I looked in. I can see he's ill. May said old age. She said it wasn't cancer.'

'He says cancer but that's just because he wants the best. What it is is congestive heart failure. And general debility. He's running down, I don't know, like a washing machine. I hope you didn't come here to try and save his life. I'm not offending you, am I? I mean, thirty-five years.'

'You're not offending me.' She was disturbing him: a thin quick woman, hair drawn back for action, teeth filed sharp, a glittering alertness in her eyes. He could see her, somehow, in the prow of a boat. Yet she seemed to be wanting to project friendliness.

'That's good. I do sometimes. Come in the kitchen while I put the kettle on. You didn't see Heather on your way in, I suppose?'

'Is that May's daughter?' He followed her out of the sitting room.

'Yes, the boss around here. She runs the orchard. Girl with a head scarf and a taste for command.'

'I didn't see her. I didn't know May had a daughter until she rang.'

'She's the only grandchild the old man's got. Unless you've got kids?'

'No.'

'You married?'

'No.'

She was quick with kettle, cups, milk – at the sink, at the fridge, back again – and her conversation jumped about. He wanted to hold her in one place.

'Tell me about David. If that's all right.'

'Is it thirty-five years for him and you too?'

'Yes.'

'You just walked out and never came back?'

'I had my life to get on with,' he said.

'You Macphersons. All looking for a life. I hope you found one. The army, wasn't it? Lieutenant-colonel? That's probably where Heather gets it from.'

He sat down at the table, keeping his resentment in control. The woman was a specialist in needling, that was plain, and yet good-humoured with it, and interested too. If she had married into the Macphersons and survived she had earned some respect.

'I'd like to know about David,' he said.

'So would I. Okay, smart talk. Let's see. You know he was a policeman, I suppose?'

'No, I didn't.'

'He wanted to be in the CIB but he never made it. Then he

was – internally disciplined.' She flashed a grin. 'It sounds like they gave him a twist in his bowel.'

'What did he do?'

'Hit someone too hard. There was no way he was going anywhere after that. So he got out. He tried, God, I don't know, this and that. I wasn't around. I didn't marry him until a couple of years ago. Milk and sugar?'

'Milk. What went wrong?'

'What didn't? May introduced us, did you know? I've known May since we were at school. She came up with this nice-looking brother – he looks like John Wayne, except he gets rosacea, and he's a bit mean in his eye. Still, passable. Nice laugh, you know, and he splashed his money around. He was no slouch in bed either. I'm pretty big on that.'

The woman was still hurting, Alan saw, but hurting, perhaps, at what she had done to herself. 'What did he do for his money? What's his job?'

'He owned a car yard. In Richmond. He sold it when we split up. What he works at now is getting me back. He doesn't like wives who get away.'

'Did he have others?'

'Girlfriends. He played the field. That's why marrying was such a big deal for him. Contracts, you know. Property. I was the one who was married before.'

'Yes?'

'To a man called Bill Prentiss, until he died. He had what old Robert in there thinks he's got.'

'Were there any children?'

'Nope. I couldn't. Because – none of your business. Hey, I'm confessing. Are you sure you're not a priest?'

For a moment, in the pause she made, she'd dropped into a hole, and he admired her agility in scrambling out. He sipped his tea and took a biscuit from the tin she offered.

'Tell me about May.'

'Ah, she's too tough. You'll have to go and see her for yourself.'

'Won't she come here? Does she come and see –' he found the word hard to say – 'Dad?'

'Not if she can help it. I won't be staying long myself. I came to pick apples and I got shoved into this.'

'Thank you.'

'I'm getting paid. It's not for love. Nursing is my job. One of them. Hear that? Listen.'

'Dad?'

'Banging his walking stick on the floor. Maybe you could buy him a bell.' She went to the door, but stopped. 'One thing, Alan –'

'Yes?'

'About David. He doesn't know I'm here and I don't want him to.' She grinned. 'I'm on the run.'

'He doesn't come either?'

'Not for months. He's – he gets violent. I've had to take an order out. Non-molestation. So . . .'

'Yes. I won't tell him. If I see him.'

'Thanks. I'll get Robert ready. Pour yourself another cup of tea.'

She padded off – pump soles – and he put more milk in his tea and swallowed it lukewarm, thinking that what he needed after all that was a Scotch. A managing woman, sharp and cross – which was her nature, he supposed – and a good deal hurt. He hoped he would not have much to do with her. Why was May not here?

He stood up and looked out the window – and all those even-featured trees, all of one size, were not so much an orchard as a factory for making apples. He felt like an alien, he felt civilised; and he told himself that he would get away as soon as he could. Decently could. See May. See David. Talk with his father. Get away. That was the plan.

He heard the stick strike the floor again. It made a sound like a branch snapping in the jungle: the woman, Freda, must be doing that. It would have been good manners to come and fetch him.

He rinsed his cup and put it on the bench; then he smoothed his hair, obeyed the call.

ALAN AGAIN

IT WAS LATE afternoon before Alan was able to leave the house. His father had talked, and had a rest, then talked again, pointing with his knotted hand at things he plainly thought were obvious; and Alan, learning them, had found his thoughts not easily contained. It was like being in a debriefing room, except that he, the listener, was the one being debriefed, discovering dangers he had passed through and never known.

Freda put a stop to it. 'Enough,' she said, 'there's always tomorrow.'

'I'm not finished,' Robert Macpherson said.

'You are for now.' She put his stick out of reach to stop him hitting her, then brought it back and fitted its handle in his palm. 'I'm taking you to the lavatory. Don't argue, Robert. I want you done before Heather gets here.'

'Alan,' Robert Macpherson said, 'it's like I told you. You're a gone goose when they get in charge.'

Alan walked on the dusty road to the packing shed. A woman halfway across the yard stopped in midstride to watch him approach. Heather, no doubt. Heather in the headscarf, who was so far unexplained. Was her father the Evan Yates who was May's partner? She looked too young to be running an orchard – looked like a schoolgirl standing in a playground. He raised his hand, acknowledging their relationship, and turned into the trees. He did not want to take on another person yet, or more information.

The apples were a sort not grown in his day: Royal Gala. Stupid name. He picked one and rubbed it with his handkerchief. Took a bite, which he enjoyed. Sweeter than a Cox's

Orange, less tough than a Granny. Not a bad invention at all. Perhaps it deserved its place in nature. Today might be a day for letting new things take their place. He considered that. Old things, more accurately. Unsuspected things. He was not troubled by them – not too much – but was overloaded, suffering a kind of input stress. When he had them settled down he would discover what they meant.

Voices called back and forth: pickers in the trees half a dozen rows away. He saw their aluminium ladders flash, and saw down a long tube made by leaves and apples a woman's bare arm reaching out of sight. A tuft of black hair gleamed in her armpit. He was several folds of reality away, in a world where faces came at him as though from under water and white arms reached out from the dark. Okay, so how do I get out? There was no need to be helpless, there were things that he could do. The story his father had told him he might have worked out for himself, so there was no need to be shaken up. Could he really, though, have worked out love?

'Your mother was the one,' Robert Macpherson said. 'There was never any other woman for me. All the rest . . . I'm a man with strong needs, Alan. I had to have a woman in my bed. I still need one, not that they'll let me, bloody nurses . . . but there's got to be an outlet for a man. No use being namby-pamby, I needed to get my end in regular. That girl's mother, what's-her-name's mother . . .'

'May?' Alan said.

'May. Fay it was. She was hot stuff. I hadn't got her here a couple of days and she was climbing all over me. Good for a while. Couldn't last. I had to get rid of her. A wife's the thing for regular. But my wives got sick. Both of them. A sick woman is no good to a man.'

'What did you ask me down here for?' Alan said.

'Her.'

'My mother?'

'Because she's the one. The others, all the others – second best.'

'Did she love you?'

'I don't use that word. That's a woman's word.' He spoke

with difficulty, wheezing. His big nose, drooping, had run all its flesh down to the tip.

'How did she feel about you, then?'

'Don't like feel either. Your mother and me – there's ways a woman lets you know. You never had a wife, did you?'

'No.'

'So you wouldn't know. She made it plain.'

Alan walked out of the apple trees and stood at the edge of the cliff. The road below him was hidden by trees. He heard cars whining up, and saw caravans and housetrucks and camper vans arranged in rows like boxes beyond the second fall of cliff. He looked out as though from a cave, and wanted to go there, into the camp, across the sea, away into the distance. Colour and light would free him; but he could make no connection. He walked along the cliff to a stand of pines left, he supposed, to hold the edge from eroding, and sat down with his back to one. He finished his apple and threw the core away. Over the Royal Gala trees he saw the red roof of the packing shed, and the roof and windows of the house. The woman Freda, his sister-in-law, walked onto the patio, only her top half showing, and raised her hand to shield her eyes as she looked west towards the mountains. Then she turned his way, but did not see him, for she scratched her ribs and yawned, working her shoulders one way then the other. She went inside again. Like her he shielded his eyes and looked at the mountains – shapes so familiar once that he could have drawn their profiles without looking: the two jags of the Twins, filed teeth, Arthur with its leftwards slant, flat-topped Crusader, a military hill. They had been his west: pale in the morning, black at night. Now they were too distant to reach. He was tangled here.

'Do I have to spell it out? Your mother was a tiger, she couldn't get enough. I sometimes think getting sick was a punishment. I don't forgive her, leaving me alone.'

'So why,' he managed to say, 'do you want me here? To tell me this?'

'You're her son, that's why. The others are – they're useless. You're an army man. I knew we'd have a good son, always knew it, Noeline and me.'

'I see.'

'You got her looks. She was a looker. The others were fatties, skinnies, you remember. I've said enough. I'm not letting you think I've gone soft. But every man should have a woman once. And a son with her.'

Love story, Alan thought, sitting with his back to the tree. He supposed he should be pleased. His mother had loved his father; and his father, in spite of his disclaimer, had loved her, he made it plain. It had been more than carnal, that was plain too. Alan laughed. He felt a little sick – but maybe that came from the apple. He closed his eyes, letting go the mother he had kept since she had died. She had been unreal for most of that time. He hoped he would be pleased to be rid of her. But who was the woman in her place? She was no one he would want for himself. Yet it seemed that she had loved. That made her mysterious, it kept her from coming clear.

The mountains grew darker and seemed to squat. Higher than Ben Alder. Higher than Ben Nevis. May was over there, on the other side, making pots. It seemed the muddy sort of thing she'd do, the child who went barefoot with road-dust on her ankles, the child with ringworm.

'She's still a fatty,' Robert Macpherson said. 'She hasn't changed. I've never been sure she's really mine. That Fay could've been in pod before she ever got here. There's no way for a man to know. But I gave her a home – twelve years it was. Until she took off with a picker. Same as her mum: after anything that had a dong. But I treated her right, Alan. I put her to school. I fed her and paid for her and I never had a word of thanks. The only good thing that ever came out of her was that girl –' gesturing at the packing shed.

'I took off too,' Alan said.

'You're a man. A man's got to make his way. The thing you did wrong was quitting the army. You could've been a general if you'd stayed.'

'We don't have many generals. I got as far as I wanted.'

'David quit too but I never had any hopes for him.'

'You shouldn't have had any for me. What is it you want me here for, Dad?'

'Water. Give me some water.' He drank. 'You know I've got this cancer?'

'I heard. What sort?'

'Doesn't matter what sort. It's spreading all over me. I'm not complaining. A man's got to die of something and I still got my brain.'

'Yes.'

'I won't let them do surgery. Or chemicals or X-rays, all that muck.'

'Good for you.'

'So – this Heather. What do you think of her?'

'I haven't met her yet.'

'Go down the shed and have a look. She's no oil painting, but by God she's got some go. She came in here one night, just walked in off the bus, told me, "You're my gran'pa. Can I have a bed?" I sent her down the pickers' hut, told her to stay there. And then we were short so she stayed on picking. Six years ago and she's still here. She's learned the orchard business better than a man. That girl. She's good.'

'You're lucky.'

'I pay her,' the old man said. 'She gets a good wage. I've told her if she stays . . .'

'Yes?'

'The thing is, you see, there's no way I can check up.'

'If she really is your granddaughter, you mean?'

'That's it. She's May's daughter all right, same looks. But how can I know if May was mine?'

'Does it matter?'

'What do you mean?'

'You brought her up as your daughter. So she is.'

'She ran away.'

'That's not Heather's fault.'

'It cancelled it. It's like she said, Stuff you, stuff your orchard.'

'Heather's not May.'

'Ah, you're soft. I thought an army man . . . You know what I'm saying: if Heather's not mine then someone's got to have it and it's you.'

'What about David? What about May?'

'They lost their chance. Anyway, this is for your mother. Except . . .'

'Heather, eh?'

'I made a kind of promise to that girl.'

'Keep your promise. I don't want it. I'll tell you, Dad, I'd sell it and then it would be gone.'

'You're not getting it unless you run it. You could keep that girl as manager. That might be enough for her.'

It would not. Alan heard her through the trees, shouting instructions at the tractor driver. I don't want any of this, he thought. I don't want a fight with her, I want to get out. The rights and wrongs were clear, there was no need to consult.

He turned his back on the sea and walked through the trees. His way took him round the back of the shed. He was grateful for that. He was not ready for her. He struck out for the boundary, through the Granny Smiths, but the trees went on and on. The old man had expanded, bought out neighbours, brought in more land. Some of these new trees, strung on wires, would be varieties he had never heard of. Did 'that girl' understand it all? How old was she? No one had said. He did not like the stretched branches and the crucified shapes; they were not trees any more but production units. He turned back, blaming her, not liking her.

The duck pond was gone, the fowl shed gone, and where the Jonathans had been more wires stretched away with more tortured saplings strung on them. I can't run this, he thought. I can't even own it. It's not mine.

He circled the house and came into the yard, and Freda, on the patio, said, 'There you are. You'd better bring your stuff in.'

He got his suitcase from the boot of the car and the bottles of wine from the back seat.

'How long are you staying?' she said.

'I don't know. I'm not sure what I'm here for yet.'

'Did he give you that eyewash about May not being his?'

He looked at her, surprised. 'Yes. Has he told – the girl?'

'Heather? No. He doesn't even know he's told me. His mind wanders a bit.'

'Then she'd know.'

'If she does she's keeping quiet. What's he want you to do about it? Hey, I'm family, I'm not prying.'

'I don't know what he wants to do. But I think May should be told.'

'You must really like trouble.'

'You think I should keep quiet? Maybe I should.'

She showed him a bedroom whose bareness he liked – wardrobe, bed and chair. 'I think this is where she wants to put you. I'm off now.'

'Don't you stay here?'

'Me, I'm in the pickers' hut. I'm nine to five. Well, eight to five. If I stayed here I'd get sucked in.'

'I see.'

'Heather looks after him at night. She's young, she's got the energy. I can't do twenty-four-hour shifts.'

'Does he need night nursing?'

'He wakes a bit. Yells out. You'll hear him. She manages all right. Heather likes him. Don't say anything against him when she's around.'

'He likes her too.'

'Yeah, he does. It's really nice to see them sometimes.'

He looked at her sharply, suspecting sarcasm – but no, she meant it. 'God knows, they both need someone in their lives. But nothing funny,' she added quickly, 'I don't mean that.'

'No, of course.'

'He tries that on with me. And any other woman that gets close.'

'I'm sorry.'

'I'm a nurse. We're used to it. Well, I'll be off. But look, Alan . . .'

'Yes?'

'This stuff about May not being his. Don't tell her, eh?'

'I don't know whether I'm even seeing her.'

'Go across. She'd like it. But she's had a lot of trouble and now she's coming right, with Evan Yates.'

'All right.'

'May and me go back a long way. We were at school.'

He nodded. Good feeling in a woman always drew him. 'Have one of these,' he said, pushing a bottle at her. 'I bought it for May but she can have the other one.'

She took it, startled, then was pleased. 'Hey, that's great. We'll open it now. I could do with a drink.'

'It's supposed to be chilled.'

'I haven't got a fridge over there. Or an opener either. Come in the kitchen.'

He opened the bottle while she found glasses.

'Okay,' she said. 'Warm white wine. What'll we drink to? There's plenty.'

'Like what?'

'Problems to get sorted out. Me and David for one. Let's drink to my happy divorce.'

'Which he doesn't want?'

'No. Drink to it anyway. Go on. You gave me the bottle so I get to make the toast.'

'Okay,' he said. 'To your divorce.' Drank a mouthful. 'What's my brother like?'

She drank too. 'He's not a nice man. I know I should let you make your own mind up, but I'm a kind of specialist on him. He's not nice.'

'That seems to cover a lot.'

'There's a lot to cover. Let's just say he got spoiled – by him in there. Maybe it should have been chilled.'

'I'm sorry.'

'You apologise a lot, don't you? I didn't think a soldier would. What do you do now?'

'I'm an office manager. I run an office.'

'Who for?'

'A firm of accountants.'

'Bean counters.'

'You could say that.'

'It must be a long way from – what do soldiers do? Guns and stuff?'

'I was behind a desk for most of the time.'

'So you didn't go out there shooting at people?'

'A couple of times. There wasn't much shooting.' Sharp was

part of her as well as soft – the dominant part? He did not like it; felt how she moved into it for control.

'You look a bit like David,' she said. 'Same eyes.'

'Yes?'

'Your mothers were different though?'

'One and two. What's rosacea?'

'Oh, redness in the face. High colour. It comes from overheating, not booze. David's an overheated character. Not that he's not a boozer too. The old man' – she jerked her thumb at the sunroom – 'seemed to go through a lot of women.'

'Two wives. And May's mother, I guess she counts.'

'You don't take after him? With wives, I mean.'

'Who told you that?'

'Robert. But he wanted me to know you're not a fairy.'

He sipped his wine. 'Do you always go jumping round like this?'

'Flea-brain, that's me.'

He suspected that her brain was good. She had learned how to move so as not to be focused on. He wondered if it was from necessity or choice. A pretty woman once, he thought, but good looks ruined now. A kind of hard bewilderment in her. She won't lie down. She's camouflaged.

'Take a good look, why don't you?' she said.

'Sorry.'

'I never heard David say that once.'

'Did he hit you? Physical violence?'

'Just black eyes and fat lips. I've got a chipped tooth, see.' She pulled down her lip. 'I'll have to get it filed one day. Do you mind, though? I don't want to talk about that.'

He stopped himself from saying sorry. Finished his wine, poured some more in her glass, then in his. 'How long is Dad going to last?'

'You should ask his doctor that, I'm just the nurse.'

'You'd have an idea though.'

'He could go on for months. He's hard – in his body, I mean. Worked hard all his life. I don't think he's ready yet either, in his mind. He has to get it worked out who's going to get the orchard. God, I hate people who play around with wills.'

'I don't want the place,' Alan said.

'Yeah? People always say that. You don't turn money down.'

'I think maybe you don't know enough about people.'

'I know about David. If Heather gets it he'll go to court. You can bet on that. It's likely to get messy round here. Anyway, I'm off to make my tea. Is it all right if I take the bottle?'

'Yes, please do. What time does Heather come in?'

'Any time. You mightn't get your dinner for a while.'

'I can cook it. I'll see what's in the fridge.'

'She wouldn't like that. She's a control freak. She doesn't need to be last over there in the shed but you try and get her out of it.'

He went with her as far as the patio and watched her walk away with her bottle down the road. The cottage was halfway to the gate, backing on to the low part of the cliff. All the pickers were locals, she had said, so she had it to herself. He wondered what would happen if David found her there.

Back in the kitchen, he looked in the fridge. The usual things: butter, cheese, milk, fruit juice, cans of beer, tubs of flavoured yoghurt; and some he would not have expected to find: capers, olives, acidophilus. Pork pieces overflowed a bowl. He could not be sure how Heather meant to cook them, and Freda's warning made him nervous, so he left them and walked through the lounge to look at his father. The old man was awake but did not see him in the door. Alan went into the sunroom and sat in the chair.

'I went around the orchard. There's been a lot of changes.'

'There would be after all the time you're gone. Alan . . .'

'Yes?'

'Down there in the cabinet. Pour me a dram.'

'Are you allowed to have it?'

'Habit of a lifetime. No one's got the right to stop me now.'

Alan took the bottle and glass and poured half an inch. 'You don't smoke your pipe any more?'

'I stopped that myself. Get yourself a glass. Have one.'

He went to the kitchen, came back with a glass and a small jug of water.

'Cheers.' Was that the sort of thing you said to a dying man?

'You've just about doubled the size of this place.'

'Thought you'd like it.'

'It's a big orchard. I see you've got some new plantings down where the fowl run used to be.'

'Fujis. That's the girl. She ripped all the Jonathans out. There's no market.'

'Does she know what she's doing?'

'She knows. Don't you try telling her what to do.'

Robert Macpherson closed his eyes. He was tired, Alan saw, and perhaps in pain. There were pills on the side table, but Freda would have seen to that. 'Are you all right?'

'Lift me up a bit. I get a sore bum.'

Alan put his glass down and took him round the shoulders. The bones were still big, they made a frame, but the flesh was gone and the skin slid as though not secured to anything. Alan was surprised at his father's lightness too. It was as if the organs in the torso had dried out. He settled him, rearranged the pillows. 'Okay?'

'Did you ever kill anyone?'

'No.'

'Ever get wounded?'

'No.'

'You were in some wars though?'

'Yes. Two.'

'I was too young for the first war. I would've gone to the second. I stayed home for your mother.'

'I thought they wouldn't let you go. Because of the tugs.'

'I could have worked it. Could've gone on merchant ships. That was war too. But I stayed home.'

He was unhappy about it, Alan saw. He was almost grieving. Again he felt wrenched around. He had never known his father not be pleased with himself. Even when brooding, when raging, there had been a glow in him, of satisfaction, of complacency, or a reaching out and grabbing of what was his, and no question.

The whisky after the warm wine freshened his mouth, but too much would go to his head. He put his glass on the table.

'You got born before the Japs came in,' the old man said.

'I know.'

'Same week as Dunkirk.'

'Yes, I know.'

'If I'd been there I could have saved a few, English or not. I would have rowed across if I'd had to.' He sipped again, then gulped and made a face. 'Even this stuff has lost its taste.'

Alan put the empty glass on the table. He wondered how long Heather would be. The nursing seemed too casual for a man as sick as his father.

'Are you getting some pain?'

'Tired is the worst thing. I can't even lift my hand sometimes. And my mind keeps going every which way. I think there's people here and there's not. Why did you go away and never write home?'

'It's a long story, Dad.' He reached for his glass again and drank. 'I'm here now.'

'You're too late if you've come for your share. You don't get anything.'

'That's all right.'

'It's going to that girl, all of it, the whole shebang. You and David can come sniffing round all you want.'

'I'll let you sleep.'

'No, sit there. You ran out once, you're not going to do it again. Sit still.'

Alan waited, and saw the old man's fierceness grow damp and shut down. A shifting and confusion started in his eyes.

'You there, Alan?'

'Yes.'

'I'll have a sleep now. Wake me up when she comes in.'

Who was 'she'? Alan wanted it to be his mother. He watched the old man drift away. It was most likely Heather, but could be Freda, May, or some woman he did not know, from any time. As Freda had said, there were enough of them.

Footsteps sounded in the lounge. Heather came in, with her head scarf in her hand. Alan stood up: ingrained habit when a woman entered. Some of them ridiculed him for it. Heather slid her eyes past and went to the other side of the bed. She laid her hand on Robert Macpherson's forehead. The old man's eyes came open. He smiled at her.

'You've finished there?'

'Kevin's doing the last bit. I'll go down later and have a look.'

She lifted one of his hands and laid it on the other. 'I see you've had your dram.'

'Alan got it for me. Alan's here.'

'I saw him walking round.' She thrust an arm across the bed. 'Hello.'

They shook hands. She's a neutral, Alan thought. There was no friendliness and no hostility. And neutral – it startled him – in her sexual nature. It was like shaking hands with May, ten-year-old May. She had the same plump face, unformed. Her hair, though, was not brown but so pale it almost had no colour. Silver hair. And she was a woman, mature. Large-thighed, big-breasted, hard in her hand. But sexless still. Her indifference was natural.

'You found your room all right?'

'Freda showed me.'

'I'll give you a towel and a face cloth.'

'Thank you.'

'Maybe you'd like to go and watch TV while I fix Robert.' Her eyes did not meet his but stayed on the level of his mouth. He went out to the lounge, taking his glass, then out to the patio, strangely agitated. There seemed to be usurpation as well as dismissal here. But he had long ago lost his right to be resentful at being turned out of his father's room. One thing was certain, he would not watch TV.

He finished his drink. The sunset was less fiery than on the previous night, although it gave flat-topped Crusader a volcanic plume. There was nothing neutral, he thought, in Heather's intentions. She meant to have the orchard, for whatever reason – profit, vocation? But she wanted – needed? – Robert Macpherson too. He should step aside and let it happen – but felt he would somehow be reduced. So, not understanding, he worked out his practical course: to stay for the four or five days he had intended; to watch and listen here, and be charitable; to see May and David, probably there (Golden Bay and Nelson), discover the situation and play things sensibly. He would help the woman Freda if he could. And it would be best, he thought, to keep out of Heather's way – although he should thank her at some point for her care of his father. His feeling of being diminished, he saw then, came from her fondness for the old man.

She was working in the kitchen when he went in.

'I'm doing a stir-fry,' she said without looking round. 'I hope that's all right.'

'Yes. Good. Is there anything I can help with?'

'No. Have another drink. There's more whisky in the cupboard.'

'No thanks.'

'Beer?'

'I'll have one with my dinner. What about you?'

'I don't drink.'

He sat at the kitchen table, forgetting his decision to keep out of her way. The contradictions in her needed understanding. Dumpy, quick. You couldn't be both – but she was plainly quick; she demonstrated it: quick, certain, in control, competent, precise. Full of knowledge, he thought, at least in the kitchen. So the other word was wrong, her shape could not be called in evidence. Then what about neutral and involved, that contradiction?

'How long have you been here?' he said.

'Six years.'

'Where were you before that?'

'Sydney.'

'Doing what? I mean – do you have a trade? Profession?'

'I did all sorts of work.'

'And now you're an orchardist. Dad says you're good at it.'

She made no answer – tipped a load of diced vegetables into the pan. I'll have to be less personal, he thought.

'How's the harvest going? Is it a good year?'

'Not bad.'

'As good as last?'

'Better. We lost a lot in the hail last year. Are you interested?'

'Not the way you are, I guess. What comes after the Galas?'

'Golden Delicious. Red Delicious.'

'Then Sturmers. Then Grannies.'

'We don't have Sturmers now. Braeburns. If you want to do some picking you can. I'm short since Freda quit.'

She surprised him, until he saw it was not friendliness. She wanted to get her crop in. And perhaps he need not be paid.

'I'm thinking of going across to see your mother tomorrow.'

'Okay.'

'I'd quite like to see Dad's doctor too.'

She turned from the stove. 'What for?'

'Well, to find out how he is. Get a report.'

'Do you think I'm not doing a good enough job?'

'No –'

'Anyway, it's none of your business. Can you look at me and honestly say it is?'

She had been ferocious, then it was gone; she asked the question in a reasonable way. But he had seen his father, seen his anger, in her face. It had put a burning in her eyes and a new contour on her forehead; unfleshed her jaw; refined her. Genetic connection. Macpherson face. The old man need not fear that she did not descend from him.

'I've been away for too long. I know I've got no rights,' he said.

She stirred the vegetables and meat, checked rice in a pan. 'I look after him as well as I can.'

'I can see.'

'There's no one else. My mother won't help.'

'Do you blame her for that?'

'No, I don't. She's got her own life. So has Freda.'

'Has May told you why she ran away from here?'

'We don't talk. But I'd run away too if he was my father.' She turned and looked at him. 'We've got a business arrangement. There's nothing personal even if he is my grandfather.' He saw her pause to consider that, and become a little puzzled by it.

'You like him though?' he said.

'I love him. But what I mean . . . it's not because we're related. He could be any old man.'

So by personal she meant having a sense of duty. Looked at

that way, his visit was personal, even though he made it without love, or even liking.

'He taught me how to run this place,' Heather said. 'There's nothing else I want to do.' She flashed a smile at him, and again he saw his father's face – although his father grinned, never smiled. 'I don't even like apples. Not to eat, I mean.'

Alan laughed. 'I'm not sure what you do is grow apples here. Not the old way.'

'What do you mean?' Her smile was gone.

'Stringing them on wires. They look as if they're chained to a wall. The inquisition.'

'You don't know what you're talking about,' she said.

'No, I probably don't.'

'If you want to help, you can set the table. Just placemats and forks. I hope you don't mind eating in the kitchen.'

'I do at home.'

'Put out that bottle of soy sauce.'

He obeyed. She had, as Freda had said, a taste for command.

'We're up with modern methods on this orchard,' she said. 'So don't you come in and criticise.'

There was no pudding, which did not displease him. He had stopped eating big meals after Phoebe – stopped doing anything to excess. There was though, he thought, something excessive about being here, about returning, and getting tangled up in people's lives.

'Is something amusing you?'

'No. Nothing,' he said. 'You needn't worry about me, you know. I've got no claim on anything here.'

'You mean the orchard?'

'Yes, I do.'

'That's the way I see it too.'

She met his eyes, showing a deep clearness in her own, and he saw that she dismissed him; had, perhaps, understood his lack of threat before he declared it. Although he was not pleased, he was amused. She was, he thought, cunning and simple; she read conditions well and knew how to move in matters of self-interest. He did not dislike her, yet would not spend much time with her if he could help it.

'I can't answer for my brother,' he said.

'David?' She dismissed him too, with a shrug. 'Let's not talk as if Robert's dead. He might be around for years yet.'

Later, when he looked into the sunroom, he saw her feeding his father mashed rice and vegetables from a porridge bowl. The old man ate like a child, pushing his mouth forward greedily. His false teeth clacked on the spoon. Heather wiped his mouth with a paper napkin.

'Nice?' she said.

'Nice,' Robert Macpherson replied.

MAY

I'M TIRED OF peaches, May thought, it's time I did some painting. She wanted to put land and sea together; paint the contest, paint the uneasy love between them – the knifing rock, the bursting wave, the overwhelming tide. Instead of fleshy orbs pumped with juice, and peonies, fat peonies, overblown, with leaves like lazy fingers holding them. Evan and she had chosen these subjects with care: committee decision. Something colourful and succulent (her word); something to sell. Maybe Junior Mott had a point.

Evan was busy at the mould with another dish – fish dish – and Sally was in the showroom, humming like a pretty little housewife, feather-dusting. No customers yet. The season was winding down and soon they would let Sally go and be by themselves and May would sit in the upstairs studio and paint, and take her sketchpad out when it was fine, down to the estuary, mud and crabs and shrimps and lapping water and trees hanging on in rocky coves, or out to Wharariki and the islands pierced through. It opened out her mind and blew clean air in all the folds to think of Wharariki in the sun.

'I'll finish now,' she said. 'I'd better do lunch.'

'What are you making?'

'A salad. And a quiche. That should be enough.'

He looked at her, head a little on one side, estimating. 'Nervous?' he said.

'No.' Then she smiled at him, because he knew. 'Just a bit.'

'I don't think this one will want to fight.'

'He'd better not. He's a soldier, though. At least, he was.'

'We'll put out a white flag. Shall I call Christine as reinforcements?'

'Leave her. Hold her in reserve.'

She walked to the house, feeling easier in her mind. She had got through half a lifetime since Alan had gone away. That was statistical, near enough, and the years stood like a block of stone and would not be moved. How many times had her cells been renewed? Those early days, the memories, were reduced and locked away and she, the new May, held the key. There was no need to let them out.

She made the quiche, made the salad – salade Nicoise – and found herself, when they were done, with time on her hands. She should go back and do another tile; or sell a vase, combat her possessiveness; but sat down with her sketchpad and drew herself rowing on the inlet. Put strength in her rigid arms and her bending back. Made it a buoyant tide, lifting the dinghy. I'll do some tile paintings, she thought, six tiles, one of them with me – no, a woman – in the boat. Red roofs over here. Rocks and trees. Mud and rushes. A cabbage tree. She roughed it in, on a grid, and looked for Evan then to show it to. He had wanted her to try this sort of thing. She crossed the yard, avoiding a car turning wide for a parking space. Then she saw the driver was a man, and at once thought, Alan, and wanted to run and be with Evan when they met. She stopped and waited, turning over the pad to hide her drawing. Running was no use. She must not turn Evan into a shelter, but manage this alone, at least the first part. Remember, she told herself, everything has changed, you're someone new.

He stepped out of the car and left the door hanging. A tall man, military of course, in a casual way – short-sleeved shirt, no tie – but over-neat for all that, too well pressed for her taste.

'May?' he said. 'I'm Alan.'

She transferred her pad, thrust out her hand. There would be no kissing. 'Hello.'

He wanted to kiss her; had expected to. She saw him readjust. But he was stubborn. He held her hand a moment before letting it go.

'I would have recognised you,' he said.

'I find that a little hard to believe.' Did not want to believe it. Surely she had changed.

'I can't tell what it is. It's no one thing.' Studying her. 'How are you, May?'

'Very well.' Better than when you saw me last, she would have liked to say. She did not care for his assumption that they would be easy with each other. Yet she did not feel the resentment she had expected and she was pleased about that, pleased with herself. He's not going to upset me, she thought, looking at him as though he were down a slope from her and must pick his way up. She could hold out her hand to help him, but would not. Not yet.

'You found the place all right?'

'Oh, yes. No trouble.' He was startled that she should want that sort of conversation, and she rather liked the sidelong look he gave, assessing her.

'It's an interesting drive over the hill.' She spoke with pleasure, almost elation, punishing him without the need to.

'Yes, it is.'

'Lovely views. Come and meet Evan.'

'Yes, I'd like to. He's your . . .'

'Partner. Both sorts. Business and – ' could not find a word – 'other things.' Her clumsiness destroyed her control. 'Come on,' she said.

'I've met your daughter, Heather. She's an interesting girl.'

'Woman,' May said. 'Yes, she is. Evan's not her father, if that's what you want to know.'

Then they were inside and the men were shaking hands, and you couldn't tell, as you sometimes could with women, whether they were going to like each other. She would prefer that they did. And she saw suddenly that Alan had not assumed she would be easy with him, but had suggested, requested it. She understood how difficult this meeting was for him.

'We built all this from scratch, Evan and me,' she said.

'It's very impressive.'

'I'll take you on a tour later on. Come across to the house.'

'Can I have a look in there first? Are those the things you make?'

She followed him into the showroom, where Sally was trying out her German on some tourists, but stopped at the entrance and let him find his way. Evan came up beside her.

'Maybe we've got a customer,' he whispered.

'I think he's nervous.'

'I don't believe in nervous lieutenant-colonels.'

'He's retired.'

She took his hand and squeezed and felt the pressure returned. They conspired in a way that made her want to grin: juvenile.

'Left turn,' Evan whispered. 'He's got a ramrod up his bum.'

'Give him a chance.'

Sally took the German couple past them to the counter and wrapped a fish plate for them, explaining how to get it home unbroken. Alan had the showroom to himself. He stopped at the end wall, where her paintings hung. She grew tense. As always, she feared interest and indifference equally. His hands were clasped behind his back – Duke of Edinburgh. He leaned forward from the hips to read her signature.

'You did these?'

'Yes,' May said.

'Are they local scenes?'

She left Evan and walked to his side. 'Most of them.'

'They're good. No one told me you painted.'

'I don't do much. Half a dozen a year.'

'Did you go to art school?'

'No. Just the polytech, for half a year. I'm a dropout.'

He went two pictures back, past the spit, past the inlet, to Wharariki beach, $650, middle-sized. 'Where's this?'

'They're the Archway Islands at Wharariki. On the coast, south of Farewell Spit.'

'I like it. It's full of – fight, I suppose.'

'Well . . .'

'I mean the sea against the land. But restful, in the end. Long term. You need a kind of tension to be still.'

'Is that what you see?'

'I think so. I'd like to buy it.'

'You don't have to.' She was embarrassed.

'It is for sale? I mean, it's got a price.'

She looked at his rounded, freckled forehead. Macpherson eyes. Macpherson jaw. And his big-lobed Robert Macpherson ears. She was not sure she wanted close connection, or her painting going off with him. Yet she could not keep down her pleasure at what he had seen.

Evan bustled up. Stop it, Evan, don't rub your hands, May pleaded. 'That's one of her best ones.'

'I didn't know I had a talented sister.'

'She's creative. She's done a really big one of Wharariki, not for sale. It's in the house. All these are for sale.'

'I'd like to see it.'

'Come and I'll make some coffee,' May said. Evan, keep quiet, stop trying to sell me, she warned with her eyes.

'Shall I pack up this painting?' he said to Alan.

'Yes. Please.'

'No. Later,' May said. 'I'll be calling you for lunch soon. Please leave it.'

She took Alan outside and waited while he fetched a bottle of wine from his car.

'I brought this. I thought you might like . . .'

'Yes. Thank you. Not with lunch or else I'll want to sleep all afternoon. How's Dad?'

He made a small grimace, surprising in a face that would normally be still. She remembered him still-faced as a boy.

'I'd managed to forget him,' he said.

'How is he?'

'I went to see his doctor. Find out the prognosis.'

'They're cagey, doctors. But it's some sort of heart degeneration, isn't it? He's running down. They can't do surgery even if he'd have it. How's Freda getting on with him?'

'She seems all right.' His gesture was surprising too: of bewilderment, in a man used, she would say, to being sure. 'There's a lot of new people to take in.'

'Don't let them get you down. Sit there. I'll get coffee. Look at the view.'

Bossy, she thought, that keeps him off. And it kept her from being agitated. There was a little hum of satisfaction in her at his response to her painting. She put the wine in the fridge, made coffee, took the tray to the lounge and asked him how he liked it.

'Black. No sugar.' He nodded at the painting on the wall. 'I like that too. But I like mine.'

'Do you?'

'This looks like an earlier one. You hadn't quite got yourself together.'

'No?'

'Still the girl slinking in the trees. See? The rocks, they're sly. And the holes in the islands don't go anywhere.'

'They don't anyway.' Girl slinking in the trees? The words rang in her and made her want to cry. Ugly and beautiful – made her want to cry. She put his coffee down and went to the bathroom, where she wet a flannel and washed her face. Be still, she said. Just talk business with him. Talk about Dad.

'I'm sorry, did I upset you?' he asked when she came back.

'No, I'm all right. How's your coffee? Tell me about Dad.'

'I think you know more than me.'

'I only found out he was sick a couple of days ago. What did he want to see you for?'

He sipped and put his mug down, slopping coffee on the table. Apologised. He did not look like a man who made mistakes; he's off balance, she thought. He's closer than he likes, closer to someone, to me. It's got him spilling things. She imagined that normally his physical movements would be sure, and economical, just sufficient but decisive with it. I've put his timing off, she thought; or is there something he's got to say that he doesn't want to? If he can say 'girl in the trees' he can say anything. If he can say 'slinking'.

'He wanted to see me and talk about things. But he's confused. He says one thing and then he says the other.'

'What about?'

'Heather. And you. I think Heather is remarkable. The way she runs the orchard and looks after Dad.'

'Is it about the orchard, who gets it when he's gone?'

'Partly that. He wants Heather to have it. I think that's in his will.'

'Do you object?'

'No, not for a moment.'

'You know it's worth millions, don't you? There's enough for everyone to have a bit.' She did not want to talk about this. She wanted him to hurt her again, with another image; and please her, uncover her childhood: give her words like slinking – so lovely, catlike, secret, promising. But she had shifted him away from that and did not know how to move him back.

'It's hard to make people understand,' he said. 'But I walked away from all that years ago. I can't walk in now and say some of it's mine.'

'Are you well off? Are you rich?'

'No. I've got enough. I get by.'

'Money overcomes all arguments. I feel the same as you, but I'd take some of it if it came my way.'

'I wouldn't.' Again he was clumsy with his mug. 'It's not for Heather's sake, although I like her. But it would cancel everything out.'

'Doesn't coming back cancel things?'

'Not completely. It makes changes.'

'Are you married?'

'No.'

'No children?'

'No. Even if I had I wouldn't want it.' He half turned away and seemed to look at the inlet, but May could tell his focus was somewhere else. He was, she thought, grave and remote in his nature: it fitted with her memory of him, although she would add a string – selfish, cold, indifferent, callous, on and on, for the time back there – but he had been pulled in close, closer than he liked, by his journey south, by his journey home, and his gravity was disturbed. A little pain perhaps? A little excitement at the promiscuity of relationships and desires?

'You see,' he said, and stopped. Could not explain. Drank some coffee. 'There are all sorts of rights and wrongs,' he said.

'I hope you've been happy away from us.'

He looked at her, trying to penetrate, then drew a reserve over himself. 'I've had a satisfactory life.' He seemed to hear the priggish tone of it and blinked his eyes. His ears went red. 'I'm sorry. I don't mean to sound . . .'

'I'm sure you don't. Is that your main memory of me, slinking in the trees?'

'Ha! It's one.'

'What are the others?'

'Well – I'd be lying if I said I thought about you often. It's only since you phoned . . .'

'Of course. I remember you going away. I followed you up the drive, about two rows of trees back. I wanted you to look at me, at least.'

'I'm sorry. I can't believe now . . .'

'What?'

'The way I was.'

'And the way you went on being?'

His redness came back – the ears had hardly faded and now they grew quite rich in colour.

'That will take a bit of sorting out,' he said at last.

'I ran away too. And never came back. What are your other memories, apart from slinking?'

'Well . . .'

'You don't have to try and please me.' I just want, she thought, something like that first one, something that makes it available. But as he spoke – the girl at the stove, the girl washing dishes and running out into the rain to let down the prop and unpeg socks and work shirts from the line – it seemed there would be no second time. She was already in possession of what he offered. Bare feet, faded print dresses? She needed something that rushed up at her from deep down, or came through a vista, through the trees, and fastened on and hurt her but made that time manageable.

'I can remember the first time I saw you. He brought you home in the car and left you sitting in it in the yard.'

'I remember.'

'He came in and said to Judith, "Go out and get her. Take a rag with you, she's peed her pants." So Judith had to go out. You were –'

'Sitting in a puddle on the back seat. I was scared to ask the woman at Newmans for the toilet. And scared to ask Dad to stop the car.'

'Judith brought you in and stood you in that old enamel basin on the lino and Dad made me go out with a bucket of soap and water and wash the seat. It was leather, that old Riley. I don't think it ever –'

'It never got rid of the smell. It soaked right in. Not the best beginning.'

'It was while I was washing it I made up my mind not to be involved. And I found I could do it.' He stood up and went to the window. Again that Duke of Edinburgh stance. 'I haven't forgotten you' – he turned – 'but I haven't remembered you either. You've been like a photograph – black and white, standing at the sink or the washtubs. You didn't move, you weren't alive. You were frozen there. So I could look and turn the page. You didn't start to move until you phoned me up.'

'How do you feel now?'

'Ashamed.'

'Don't be. Don't bother. There's really nothing you can do for us. And we don't need it. At least I don't. I can't speak for David. But me – I don't need you. I needed you once, you could have helped.'

'May – '

'I'm not trying to get my own back. I don't want to hurt you.'

'I can go away if you like.'

'No. I think you're probably a nice man. We'll try and forget how things used to be. Are you a Christian? Is that why you're feeling so bad?'

'I'd feel bad without that. But yes, I am.'

'It doesn't make me like you more. It's always seemed a crime against good sense. Do you want to argue about religion?'

'No.'

'Nor do I. I'm sorry, Alan. I probably seem a bit mad to you, but it's hard to keep my mind still, someone coming back after so long. Do you pray?'

'Yes, I do.'

'I knew a man who prayed once. I used to live with him. I

caught him trying to teach Heather things. Sex, you know. She was about nine. So we all had to get down on our knees and pray the sin out, not just out of him, out of ourselves.'

'Do you blame that on me too?'

'I used to. You and Dad. Not any more. I'm sorry, I'm sorry. I meant to be so all together and laid back. You were going to see a happy woman. I didn't mean to come apart like this. Drink your coffee. Get yourself another cup.'

She went to the bedroom and lay on the bed. All it is is a bit of shifting, she thought. I'm not damaged, I'm rearranged. She imagined a sliding of parts, edge moving on edge like the shutter of a camera, and a space appearing in the centre, into which fitted the girl slinking in the trees, and, yes, another bit, the child sitting in a warm puddle on the back seat of the Riley car. And more, that she had not known, but knew now: a boy with a bucket and soap, washing down the leather. It's someone seeing me, and giving me a word, giving me 'slinking'. And me seeing him. He was out there washing the seat. I wasn't alone. She heard her blood throbbing, moving in her, and felt plump and energetic, whole.

Voices came from the living room. Evan's voice, Alan's voice, then a laugh with that East End guttural, that sound so lovely to her, Evan's laugh. She got up and smoothed the bed and was at the mirror tidying her hair when he looked in. She smiled at him.

'I'll be there in a minute. Oh, Evan, there's a bottle of wine in the fridge. Open it. We'll have it with lunch.'

They ate and drank and Alan praised the salad and the quiche. Evan praised the wine. He told stories about growing up in Bermondsey, failing his eleven-plus, and running with a ratpack, scavenging the docklands; then about opal mining at Coober Pedy; and May could not understand where his good health came from. How had he survived the deprivation, the mud and dust, and kept his good cheer and his generosity? She had barely survived her own mud and dust; had needed him to lift her up; and now, it seemed, needed Alan too.

'Sally and I can handle things,' Evan said. 'Take him out and show him a bit of Golden Bay.'

'All right. Would you like to see Collingwood, Alan?'

'That'll take two minutes. Take him to Wharariki,' Evan said.

No, she thought, don't go too fast. Keep it close to home. She did not think Alan was a man who would be pushed, and she did not want to push herself.

When Evan had gone she took Alan up the hill to the water tank; showed him the pond with its floating ducks; showed him Woods Inlet and the sea and Farewell Spit. Felt herself expand to cover things: this was hers. She tried not to say too much about it, knowing she would say something foolish, and feeling, still, that he might draw back. He was a man who would keep part of himself in reserve. You would not fully trust him and relax as you did with Evan. They went down to her car and drove to Collingwood – cruised the main street, cruised the beach front, and it was done. 'Come and see some swans.' She drove around the estuary, where the swamps and mud-flats drowned in the rising tide, and under the black Burnett Hills; broke out on the coast again and found the birds in their thousands, floating in the shallows by Pakawau.

'God,' he said, 'black ones. There can't be so many.'

'They're an army. They came from Australia and they've taken over here. And out on the Spit there's all the godwits from Siberia. There's the Spit.'

'And this just empties out?'

'Thousands of acres of mud. I love the mud. You can keep your sand.'

'What about Wharariki beach?'

'That's different.'

She turned the car and drove home, but parked by the gate and said, 'Come and have a ride in my dinghy.' She led him on the path through the rushes. 'Take off your shoes. Leave them here.' He obeyed. 'Roll up your pants.'

She could not tell whether he cared to be bossed. Army officers probably didn't get enough of it. She felt sure enough of herself to risk his displeasure, but saw that he was interested as she launched the dinghy.

'It's not made for two.'

'You won't get wet.'

It was not easy to row with a man sitting in the stern. She had wished to show off her skill, but his knees got in her way and she had to shorten her stroke. She took the dinghy round the western shore, under hanging trees and slabs of rock, wishing to impress him again. Went slowly over green deeps in the shade. The dinghy floated low, the upward pressure seemed increased, there was a heavier life in the water. She made little dips with the oars, not wanting to go deep. Alan faced her, a metre away. This, she thought, could get embarrassing.

'Rowing is my pastime,' she said.

'You're good at it.'

'Your knees get in the way.'

'Sorry.' He angled them to one side, which shifted his weight and made the dinghy tip.

'I've got a runabout,' he said. 'On the Auckland harbour.' He looked around, then smiled at her. 'It's more crowded than this.'

'It would be. Tell me – ' they lowered their heads under an overhanging branch – 'have you always been religious? I mean, we didn't get any at home. There was a bit at school, of course. Your one too, I suppose. Did they get you there?'

He frowned: surprised perhaps, and putting up his reserve. 'I wouldn't say anyone "got me". Non-believers think there's a conspiracy . . . What are you?'

'Nothing. An atheist, I suppose.'

'You don't know?'

'No, I don't. I don't think about it. It seems so remote from real life.'

'Oh no. It is life.' He put on a smile, tried to lighten things, but could not. 'Have you heard of the Covenanters? No? I got interested in Scottish history. Because of Robert Louis Stevenson. *Kidnapped*, remember? Did you get that?'

'Not as much as you and David. You got your names.'

'Yes, Alan Breck. But I went off the Jacobites. Bonnie Prince Charlie, that seemed kid stuff. I went on to the Covenanters.'

'Who were they?'

'Religious reformers. They rebelled against the church and

got persecuted for it. And they did a bit of killing and burning for themselves. It's a long story. But the point is, try telling them that religion isn't life.'

'So you're a Presbyterian?'

'No, I didn't say that. I'm Church of England. That was what I went to in Duntroon. Church was compulsory first year. After that I got out of it and it wasn't till years later, after the army, that I went back. And I saw it was . . .'

'Real life?'

He smiled at her. 'I'm not trying to convert you, May.'

'You couldn't.' The dinghy bumped on a rock and she pushed away with an oar. 'What made you go back?' She would not, she thought, ask him questions like this again. The combination of newness, their surprise in each other, and the place, the stillness, the uplifting water, the heavy buoyancy of the boat, gave her a sanction that would be withdrawn. 'Was it something that happened?'

'Yes.' He was reluctant. 'It was.'

'Something you can't talk about?'

'No. I never have. I just got to a point – no, it wasn't a point, it was an event. It came on me. I saw something. It could have ended me. And I had to have somewhere to stand.' He smiled, still polite. 'All this must be double Dutch to you.'

'Was there a woman in it?'

'Yes, there was. But much more too. More than a woman. I don't think I want to talk about this, May.'

'No. All right.'

She pulled the dinghy out into water that moved, then headed along towards the Woods Inlet wharf – a few rotten piles with weeds growing on them.

'I never liked Alan Breck,' she said.

'I did. I had to, with my name.'

'There was just one part, where Alan Breck and this man are going to fight but instead they settle it with a bagpipe competition.'

'Robin Macgregor.'

'I don't remember his name. But Alan Breck plays, and then this man plays, and he's a master, and it says something like –

his anger died, Alan Breck's, and he could only think of the music.'

'I remember.'

'And he says, "I'm not fit to blow in the same kingdom as you." I liked him then. He wasn't just a silly little man waving a sword.'

Alan laughed, a bit mystified. 'You think it's all sword-waving in the army? Most people do.'

'I've never thought it was an honourable trade. I'm sorry, I've offended you –' seeing him flush. 'You're out now, aren't you?'

'Yes. Fifteen years,' he said stiffly.

'I have offended you. We've had different lives, Alan. We don't have to agree.'

She let the dinghy glide past the piles, then turned across the tide, letting it carry them towards the causeway.

'Come and see Woods Inlet. It's all sand, you can walk in bare feet.'

She pulled strongly for five minutes and beached at the foot of the settlement track. Alan climbed out and helped her lift the boat clear of the water. They walked past George and Daphne's house, where the curtains moved and a face looked out – Daphne alone. Further on, Junior Mott was sitting on his doorstep smoking a joint. He did not notice them go by.

'It's legal here. Smoking pot. We like to think,' May said.

'Do you smoke it?'

'I gave it up twenty-five years ago. Artie, Heather's father, was so zonked out on it he never knew what day of the week it was. I didn't want my brain going soft. You all right now? I didn't mean it as an insult.'

'Forget it. Tell me about Heather. And Freda. I like them.'

'You're not one of those people who likes everyone?'

He smiled, with difficulty still. 'Just those two. They seem to be battlers.'

'Gutsy women. Me too?'

In spite of the time he was taking to come back, she felt at ease. He'd sat, as they crossed the tide, with his knees cemented, while she had had her legs thrust out on either side, and it had seemed a fitting was accomplished, a sibling connection that they had not known when they were young, and they would stay together now even when their differences held them apart.

'That's lesbian alley,' she said, pointing at the cottages and shacks at the back of the sandhills. 'There's a dozen of them. There's some battlers there.'

'Lesbians?'

'Yes. Sally's one. In the showroom.'

'The girl? But she's . . .'

'Pretty? Some of them are, some are not. Just like all the rest of us.' She wondered if the army made men monkish, disconnected them from the world. Or was it religion had done that? And the army that had given him his stillness, and the feeling that he might break into action at any time? It could be just a Macpherson trait.

They walked on the beach and she told him about her life with Heather – up until the slap, which she left out. 'She left home the way I left and didn't come back. No letters, nothing like that. Typical Macpherson behaviour. I couldn't complain. I didn't see her again until she turned up at Dad's, and she'd been there three months before I found out.' She told him how she had stayed in Auckland when Heather left, sharing house with Freda; and had done two half-papers at the university; then drifted to Nelson and her polytechnic course. 'I always did things by halves. Came across to Golden Bay. Lived in a shack. Possums and hares and eels, that's what I ate. I was the wild woman of Woods Inlet. Then I met Evan and came right. You don't want to know all that. Freda came to Nelson and got married to Bill Prentiss.'

'Who died.'

'Who died. Then our brother David came along. That little story is still going on.'

'I've got to see David.'

'Tell him to lay off her. Not that he will. It's a pity you and Freda can't get together.'

He almost jumped. He stepped sideways and looked at her. 'Do you always say the first thing that comes into your head?'

'Not always. It just sort of presented itself. A solution. But of course it leaves David out.'

'May, don't. Don't push too hard. All right?'

She felt herself blushing, and felt stupid and clumsy and somehow gross. My thick fingers, she thought. It was due to euphoria, having a brother suddenly. 'I'm sorry,' she said. 'I get silly sometimes. You're not going to go away, are you?'

'No, I'm not. But I will.'

'Please stay. I was hoping you'd stay the night. And come to dinner at the Snapper Inn.'

'I didn't bring anything.'

'You don't need anything. There's a spare toothbrush. Unused. I'll wash your shirt and underpants overnight. Your socks too.'

'Heather, though? She's expecting me.'

'I'll phone her. You can go back in the morning. Say yes.'

'All right. Yes.'

They turned back, climbed the sandhills, walked up the road, past Junior Mott dozing in the sun with his dog sleeping across his feet, and Daphne Otway twitching her curtain; crossed the inlet, tied up the dinghy; and that night drove down the highway to the Snapper Inn, where May was delighted at Alan's confusion in the big bare room with its manor-house tables and cats by the fireplace and children running, guitars playing, people singing, and the mugs of beer and slabs of bread and plates of food.

'I'm having fish stew. Have the fish stew.'

'Yes, all right.'

'I'll get some beer,' Evan said. 'Beer for you, Alan?'

'Yes. Beer.'

'Relax, Alan. Go with the flow. Can't you feel it? It all comes together in this place. Take your jacket off.'

She waved at Sally, sitting with the two guitarists at the lesbian table.

'That one bringing beer, that's her partner, see?'

'Partner?'

'Her hubby. Except that they don't use that word.'

Alan hung his jacket on the back of his chair. He could not, it seemed, look at Sally and Christine, but glanced at them, then looked at the blazing logs, the cats and the children, and back again.

'I think she was in the army. At Waiouru. A corporal.'

'Christine?'

'I think it's her. It's twenty years.'

'She passes for thirty-five round here.'

Evan brought the beer back and sat down.

'Christine's a corporal,' May said.

'She's a sergeant-major. She's a bloody field marshall,' Evan said.

'She recognises you, Alan. See the way she's looking everywhere else? Don't say anything, it wouldn't be fair.'

George Otway came in, wearing a plaster on his forehead. He got himself a drink and joined their table. May introduced him to Alan.

'We don't see you here often, George. Are you eating?'

'I'm not hungry. I ate an apple walking up the beach.'

'You came on the beach? Is it bad times again?'

'A little bit of argy-bargy.' He touched the plaster on his head. 'Nothing serious.'

'It's swollen pretty badly under that.'

George shrugged and turned to Alan. 'I didn't know May had any brothers,' he said.

May watched them find each other out. She was pleased that Alan and Evan would get on, and surprised at it: East End boy turned potter, and soldier turned office manager. The gap was huge – but some direct way with experience was involved and a basic seriousness. George Otway should fit in; but never had with Evan, and now, it seemed, would not with Alan either. Liking was mysterious, friendship too. The chances of her liking Alan had been so reduced that their sitting here like this could be seen as a miracle. She was so sure of it that she was able to break into the conversation and turn away from Alan, even though he was not enjoying the Snapper Inn. She talked with George, who described Daphne's latest assault. It was, she thought, less serious than the last. It sounded tired. George thought so too, and worried that Daphne was sinking under, getting remote. 'I've got to find a way to save her, May.'

It's almost comic, May thought, except there's death in it. There was something unhealthy, too, in their agony. It seemed too snug and too contrived. Why couldn't they just go off in different directions?

'You'll sort it out,' she said, not believing it.

'Not much time left,' George said.

Evan stood up. 'Junior. Junior. Over here,' he called.

'Leave him, Evan,' May said, looking at Junior Mott, who had somehow got into the room.

'If he sits down I'm leaving. No offence, May, but he never washes,' George said.

'He won't sit down.'

'Look at the cats. They should keep that dog out of here.'

'They will. They'll make him tie it up in the yard.' She watched Evan cross the room and talk with Junior: a short thick man, bald and bearded, and a six-foot one like a scrawny tree, bending down, but not in friendship or with any wish to hear. Bending with a spitting hatred, close. It stopped her seeing them as a comedy team. 'I don't know why Evan keeps on trying.'

'That's the fellow who was smoking marijuana,' Alan said. He half rose. 'That dog will bite Evan if he doesn't watch out.'

'No it won't. He's all right.'

'Who is he?'

'Junior Mott. He and Evan were friends once. He thinks he taught Evan how to pot, but really Evan taught himself. Now he hates him because of me, because we shacked up and left him out. And we make money too. That's the cardinal sin.' She tried to lighten it. 'He's just a sad old hippy out of the sixties. Evan keeps on trying to prop him up.'

Junior Mott spun away from Evan and walked out. His arm came back inside, opening the door for his dog. May went to the counter for the tray of fish stew and carried it to the table.

'Did you tell him he was colour blind?' Evan said.

'I asked him if he was.'

'Well, he is. He thinks I told you.'

'I only guessed it. How could he make all those cacky pots otherwise?'

'May, May, give him a chance. He was okay once.'

'He won't give me a chance. Domestic dispute, Alan. It's our only one.' Then she smiled at Evan, feeling sorry for him. 'I don't hate Junior, Junior hates me.'

'He hates us too,' George Otway said. 'Our house lets the neighbourhood down. It's too neat,' he explained to Alan.

'Let's have some food,' May said, putting out the stew. She sat down and laid her hand on Evan's, and was overcome by her love for him; played her fingertips on his knuckles, a tune. You're the cream in my coffee – stupid words but she wanted to say them. 'Don't worry,' she said. 'Don't worry about him.' Alan watched them. He sees how much I love Evan, she thought, and wondered if he could see how much Evan loved her.

George Otway finished his beer and left, refusing a ride. The Snapper Inn grew noisier as the tables filled. Alan would not, could not, enjoy himself. A guitarist with an amplifier started performing from the stage by the servery. Someone trod on a cat and a woman changed her baby's nappy on the floor by the fireplace.

'Had enough, Alan?' May shouted. He signalled that he could not hear. 'Come on,' she said to Evan, 'let's get him home.' In the car she said, 'I'm sorry, it's not usually so loud.'

'The food was good,' he said.

'But you'd rather have a candlelight supper?'

'I like a place where you can talk.'

'Me too,' Evan said. 'It's always best to eat at home. You can be in control.'

She patted his thigh, and let her hand rest there. In bed, when he was sleeping, she remembered Alan's washing and padded out through the house and put it in the machine. Back in bed she heard, distantly, the beating and spinning. She would send Alan back to the orchard as clean as when he had arrived; which, she thought, was pretty clean. There was, perhaps, too much soap and water in his life, for which – she grinned into the dark – she might be held responsible. And there were areas fenced off – no trespassers. But that was better, she thought, than slopping all over the place; letting it all hang out, as they used to say. He asked for nothing, but offered to pay what he owed. I like him, I like him, she thought, her mind sliding but returning to that – from girl slinking in the trees, and boy with his bucket and rags, and boat on green water and man with locked knees – I like him. I've got a brother now, isn't that nice? She heard faint beeps as the machine finished its work; and she slept . . .

Woke with the sun streaming in, left Evan sleeping, put Alan's shirt and socks and underpants in the drier, made tea and took it to them in the bedrooms. She ironed the shirt – never ironed underwear – got the last bit of dampness out. A quality shirt, as far as she could tell. He would buy the best, and treat his possessions well, make them last. There would be both snobbery and morality in that. She laughed, inclined more to judge him in the morning.

'Room service,' she said. 'Would you like more tea?'

'No thanks.' He was naked in bed, which made him uneasy. Probably, she thought, a bit tumescent in there. She hoped he was, it made him less perfect; and she wanted to go back and see if Evan was that way too.

'I usually go for a run before breakfast,' Alan said. 'But if it's all right with you I'll go for a row in your dinghy.'

'Help yourself. You know where it is.'

Evan was in the shower. She made porridge for him and they were eating when Alan strode back underneath the windows.

'Someone's had a go at your dinghy,' he cried.

'What have they done?'

'Chopped holes in it with an axe.'

She rose from the table.

'No, May, wait here,' Evan said.

'I want to see.'

They went down the drive, along the road, through the rushes. The dinghy was lying bottom up on the mud, still tied to the waratah. There had been no method in the chopping. The cuts went every way and three blows, crosswise, had severed the spine.

Rage first, then grief, made May cry out.

'Easy, May,' Evan said.

'You know who this is?' She wiped her cheeks, and said to Alan, 'This is our resident madman.'

'You can't tell,' Evan said.

'Who else would it be? I'm calling the police.'

'No, May. Let's not have any trouble.'

'What do you call this if it's not trouble? Oh, my boat.' The cuts made her shrink and tremble.

'The tide's been in. There's no footprints,' Alan said. He put his fingers under the dinghy and flipped it over. The edges of the holes curled up like skin.

'Look what he's done to it,' May wept.

Evan put his arms around her. 'Come on. Let's go home. Leave it, Alan, just leave it there.'

'He's had a go at the oars too.'

'Leave them.'

They went back to the house. May sat in the bedroom, on the bed, and listened to the men at breakfast, talking quietly: about her, probably, when they should be talking about Junior Mott, getting him certified and locked up. I won't let that crazy spoil it for me, she thought. I've got Evan and we've got this place and no one's spoiling it for me. It seemed even more important now that Alan had come into her life. But oh, she thought, my boat, my boat.

She went to the bathroom and showered. Evan came in while she was towelling herself.

'All right, love?'

'I'm all right. He's mad, you know.'

'I know. I'll go and have a talk with him. Prison's not the thing, May. He'd go mad in there.'

I thought we agreed that he was mad already, she wanted to say; but let him hold her for a moment and kiss her. 'You be careful if you see him,' she said.

'I will. Junior won't hurt me.'

When she went into the kitchen only Alan was there. 'There's some coffee in the pot,' he said.

'Thanks.'

'Evan's wrapping my picture.'

'Do you still want it?'

'Of course I do. It's a great picture, May.'

'Did he make you pay?'

'I gave him a cheque. I wouldn't take it for nothing, so don't offer. You can buy another dinghy with it.'

'I might do that.'

Later on, at the car, he kissed her on the cheek and she kissed him.

'Come again before you go home,' she said.

He drove away with the painting laid flat in the boot.

She climbed to the water tank and watched his car cross the causeway and turn out of sight through the cutting.

Interlude

ROBERT MACPHERSON

NEVER LIKED DAD, never liked it. Wanted Mister but she laughed at me. You're not playing captain in my house, Bob Macpherson. You'll be wanting him to salute you next.

Little woman, shrimp, I used to say. Big chin, never let her chin put me off. Like the counter on the *J. C. Rumbold*, told her once. Did she laugh? She could laugh, whoop, whoop, like a scuttleboat siren when I took my trousers off and the door blew open, there in my underpants, all those picnic women, lady women, looking in, like some bird in the swamp she was. Not about her chin though, almost cried, thought she'd cry. Started with the waterworks that time I smacked the boy. But she was sick then. Sick women.

Judith, number two, off colour she called it. She was the crier. Things she thought I didn't do for her. Didn't hold the door open, let her go through. Forgot in the hotel, only once, standing there outside the door, waits for me to walk back, I'm not starting that way, no fear, tears on her face, snail tracks. Wash your face, I said, you look repulsive. Licked them once, Noeline's, saltwater toffee. Bloody mad.

Too much crying. Women cry. Never laugh. Only Noeline. Laughed at me. Fist I had, opened it in time, she went across the room, got tangled in the chair, sat in the corner, legs all skew, bleeding mouth. Didn't mean it, blood. Like a baby, picked her up, Just a small one, Noly, only a tap, flapping like a kingfish she was, locked the door, the boy in there, made me mad in there. I said, Open, open, and she, Go on, I dare you, break it down. Wanted me to, I think she wanted . . . Fat lip in the morning. Wouldn't let me touch her seven days.

Week away after that, salvaging the *Florence E*, too long, they didn't like it, but couldn't get the anchors fixed and the set was tricky, got a veer, did they want me aground as well, and still she wouldn't, two weeks, still she wouldn't, I had to . . . apologising is a woman's game.

Noeline. Noly. Shortens nice. Don't call me Bob. Okay, Roberto. Roberto Mac. Listen you, I said, but she laughed. Captain Roberto Mac puts a woman on her back. Things she'd say. Cunt and stuff. I never heard . . . even with . . . but only then, only when we . . . A woman is pure or else there's no place we can go.

Arrgh, sore bum. Why can't she. I need oil. Can't be any fun for her, old man's bum. Skin sliding; feel it slide. Dead bum. Gangrene of the bum. That would be something to die of. Or, God, of your family, holding your hand. I could still squeeze, I crack bones, that army man, colonel with his troops, I thought he'd have a moustache or is that RAF? Soft hands, office work, he should be fighting wars, that's what they're for, killing people, saving the nation, empire and the king, queen, is it king or queen. That one, George the sixth, wanted to squeeze, hear his little bones crack. English. God save the boy, bonny prince, that's what I'd say. And that Elizabeth Regina, she's a tug. Never smiles. Never laughs. Noeline, God she laughs, lying on top. Towline, she called it. Pull your towline in I'm casting off.

Never had. Told me she never. How many men before. I'll kill . . . Only one, one, he was just a boy. Liar. You're a bloody liar. Liar, I said.

'What?'

'None of your business. I was talking to my wife.'

'I'm sorry if I woke you. It's time for your pill.'

'Where's Alan? Where's he gone?'

'To see David.'

'What's he want to see him for? He came to see me.'

'He spent an hour with you this morning. Open.'

'I've got a sore behind.'

'I'll shift you in a minute. Open please. Swallow.'

'These things are not going to save my life.'

'They're not meant to, Robert. They're meant to make things easier, that's all.'

'I like it better when that girl . . .'

'I know. But she's busy looking after your orchard. Now, you'd like some oil on your bottom? Don't look so helpless, you can turn.'

Why do they give me this one. A woman should be soft, a nurse. It's like she's stowing goods. Wool bale. In the old *Phyllis*, high tide through the mangroves, bang, bang, engine going slower than an engine's got a right. Sails stowed. I liked the scows. Warm deck in the sun. Mud all sunk, ten feet under, green treetops like a cabbage garden to the shore. Best time. Bales on the jetty. Slack water, ease out on the ebb. The sun always shines. She's got good hands. Putty it must be like, working it in, oil in the joints, that's where I need, crank oil, vaseline like that whore in Sydney, made me come before I, wouldn't pay so she called her pimp and I gave him ten bob, That's more than it's worth, try it on, I said, seeing if he'd pull a knife . . . Ah, that's good. Slapping dough.

Suffocate in this pillow. Wouldn't give a damn any of them. That girl would. Old feller. Warms me. Nothing in it. Hot water bottle is all.

Arms looped in a bight, hard as ropes. Turning o-o-ver. Pyjamas up, ties a bow, wrapping for Christmas.

'This arm. Lift. I want to put some oil on your elbows.'

Skin will come off. Like she's sanding four by two, clumsy bitch, ow. Scraping paint. Tarring the deck, waiting for the tide to turn. It lies still or it's pulling you, half an hour's slack and then it's moving. Never gets anywhere, in, out, senseless thing. You're either beating it or it beats you. Shallow water is the worst, nothing to trust, drag your towline, watch out for the override. Glad to be in harbour, they told me personally because she'd only, two weeks dead when I went out, I'm sorry Robert . . . English bastard, all the way from, what would he know. Job was mine. Never let them see how . . . Get out of my way you buggers, I'm leaving. Out the door, down the steps, straight up the wharf, don't look back. I phoned that night. That's the way: think it, do it. Settled. Signed. Don't like the sea, always shifting, mindless, never gets anywhere. My job. It was. Captain Macpherson, harbour master. I promised you, Noeline . . .

There are things you've got to do. Chafing gear. Doesn't even know to get the chafing gear on. You're fired. Get up the office and get your pay. Fired 'em like that, one two. Belly out, bulging eyes. Have a go at me I'll flatten you. Fuck your union. The strike was what they didn't like, counted against me. Crew trouble, Robert. I never had crew trouble, what I had, bastards that didn't know their job. Didn't know a Sturmer from a Granny, but she could learn. Say it once she knows it. Petal fall. What's petal fall. Thought it was some sort of disease. See her now, think it, do it. Down the road that Dutchman, you're fired.

Where's she gone. She was here. Feel like a dead fish in the bilges. Watching the gut boat empty out. Gulls like maggots. Fish like maggots, eating. Big grey kingis follow it down. Years of rubbish after Noly. Not one thing has happened, rubbish dump. I hear gulls. Hate bloody scavengers, hate gulls. And people hanging on to me licking their chops. No one's getting anything. Except that girl.

No oil painting. She's too fat for seventeen. Is it. Twenty-seven. Sack of wheat. Feel her innards shifting. But warm when she gets in. Keep your back to me old feller, that's right. All one piece, all the way down, belly and breasts, lying in the mud, sun shining on you, warm water, tide coming in over the mud. I like the sky, clouds moving, I should have flown an aeroplane instead of the sea. Sea always rocking, it's like your blood, flows in, flows out, little fish, crabs eat you, cold turns you numb. There's no air . . .

'Easy does it. You're okay.'

'I thought I was drowning.'

'It's the pill working. Go back to sleep.'

'No.'

'It won't happen again. You'll sleep now. Do you want me to hold your hand a while?'

'What did I say?'

'Help, help.'

Sailor drowning. Throw me a line. Who's laughing. Is that me.

'Is Alan home?'

'Not yet.'

'What's the time?'

'It's eighteen minutes to three.'

'Is that all?'

'Go to sleep.'

Don't want my hand held, not by this. Pushes like she's getting me berthed. Hawser arms. Close eyes she'll go away. Thinks she's hard, hard as nails. Spit tacks. Spitting tacks. David will get her. They've got small bones like fish. When he gets her, crackle, snap. Could have been all right. Half of him was Judith, half was soft. He'll break her though, where she runs. I'm not looking after, no place here. She thinks I'll, from my own . . . David Balfour on that island, didn't even know the tide went out. Eating shellfish, chasing gulls, thought he was stuck and all the time . . . Mummy's boy, in the kitchen, giving him brown bits from the roast and hot scones. Put a stop to that. Apple stick from the prunings, not as good as willow, use my belt. Screamed as if I was hitting her. Sat down with him on the floor, held him by the head. Couldn't believe . . . I don't want a pansy for a son.

Arms as soft as. Softer than that Fay. Judy she wanted to be called. I married Judith I said. Fay screaming too, You promised me. I promised nothing. I said if. She couldn't even keep the dunny clean. I get them mixed. Judith. Fay. Sacks of flour both of them. But soft where you put your hand. Silk it is. Fay opened up, the other closed. Should have known, from her mouth, turkey's bum. You can light them up, they surprise you, not her. You knew what getting married meant, I said. Drowned woman would be better. Sick is no good to a man, damaged goods. I'm off colour Robert. Outside she was good enough, fat when she was dying, inside, won't think, watery core.

'How are you, old feller?'

'No good.'

'Hurting?'

'Just tired.'

'Is she looking after you okay?'

'I sleep all the time.'

'Sleep's good for you.'

'Who says?'

'I say. Nice?'

'I don't like people touching my face.'

Fingers rough. She works too hard. Women doing men's jobs, hard. Hair up in a scarf. Where'd she get. No hair like that in the Macphersons. Fay had black. May black. Ringworms in her hair with the cat all over, screech like a block and tackle, biting herself. Good shot, that boy, broke her hips. Cats. I never had time. Dogs. No time. Tied to the mangroves, teeth all showing, when the tide, what a way . . .

'What is it?'

'Thinking all the time.'

'You were dreaming.'

'It's the same. Can't stop my mind . . . What I want to do . . . stay awake.'

'I'll pull the curtains back some more. We're out of the Galas, Robert, into the reds. You can watch.'

'What are they like?'

'It's the export pick. It's the best I've seen.'

'That's why you're grinning?'

Teeth like a broken cup, poor little bitch. No wonder there's no boyfriends hanging round. Bounce them off, she'd bounce. Show them her teeth, run a mile. No fat Macphersons, who's she. Walks in, I'm your, how am I to know. Anyone. May would put her up to it. Split the proceeds, live in clover, think I'm dumb. Alan, did Alan, I never asked. Did he ask. How can you ask. Mother was a slut, a whore, climbing all over. Where'd she learn. With her mouth. Dozens of men. I would have had her back though when I got that Judith . . .

'I'm going now. We've got some pretty dumb pickers this year. You should see what they pick.'

I never ate an apple. Never all my life ate an apple. Sour like wine. Liked peaches, nectarines. Drown in apples. Too many. Slice them, quarter, look inside. Chewed, spat them out. Like those fairies tasting wine, make you puke. Wouldn't have known an apple if I saw one in '47. Get as far from Auckland as I can, from that Pom. Southampton like it's on the right hand of God. It's not as if it's even the Clyde. Never saw the Clyde. I never was in Scotland and nor was my father. Macphersons everywhere, all over the world. Heather Macpherson. I don't know her father's name. Here on my orchard she was got, in the grass, I saw them go, she looked back and pulled him by the hand and they sank like water and no one there when I ran, he was gone, I got the gun, would have, by God, I would have shot, with my daughter, must have waited for her down in Ruby Bay when she, fat lip, I slapped, playing slut on my place, If you go you never come back, leave that money, you don't take anything from here . . . Is that what I, down the drive, was it May going, was it Fay?

Hiding somewhere. Where is, where. Dumping on me. Down the street, doorways, cars, I can follow the bus, pull her off. This is yours. Thinks she can dump her by-blows on me. Child with my, see her in the mirror, there's nothing I can, mine and I, what can I do. Never had, not daughters, sons, girls can turn bad. In the grass with, white hair, rotten teeth, I knew. Ever since, in the car, soaked right through the leather. Ruined with piss. And walking in, half her life and no knock on the door. Well Dad, it's May, I've come to see how you're getting on. I thought it was Fay come home, blood went dropping out, years got lost, I thought you were your mother, I said, where's she. Wouldn't know, she said, wouldn't care, last time I saw her she was leaving on the bus. This is Evan. Englishman. Always the English taking things. Is he your . . . Partner, she said, only partner, like you and Mum. Slapping my face with it, she knew.

I want to be back, I want to be there. With Noeline. I'll build a house for you one day, I said. It'll have a sunroom, in the sun. For you to lie. You can see the hills or the sea. What do you choose. Not the sea, she said, an orchard, Robert. You can pick an apple for me. Captain Roberto. Hold my hand. Don't cry, she said.

I never cry. Men don't cry. I'll smash, I'll smash anyone who. Blood in his mouth, in his ears, knew I'd hurt him bad, in his ears. Run. Shadows growing long and short, run along my shadow. Jump. Water, oil. Come up in the piles, cut my hands, mussels sharp as razors, out the other side, see them there, backs all, razor in his hand. Soft. Schveet. Water in my shoes. Easy. Don't run. Walk a mile. Walk two. He'll never. Geordie bastard, he said. Scouse louse, I said. Never had a country of your own.

Ship out. Shouldn't leave your own country ever, never leave. Give me, give me. Where do I go. Mangrove creeks. Give me Noeline, see her dive, yellow water, swimming in the treetops, floating in, soles of her feet so white I can't believe. Swim close, grab, she's like a possum on my back. Do you have a woman, do they have you. Bar harbour girl. Opotiki girl. Never knew her then, when I, in on the tide, load the cattle, sling under, dripping shit and water when one goes off the wharf, moo, like a fish we'd caught. Baby then Noly you were, sleeping in a cot in the town, girl on the wharf, barefoot, thumb in her mouth, was that you, saw you then. Cow like a big fish saying moo, took your thumb out, pointed, see, was that . . . Same day I saw. Drowned woman. Lying on the mudflats. Sack. No. Man. No. Woman. Teeth all bare. Crabs. Eaten off. Leave her, police will. Not on my deck, over. Warm sick in the tide. Fillings there, black teeth. Crabs run for their holes.

'Sorry, did I wake you?'

'Leave them.'

'There's a strong draught, Robert.'

'Leave.'

'There's people picking right here by the window.'

'Let them look.'

'You were dreaming again. Bad dreams?'

Hand on forehead. Cool. Woman. Don't let me cry.

'I'm scared of . . .'

'What?'

'Things getting in my mouth.'

'Like what?'

'Cockroaches.'

'There's no cockroaches here. We run a clean house.'

'I saw . . .'

'What?'

'Saw.'

'There's nothing here, Robert. You were having dreams. Alan's home now if you'd like to see him.'

'Yes.'

'Dad. Having a bit of a bad time, eh?'

'It's the pills. They make me . . .'

'What? Hallucinate a bit?'

'I keep on remembering when I was on the scows.'

'When was that? I never knew you were on scows.'

'Before the tugs. My father owned a scow. *Phyllis*. We did the creeks. Bar harbours. From the Hokianga right round to Opotiki.'

'What did you carry?'

'Coal. Timber. Cattle. Sheep. Everything.'

'The scows are gone now.'

'Gone a long time. Gone before the war.'

'Is that why you changed to tugs?'

'Went on merchant ships. You never knew that. See the world. 1924. But I came home. Nearest I got to Scotland, Liverpool. I was . . .'

'What?'

'Thirty-six when I married your mother. She was – half.'

'Eighteen?'

'Strong woman. She could beat me. In a fight. She was no girl. Did you . . .'

'What?'

'See David?'

'He wasn't there.'

'Did you . . .'

'What, Dad?'

'Find out about . . .'

'Dad, May's your daughter. You only have to look at her face.'

'I knew . . . she was . . .'

Didn't want her. Not a girl. Why couldn't that Judith look after. Woman's job. Put some shoes on her feet, I said. Give me some money then, she said. Twenty dollars. Sent a cheque. No more so don't ask. Your daughter doesn't live, she's gone. Thirteen years and she never looked at me one time. Look at me, I said. Lift her up, hand under her chin, look at me. Robert you're hurting her. Look at me. Am I your father. Take her away for God's sake. Wipe her nose. Rags. Blood. She can't come to me with that, ask at school, there's women teachers for, I need to get out of this, I want to be . . . Orchard's no good, apples no job for a man, I've got that girl, it's her job, I want to, running down to leeward, to the light, and rounding to and taking in the sails, that's for a man, up the rivers with the motor beating and Mr Macpherson there, hard hand, didn't see it coming, into the coal. I said, You hit me one more time Mr Macpherson I'll pick you up and throw you over the side. Settled it. Walked around me then, knew I could. His father too, Macpherson too, couldn't understand, thought he was joking, voice like that, och, aye, like he's cracking jokes all the time, only once, saw him once, Dunedin, and he's dead, but tells me, aye, Stevenson, just a wee laddie when I saw him in Kirkcaldy, father was an engineer, Thomas Stevenson, inspecting the harbour, and this wee laddie, like a wind would blow him away, face like a knife-edge and eyes like a Mexican or a Pole. Aye but the spirit in him, standing in the storm. And gives me, he gives, There's a Macpherson, that's a tale to beat them all. I don't read books, but Cluny Macpherson. Our name in a book.

Wasted it. Chose the wrong . . . cries all the time. He wants his mother. The older boy never cried, stood up, made a fist. You hit once more . . . Noeline's son. I built, I said I'll, one day, a sunroom, built this house. For . . . Housekeepers only. Need apply. There's a sunroom, Noly, with the sun. Yellow curtains. Apples outside. Slices thin as paper. You've got to eat.

Could have been her daughter. Except. Teeth all wrong. Plain jane. I want to cry for her. No one sees. No one must. I'll never cry. Never cried for Noeline. Never will. Held her hand. She said, They'll give you the job 'cause you're the best. She said. So how . . . Get out now. Do it. South. But I don't, how do I. Don't know what to do. They watch while I, laughing at. No one laughs, I'll smash . . . Kill myself here forty years. Drowning. Apples. The tourist buses stop. Best, they say. No one else gets it, for that girl.

Open up the branches, face looks out, pretty girls. I don't

mind, nothing to see, curtains make the sun go red, you swim underwater, light in water, see her frogkick, yellow skin, lies on her side, pearls from her mouth, hair bouncing, water-bouncing, one kick, two, she goes up. I follow. Follow, follow. Follow Noeline. Hand on shoulder, hand on breast, she turns and swims. I follow.

Curtains. Soldier. Closing. Leaves me in the water, yellow tide, now I breathe. Got to have air. First thing you learn, suck in air and you never stop, they must get tired, never stop, heart never, beats away, making time, you can give it rests but you can't stop, it's like the sea. I feel, I know I've got, all your life you don't know, you don't care, but now I know, it's like I've got it shored instead of tommed and it's starting to lift, cargo shifts, we're in trouble now, go down there you're smashed to bits, she'll roll, if there's one thing it's being trapped inside, thousands thousands of men have died that way and I can't stand . . . Don't think about, put unpleasant thoughts, think of Jesus, hand on my hair, my fingers in the cord of her apron as she stirs, don't be under my feet child, never wrote to her, wrote from Sydney, Dear mother, your son, never got, he tore it up that bastard, tore, I walk off the *Phyllis*, it's leaving home, so I'll leave and he can, old bastard, hard old bastard, she had to with her Bible be with him, No Mum I don't, not any more, how can anyone believe that stuff, it's like I stick a knife in her she holds her heart, like fenders, rubber fenders, her front, she's soft all round. Sink into her, Go to sleep, hand on my hair, Jesus loves you child . . .

'Who're you?'

'Quiet, old feller. I'm just sitting here.'

'Where's everyone?'

'Gone to bed.'

'What time is it?'

'After twelve. It's tomorrow.'

'The sun was shining. I can't . . .'

'What?'

'I can't be gone that long.'

'You had a good sleep, that's all. You slept like a baby.'

'That's too long.'

'Don't worry. Take it as it comes. What are you doing?'

'I need to have a piss.'

'We're not taking you out there any more. We're using a bottle.'

'No . . .'

'Yes. Don't worry, old feller, it's all the same to me. You know me.'

'Yes, I know.'

'Sit there. That's right. Now just let it go.'

Never thought I'd. In a bottle. Woman helping me. It doesn't matter. Nothing matters. How did I. Lucky, what I am. Here she's back, flushed it down. Round, she's soft, she's all . . . who is. I don't know, that girl.

'Shall I get in with you? A little while?'

'Yes.'

'Don't shift. I'll lie on the side. That nice?'

All of them. This one is the best. Noeline's girl.

A *death*

DAVID

HE THOUGHT it might be a note from Freda and he read it by the door as soon as the light was on. *Dear David*, it said. Not her. His eyes went to the bottom. *Alan (your brother)*. How'd he get here?

I called in to see you today but you weren't home. I'm staying with Dad in Ruby Bay. I'll phone you tonight and maybe we can meet tomorrow. I think we should talk. It's been a long time. All the best. Alan (your brother).

He sat down at the table and read it again. A page torn from a notebook, an arty-farty handwriting they didn't teach at school. He had no connection with it, could not see a brother who had grown into a man. David looked at his watch: five to twelve. If Alan had phoned the way he'd said he was shit out of luck. He pictured someone in a uniform dialling, a man at a desk, no one he knew. *All the best*. After thirty-five years, *all the best*. David laughed. You couldn't beat the cheek some people had. Thought he'd walk in and say, How have you been? After being gone for thirty-five years.

But I want to see the bastard, I want to see him. He's down here for the orchard, he's after the old man's property, that's what it is.

He read the note a third time, trying to make it say more. *We should talk*. Fucking oath we should, and get it worked out who gets what. He's oldest so he reckons maybe he can have it all. David poured a drink. He tried to work out how to look after his interests. If Alan put the skids under May's girl by himself it would leave him in control. The old man didn't like his children, no doubt about that, but if he had a favourite it was Alan, you could tell by how often he said lieutenant-colonel, even though he made it sound like office boy.

David sat drinking, turning things over. The old man had to die soon, he was ninety-one. Alan had chosen a good time to show up. Maybe he would give the old bugger a nudge, tip him over one of those cliffs out there. David laughed, but he was agitated, he could not keep still, it was no joke. His share, if he could get it, would be . . . say it was worth a million and say he got a third, he had to get a third at the worst . . . $333,000, say $350,000. He could get Freda back: she would come for that much. Freda liked money.

'Freda,' he said. She returned to his mind differently from the time when he had been certain of her, when she was at the centre, fixed in place. Now she moved, she hurt him, and he could not see her face: it flashed on and off like a light. He struggled to hold her still, and he grew angry; said, 'I'm not buying you, you bitch, you'll come for nothing.' He poured another whisky, draining the bottle, and when he had downed it opened a vodka warm from the cupboard. May had given it to Freda for Christmas, Polish muck. The first gulp took his breath away. Jet fuel, he thought, and he remembered drinking Bloody Marys with her in the Rat Trap Hotel before it was burned. They were driving home from Woods Inlet, where May had given Freda the plate that weighed a ton, with a fish on it like no fish that ever came out of the sea, and Evan Yates had turned green because he wanted money. The plate was a present for him and Freda getting married. He saw a spasm of alarm cross May's face when they told her. He stopped at the Rat Trap because of it, although Freda wanted to keep going. She asked to drive when they came out because he'd had too many. They argued in the carpark and he got her by the arm and shoved her in the car: showing him up in front of people, it made him mad. Halfway up the hill she said, 'Stop, Dave. I need a pee.'

'You should have had one there.'

'Well, I didn't. I'll go in the bushes.'

He stopped the car and she got out, but walked round to the driver's side instead of the trees. She rapped on the window and he opened it.

'Shift over, Dave. I'm driving.'

'No you're bloody not.'

'If you don't let me drive, everything's over. I'm not being smashed up by you or anyone else.'

'I can drive. I'm all right –'

'Kill yourself then. I'll hitch.' She walked away down the road. He saw the calves of her legs luminous in the dark.

'Freda,' he shouted, climbing out.

She ran. Her light shoes went pitpat on the seal. He knew she was running out of his life.

'Freda, stop. Come back. You can drive.'

Silence in the night.

'Freda.'

'What?' – distantly.

'Here's the keys. You can drive.'

She walked back out of the dark and stopped short of him. 'No funny stuff, Dave.'

'No, it's all right. I have had a bit too much. Here.' He was close, when she took the keys, to grabbing her arm and twisting it up her back – there was a moment when he would do it: throw her in the car, push her in the footwell, keep his boot on her.

She said, 'Don't you ever make me do this again.'

'No, I won't.' He did not know how he kept from hitting her. But watching her drive, God I nearly lost her, he thought. He turned away and wiped his eyes and she grinned at him.

'Vodka tears.'

'I'm not crying.'

'If you say so. Cheer up, Davey boy. We can be all right.'

She was so compliant then, in bed, doing what he wanted, that he believed he would always have her and she would always do what he said, no more arguing. He laid an arm across her waist and held her as she slept. This is the night I got her. She's my wife.

The vodka, straight, made his eyes fill with tears again. I'll end up a bloody woman, he thought, and he went to bed and slept heavily until dawn, when his bladder woke him. Back from the toilet, he could do no more than doze, suffering half-dreams that made him groan with anger and fright. He made a cup of tea and brought it to bed, where he sat and smoked. Brother, eh, he's no brother. The bastard might turn out useful though. Freda and the money he might get would not separate in his head and the man with no face, lieutenant-colonel, was a khaki presence, insubstantial at the back of things. Then a sentence from the note detached itself, making him sit higher and find a place for his cup on the bedside table. *Called in to see you*. How did he know where to call?

David got up and went to the kitchen. He found the note on the floor by the table leg and read it again. *Called in*. David had only been in the flat three weeks. May's girl and his father did not know the address. Freda was the only one who knew.

He's seen her, David thought. He became so certain of it that he almost went to the phone to demand from Alan where she was, but stopped in the doorway; grew cunning; thought it out. He grinned through the lather as he shaved. He was pleased at the way he had slowed himself down, and he felt a new solidity and weight, as if he had qualified and was licensed now. When he was showered and dressed he rang the orchard number. It wasn't half past seven yet: blow a bugle in the colonel's ear.

A voice said, 'Who's that?'

'I want to speak to Alan Macpherson,' he said.

'He's not out of bed yet. You know what time it is?'

'Some of us have got to work.' He liked that. 'Say it's his brother.'

'Oh, it's you. Hold on.'

He waited and in a moment a man's voice said, 'David?'

'Yeah. Was that May's girl?'

'Yes. Heather.'

'She's a beaut, isn't she? Likes to have your balls.'

There was a short silence while the brother, lieutenant-colonel, sorted himself out.

'David,' starting again, 'I came to see you.'

'I got your note. That's what I'm phoning about. I'm busy this morning so how about we meet this afternoon.'

'Yes, all right.'

'What say two thirty?'

'Yes, I can make that.'

'And you know where to find me?'

'I know.'

'What do you drive?'

'What?'

'What sort of car? It's the cop in me.'

'Ah. A Toyota. A Camry.'

'Plate number? So I'll know it's you.'

'It's – RN7267.'

'Thanks. I'll see you.'

He hung up. Got him on the back foot, he thought. I'll throttle Freda out of the bastard if I have to. But with any luck he'd get her easier than that. They should have taken me in the CIB. He felt so ready to go that he did some housework: shook the mats, did his washing, pegged it on the line. Soon he wouldn't have to do this sort of female stuff. Get Freda and talk to her, she was his again. And with money coming when the old man snuffed it he'd buy into a business, dealing in cars, that's what he knew. Things were going to be all right again.

Late in the morning he drove to Ruby Bay. Toyota, he thought. In the army all his life and he drives a Jap car. He bought a pie and a can of drink at the store and drove up the hill and along towards Tasman, passing the orchard but giving it no more than a glance. At the intersection with Marriages Road he turned back, passed the packhouse again, and pulled off the road, finding a place where the Silverado sat level. Up the slope two hundred metres away the roofs of the house and the packing shed rose above the trees. Pine trees stood beyond them – king pines, thick, bent-branched, that hadn't changed in all the years he'd known. He felt, although he could not see, the cliff that fell away to the road and the camping ground; and wondered if his track was still there, with the footholds carved in, and whether he would still be able to climb it. He took his binoculars from the glovebox and looked at the trees, at the house, the packing shed, the roof of the cottage the old man had built for pickers in 1961 or '2. Called it a cottage, the mean old prick, when all it was was a tin shed. May's boyfriend –

Jesus, boyfriend?, poxy hippy was more like it – had spent half a season there. They had sneaked away fucking up the back of the pines. He'd spied on them, could have hit the boyfriend's arse with a pine cone if he'd tried. He had known even then that she didn't like it, known that all she was was desperate.

'Poor bitch,' he said.

He swung the glasses to the orchard sign, but was at a narrow angle and could not read it. Ben Alder though, he had seen it go up in the same year that he'd left. It was from the book: the old man playing games. Cluny fucking Macpherson lived on Ben Alder. That should make the orchard mine, David thought.

He watched a girl up a ladder picking Red Delicious half a dozen rows back from the road, and wondered what she'd do if he yelled out. Don't you eat my apples, he could yell. No bra, Christ, and just a singlet. He sharpened the focus and saw her brown breast slide out each time she picked an apple. She was no girl though, she was a grandma, no good to him. He ate his pie and drank his can of juice, wanting a beer. Later he saw May's girl, fat Heather, march through the trees and grab two apples, one in each fist, from the picker's bag and hold them in her face and shout at her. He grinned with pleasure. He did not mind how long this went on. Then pictured the old man too, watching from his patio, drinking beer in the sun and looking like he'd go on for ever. Didn't like that. He wished that Alan would come out. He'd have to come soon if the plan was going to work.

A white car, a Camry, nosed out past the sign at a few minutes after one. David didn't need to read the plate but got the glasses on it as the car turned towards Ruby Bay, and got the driver too, sitting up, long-armed, well back from the wheel. No proper face yet: he saw him with a boy's face, then wiped it out for a blimpy colonel, even though he sat in a skinny way. He started the Silverado and followed down the hill. 'Okay,' he said, 'now lead me to my wife.' Alan had to be visiting somewhere. The drive to Nelson didn't take an hour and a half.

He followed several hundred metres back, letting cars pass him. The soldier up ahead didn't drive at much over 80 and on the straights through Appleby, David found it hard to stay back. He was used to travelling at 120 k, 130, and he couldn't believe in a grown man puttering along like some old dame out on a Sunday drive. He trailed a tourist bus up to the Camry's tail and kept close into Richmond, feeling as if a rod had extruded from their cars and joined in the middle and they were locked together, he and his brother, and Freda was in a blind street at the end of their journey and would not be able to get out. He did not know what he would do when he found her. That would look after itself.

They passed the meatworks, with its savoury smell. He liked it although it had the rotten edge – bad meat and ripped-out guts – that always had Freda winding her window up and saying it was enough to turn a person into a vegetarian. He didn't mind her bullshit, or her arty talk and stuck-up music and books from the library on tapestry, for God's sake, and astronomy, and monks in monasteries, and candle making, and female diseases, as long as she didn't hit it heavy when he was around. She could play her games in her own time. Call him a barbarian? The way she said it made it plain it was what she liked. She didn't mind a bit of rough – and he found the question back in his mind: where did she get it from before he came along? Not Prentiss, whose photo made him look like a nancyboy. And where was she getting it now? The Silverado leaped as his foot came down and he was only two metres back from the soldier's car. He felt the rod that linked them thicken and compress and he wanted to push harder, shunt the Camry forward and flip it on its side; but made himself fall back and felt their connection thin as his rage reduced. Easy, he told himself. Easy goes.

Alan took the inland road. David followed, three cars back. They passed the hospital and Nelson College and Alan made a right turn on the corner by the Girls' College and went along at grandma speed through the intersections to Collingwood Street. He turned right, went up the hill and pulled up in the shade of trees at the kerb. David stopped on the corner. He watched his brother get out of his car and fit a green cloth hat on his head. A big guy, David thought, as tall as me. He stood straight, which might have been the army, and didn't stoop even when he started up the steep part of the hill where the trolley derby used to start, just put his body on a forward slant. He went behind trees and David drove his wagon past the Camry and brought him into sight again, still climbing, past the fences and the letter boxes, towards the walking path that zig-zagged to the lookout on the summit.

'The bastard's having a walk,' David said. He watched with disbelief. Walking. Up the steepest hill in Nelson. With the heat at damn near thirty degrees. The guy must be some sort of crazy.

Alan climbed the stile and vanished into oak trees and came out in a moment on the elbowed path. David got out of his car, then reached back for his binoculars. Maybe they were meeting on top. Freda went for walks, she had even tried jogging once or twice. She could be up there waiting. He got the hilltop in view, the wooden bench with the donor's plaque fixed on the back. A few trees, a bit of sky. The bareness emptied him out and he knew it made no sense following Alan; then thought, But he knew, how did he know where I live, she's the only one.

He watched Alan walking back and forth on the bare hill. At the top he turned and faced the town and the boulder bank. That was why he had gone, to look at the view. David's anger came back. She had told him he was unfit, he was getting a pot, he should walk with her and not take his car, or go and play squash if that was what macho fellers did. You're going to seed, Davey boy. 'Bitch,' he said, and got in the Silverado. She was always there, never a moment when she wasn't there, telling him he wasn't good enough. Using his brother now, that fucking officer-type on top of the hill, to get at him.

'By God, he's going to tell me where you are.'

He waited until Alan started down, then he turned and drove down Collingwood Street. Parked where he could keep the Camry in sight. Waited until it passed, with the soldier at the wheel, sitting up, shoulders back, like some kid at school, the teacher's pet. He followed to his own street, then drove around the block and came in from the other end. Alan was inside the gate, closing it.

David pulled up, climbed out and slammed the door. He put on his good-mates grin. 'Alan, I just about missed you.' They shook hands across the gate, and David believed at once that he could take this guy, bend him, break him. Alan was taller, that was all, but thinner in his body and his arms – womanish in the way his shoulders sloped; and looked as if he got a lot of practice apologising. David broadened his smile.

'Come inside, you're sweating. We'll have a beer.' They went in. 'The kitchen okay?' Bared his teeth again. 'Near the beer.' He took two cans from the fridge and handed one to Alan, opened his own, said, 'Cheers,' drank, and saw that the guy wasn't used to drinking out of cans and wanted a glass. He sat down. 'Have a seat.' Face more like the old man's than he had. Dents in his temples, long nose, big red ears. Beads of sweat. David felt healthy, felt in charge.

'You been running or something?'

'I've been walking. I went up the Grampians to look at the view.'

'View?'

'I haven't seen it since I left. We used to run up there, the first fifteen, getting fit.'

'Yeah, me too. I played for them. I was a forward. What were you?'

'Fullback.'

'The fancy stuff, eh? Booting for touch. I liked to mix in there. You want to go in the bathroom and clean up?'

'No, I'm all right. You wouldn't have a glass would you?'

'Sure.' David got one. 'So how's the old man? I haven't been out there for a while.'

'He's sick.'

'Yeah?'

'Worse than sick. The doctor came this morning. I don't think he's got long, David. He's running down pretty fast.'

So that's why the bastard's here. He's in for his chop. 'What's wrong with him?'

'Congestive heart failure, the doctor says. It's just going to stop beating one day.'

'You got to die of something,' David said. 'At ninety-one.' He drank, and thought, Just go for it, this guy will fold up. 'So what's the story with the property?'

'What?'

'The orchard. Who gets it?'

The soldier pulled his head back like he'd smelled a fart. 'I haven't asked him that. That's not why I came.'

'Why did you come? It's not like you visit down here often.'

'He asked May to ring me. I came when I heard.'

'To see if your name was in the will?'

Alan drank a mouthful. He seemed pretty good at keeping control. 'No,' he said, and left it there although David waited.

'We've got to talk about this,' David said. 'That girl of May's has played the whole thing clever. If we don't watch out she'll get the lot.'

'She probably will. I don't mind. Nor does May, I think.'

'May wouldn't. Look, we're the sons, you and me. I'm not going to let some little tart from God knows where . . . I'll contest it.' He felt control slipping away, felt again the lurch to one side that brought an oily wave of nausea with it. It started with Freda and it all came back to her. He was on the point of leaning across the table and grabbing the soldier by his shirtfront, demanding to know where she was, but made an effort, held himself in check. 'You've seen May?'

'I went across.'

'She told you all about me, I'll bet.'

'No, not much. Just you and your wife are separated.'

'Freda's separated. I'm not.'

'Well' – the soldier shrugged – 'I didn't come to talk about that.'

'Why did you come?'

'Just to see you. Say hello.'

'All the best, eh, after thirty-five years? All we've got to talk about, you and me, is who gets the orchard. I'm the one who stuck by the old man. I been going out there the last ten years, before fat Heather turned up. I'm not going to sit still and see . . . Look, I don't mind you and May getting a share, and May can halve hers with the girl if she likes. But I'm having one third and the courts will back me up. If you and me work together it should be easy.'

'No,' the soldier said.

'Why, for Chrissake?'

'I don't want it.' He looked out the window to be finished with the topic, and David saw the back of his skull rounded like an apple. He felt how it would break with one good hit, and he remembered shooting with a friend from Police College, Stan something, in the hills out the back of Belmont – going after rabbits with .22s, and nothing was there, no rabbits in sight, and they were getting ratty with each other, and then he saw one across the gully, right by its hole, looking at them, and if they moved it would be gone. Stan was sitting on his haunches, lighting a smoke, he hadn't seen it. David, behind him, raised his rifle and the line of sight was under the curve at the back of Stan's skull, and David took it, made the shot, and saw Stan jumping, holding his neck where the bullet had nicked his hair, and saw the rabbit rolling, heard it scream . . . I took the shot and stuff him, David thought. The prick said he'd report me, careless use, but by Christ we came down with a rabbit, I had blood dripping on my boots.

'Are you all right?' the soldier was saying.

'How did you know where I lived?'

'Ah. May told me.'

David lifted his beer and rattled it. He drank the last mouthful, crushed the can in his fist and laid it on the table. A lie. He felt calm. Here was the lie. So he was right, the soldier knew where Freda was. He got another can from the fridge. 'Want one?'

'No thanks,' the soldier said. 'I think I'll go.'

'You just got here.'

'You don't seem to want me, David. So I'll be on my way. I'm not going to talk about Dad's property.'

'Don't then.' David opened his beer and drank. 'But I guess there's not much point in you staying. You and me wouldn't agree on much.'

'I don't think we would.'

'So piss off then. Tell the old man I'll be out.'

'What?'

'I'll come and see him. He's sick, isn't he? So I'll make a visit. Hold his hand.'

'You can't talk to him about a will.'

'Who says I can't?'

'He's not well enough.'

'Yeah? He's well enough for you. How do I know you haven't got the orchard all sewn up?'

'You don't believe me. I don't want it.'

'We'll see. I'll be out tomorrow. I suppose there's someone looking after him?'

'Yes. A nurse.' Alan picked his glass up from the table and emptied it. 'Tomorrow's all right. It's her day off.'

Freda, David thought, my God, it's her. He had an extra sense of her, he *knew*. The soldier had tried to hide her but had put her in his hands and what he did next was all laid down. I could sort this prick out now. I could go and get her. But he was confirmed in everything he chose, he was licensed again, and it did not matter, fast or slow. He would follow the soldier and see him and Freda together – find out what had been going on. She's out there and she can't get away.

'How long are you staying?' he said.

'I don't know. The end of the week.'

'You got a job to go back to?'

'Yes.'

'Wife and kids? All that?'

'No.'

'No wife? Couldn't you get one?'

'It's hard to keep track of you. You don't know where you're going,' the soldier said.

'I know all right. You'll see. Tell the old man I'll be out.'

'Tomorrow?'

'Like I said.'

'I'll get him ready. I'll see you then.'

'Sure, brother. Thanks for visiting, eh. All the best.'

The soldier left. There was no need to follow him, no hurry. David sat at the table and finished his beer. When he stood up he could smell himself and did not like it. He wanted to be clean for getting her. He went to the bathroom and showered and brushed his teeth, then laid out a clean shirt and socks. Clean underpants. Alan should have been the one who left his smell behind. He looked at himself in the wardrobe mirror and saw how thick his chest was, and his arms, he could break that soldier. His belly was starting to spread though and his cock looked shrunken, it looked old. He pulled on his underpants. It would be big enough soon enough, when he needed it.

He put on jeans and sneakers, threw a jacket in the car, and put on his baseball cap, which he had worn like a kid, back to front, to make her laugh. But he was through with clowning. It gave him sudden enormous enjoyment that he was coming for her and she did not know; that he was moving up the way someone's death moved up and stood behind and the person kept on as though she had for ever. He would reach out and put his hand on her.

Ninety ks an hour, with his window open and his elbow on the sill: he ambled along. Freda, you'll be all right, but you've got to learn a lesson, sorry, dear. He did not know what he would do with the soldier – break his arms, stamp on his throat? – trying to keep a man from his wife. David felt his body thicken up. 'I've got a right to this,' he said. Then he saw Alan, not where he was meant to be, back at the orchard, but good enough, behaving as though he had all day: walking to his car from the wine shop at Seifried's with a bottle in his hand. David understood at once – a bottle for Freda. He liked that. The bastard fancied her.

He turned into the road to Rabbit Island, made a U turn, pulled up off the shoulder and waited until the Camry went past. He let it get almost to the end of the straight before moving out and following. The rod connecting them was in place, elastic and unbreakable. He felt he could take his foot off the accelerator and he would be pulled along.

They went around the inlet and David let the soldier go from sight up the hill. He did not want to rush things but meant to give them time to get in position before he came. Drive past the orchard, turn back, come in slow. He read the sign, *Ben Alder Orchard*, and looked up the drive. And the bastard was there, the soldier was there, where he wasn't meant to be, standing by his car and looking back. David accelerated, watching in his mirror, and saw Alan lean out at the side of the road and stare after him, with his hand shading his face from the sun. Okay, okay, David thought, change the plan. Get where you can watch them; play it cool. Maybe he didn't see who it was.

He turned up Marriages Road and drove fast along the five-k loop through the hills; came out again in Ruby Bay. He had circled them; he had them cornered. He drove along the beach front and into the camping ground, where he parked facing inland, under trees by the bottom of the cliff. Now he was deep down and he could surface; come up and they would never know. He put on his jacket and strung his binoculars round his neck. Trees hid him as he climbed to the road. He stood well back in the trunks, his head on the level of the seal, and watched cars flash by; a bus; a loaded truck easing down in low gear from the packhouse. When the road was empty he crossed and pushed into the scrub at the foot of the big cliff. It was gorse and broom, which he broke through, and came to native growth and rested there. The cliff was less steep than he remembered. He could not find where his path had been, but it did not matter; he could go up in the tree trunks, they were steps, and the branches would hide him from the camp and the beach.

He climbed on an angle equalling the downward slope of the road – enjoyed the evenness of things, the way they worked out as if by rule. There were few large trees; most were no thicker than his arm. He put his foot, each time, in the crotch they made with the ground, and went up steadily. It was less a cliff here than a slope, and no risk of falling or being seen. He broke into a sweat and laboured in his breathing but was pleased that his body answered him. Resting was a weakness; he meant to reach the top without a break. The binoculars, banging on his chest, made moving awkward, so he zipped up his jacket to hold them tight. I've earned a smoke when I get to the top, he thought – but no, cancelled it: he would not have one, not until he had them in sight.

The slope became a cliff again as it reached higher. Scrub came down to meet the trees. David came to a bare place and had to lose height as he worked along. It seemed he might come out in a neighbouring orchard. But the thought of turning back filled him with rage: if he had to, he would go in by the gate and straight up the drive and get her in the house, get him too, one in each hand, and beat their fucking heads on the wall.

He stopped and squatted but it strained his thighs so he put his legs one on each side of a small tree and had a smoke. Sweat was running on his face, dripping from his nose. It fell on the cigarette and hissed. 'They'll pay,' he said. 'By Christ they'll pay.'

The tree was hurting him in his crotch. He ground out the cigarette on the trunk and pushed himself upright, looking for a way. Went a further step, and saw at once a path laid out for him. A slip had scooped a piece from the cliff edge, neat as a spoon, and he made his way across it, holding on to new-grown broom, and went back, more easily, on a higher angle, and pulled himself into the scrub on top, burrowed in and lay down on his stomach and was there. He was filled with elation: he was there. He pushed himself up and went on hands and knees, butting the foliage with his head, breaking through. It scratched his face. He did not mind. He broke out onto trampled bracken, with picked apple trees in front and pines on his right and a road of grass running between. It seemed to him he'd come into a world he had created with his climb. 'Now I'm the one who says how things will be.' His voice had a sound he had never heard before. Again he knew it did not matter how fast things happened or how slow.

He walked on the trampled grass beside the apple trees. This part of the orchard had been planted since he left. The pines though were the same, on their fist of land above the cliff. He went into them and passed through, crossing the flat place, darker now, where May and her boyfriend had fucked; looked back from the other side and saw her clenched-up face and his white bum, and laughed at them. He picked up a cone and threw it skidding across the needles, and went on. The main part of the orchard threw light into the pines; strips of it fell like planks painted in colours, rust and yellow and green. He sat down with his back to a trunk, several trees back, and lit a smoke. Then he unzipped his jacket, took out the binoculars and focused them on the house.

At once he saw her: Freda, his wife. She sat in a chair side-on to the window, sipping tea from a mug and listening to someone – the soldier, it had to be, out of sight. Her ponytail gave a flick as she shook her head. He did not like her in a ponytail; had told her to get it cut and styled properly. He smiled at it, not minding now that she built her betrayals up. Everything would be paid for in the end. He felt a hunger for betrayal; it was part of the new world he was in. He smoked and watched her; watched the soldier too as he walked into sight and stood at the window looking out. They went into the sunroom and talked down to someone in a bed. It must be the old man. David could not see him. He saw the pickers leave in their cars, saw Heather walk to the house, and the sun go down. He went to the back of the shed and had a drink of water from a tap. Back in the pines he smelled himself, heavy, sour. He did not mind, it was him.

In the dusk Freda walked out to the patio. The soldier followed. They looked at the sunset over the mountains. She put her hand lightly on his arm and rose on her toes and kissed his cheek. Up, down, like a ballet dancer. David knew that step and kiss, it meant I'll see you soon. He watched her go down the steps and walk in the drive; vanish; reappear; open the door of the pickers' cottage and go inside. A light went on, the door closed.

The soldier had watched too – had waited for the closing of the door. He touched his cheek; folded one of his ears and rubbed behind it. Then he went into the house.

David smoked another cigarette. He rehearsed how he would reach out and hold her. She liked that sort of thing, being locked inside. He would feel her ribs, elastic at first but brittle beyond that, and her heart beating under them. He knew how much he loved her when he felt her heart. But the more he loved her the more he knew she had to be punished. An idea was coming what the punishment would be. First he had to have the full betrayal.

The soldier came out of the house with his bottle of wine. He walked to the cottage and knocked on the door. She opened it. She had changed into a dress. She had taken out her ponytail and brushed her hair. David saw the gleam of an earring as it swung. The soldier followed her inside.

David sat waiting. He lay down for a while, then got up and walked to the cottage and stood outside. The curtain on the window was glowing with light. He heard the sound of plates and cutlery. Voices talked but made only a murmur, no words. David yawned. His smell had drifted on the air like smoke. He withdrew. He did not want them knowing him. Not yet. He went back past the packing shed into the pines and sat down by the tree – his tree. He smoked his last cigarette, cupping the red tip in his hands.

In the house the sunroom light went out. Heather arranged cushions in Freda's chair. She read the newspaper. Soon she went to the bathroom, then to the room where she must sleep. It was on the back side of the house, but light from her window spread into the trees and brought apples forward, curved like cheeks. He went down quietly, padding in the road, and picked one and brought it back and ate it in the pines. Her light went out.

David zipped his jacket tight. A breeze rustled the orchard and made the pine grove sigh. Far away, deep down, where he had come from, the sea made a whisper on the beach. He waited for the end of the betrayal but the cottage spread its green glow on the road. He stood up and pissed at the back of his tree, splashing the trunk, and smelled the chemicals of urine, sharp as knives, then picked up pine needles and cleaned his hands. No moisture, none in the ground. Pine trees sucked the soil dry like no other tree. A pick-axe would be needed to go deep.

He made a cushion for himself and sat down again, but was only there a moment when the cottage door opened and the soldier came out. He stood in a fuzzy glow and stretched, then became a shadow as the light went out. A second figure, Freda, closed the door. She walked in the drive with him, carrying what? David got out the binoculars but they were not night glasses and he could not see. Alan and Freda went from sight. He pointed the binoculars at the house, waiting for them. A little hum of expectation started in his throat. They were about to be revealed. He saw them cross the patio and the soldier open the sliding door. He went inside and flicked a switch and Freda was caught: Freda, coloured, in her dress, with bedding in her bare arms and her floral toilet bag on top.

'Freddie,' David whispered, 'you've done it now.' Again he felt the jolt, the sideways shift. It took him to a place he already knew.

He saw them in the room. The soldier pulled the curtains shut. The bathroom light went on, then a light in another room at the back of the house. David waited. He felt tears on his face and did not know for a moment what they were. He wiped them, cooled his cheeks with them.

One by one the lights went out. The house was dark, but was alive – had subtle movements in it and a pale luminosity in the roof. David stood up and dropped the glasses on his chest. He walked by the packing shed and along the drive past the cottage. He opened the gate, went out, shut it behind him, and walked under the sign and down the road, with the cliff on his right and the sea on his left. He found his car in the camping ground.

He drove to Nelson. The road had no corners and no hills. He was filled with a new bleak painful happiness. What he would do was laid out, each step like a new scene in a movie. He saw how it went ahead, moving fast and slow, but always at the same speed, to complete itself.

He saw the end.

ALAN

PRAYER WAS NOT demand, or bargaining, or coercion, nor was it invocation, either magical or spiritual. He experienced it in a smaller scale, as conversation, muted by his temperament, undemanding, friendly but not intimate, as though with someone in a chair set on an angle from his own, and conducted in the dark, so that one never saw who was there. No voice came in reply; only the silence of attention, which was His way of speaking, Alan knew.

Sometimes he asked, but more often he simply made suggestions. And now and then, when he prayed lying in bed at night, an exchange was made, an understanding reached, that for a moment he believed was sacramental. He had a sense of God in the world that rarely came to him in the day, when it was the idea of the Son, the one perfect man, His perfect love, that sustained him – and his knowledge that once He was here in that shape. He did not try to worry these two, these states of knowledge and of faith, together. In his life they looked after themselves, and wider than that he was not equipped to go – had no desire to go.

The word he most disliked was supplication. In his relationship with God supplication had no place, was not the thing at all. Perhaps it was pride that made him unwilling to beg. He would not bother God with requests for himself, but would deny self. He could not see that as prideful or sinful. It did not damage him, and damaged no one else. All he wanted was the ability to work in the narrow place where one was free to do better or do worse, and sufficient knowledge to make the choice. That was what he asked, that was enough. And happiness for others: he was foolish enough to ask for that – do more than suggest.

It had not brought him close to people, had not made him a worker. He stood off and could not speak to them, and could not repair the damage he had done. Self still had the larger part of his life and knocked his good intentions to one side; turned his faith into a private thing, kept behind doors. He saw how small and mean he was. The trip south brought it home to him.

'Lord,' he whispered, 'make me a better man. And let me help them now. Keep me from hurting them any more.' That was supplication. He would surrender, to that extent, his dislike of it.

He turned on to his side. The sofa bed that he and Freda had opened out was too short for him, so he lay diagonally, which upset the arrangement of springs and pressed a bar into his hip. He would do better lying on his back, but he had never been able to sleep that way. Did he want to sleep? Had he finished praying? Although he had kept at it longer than was usual, he had gained no sense of God tonight. The fault lay with him; too many things intruded, small worries, small desires, and took the simplicity away – that condition of being naked in one's mind that one had to reach before His attention was engaged.

A wind had risen outside and was causing a small persistent rattle in the door. He got up, making the springs twang, and found the newspaper on the arm of the easy chair. He tore a piece off, folded it, wedged it in a crack and stopped the rattle; was pleased with himself and felt that he would sleep now, but was no sooner back in bed than his father called out.

'Noeline,' he called.

Alan went to the sunroom door, which was propped open with a slipper, and looked in. The long windows made the room lighter than the lounge, and he made out his father's bed centred on the wall and his head dark on the pillow.

'Who's that?' the old man said.

'It's me. Alan.'

'What do you want?'

'Nothing. You were calling out. Can I get you anything?'

'What did I say?'

'Noeline. Her name.'

'She locked the door.'

'Shall I call Heather?'

'Help me out. I need the dunny.'

'No you don't, old feller,' Heather's voice said. She pushed by Alan and turned on the night light. The room became white, yellow, brown, and Heather, with her silver hair in a plait and a summer dressing gown open at the front and thick brown legs and bare feet, bare arms, pale eyes, snaggle teeth, was nightmarish in the sudden light. He wondered if he should trust her with his father.

'Close the door. I'll do this,' she said.

He closed it and went back to his bed. Their voices came, hers bossy, his perhaps distressed – Alan could not tell, could hear no words. He would ask about a night nurse tomorrow, surely it was time for that. And a new day nurse too. Freda had to leave. I might have to stay down here, Alan thought. He heard a glassy clunk as Heather put the bottle on the floor. Voices again as she arranged him. In a moment she came out and took the bottle to the toilet. She brought it back empty and stopped by Alan's bed.

'What are you in there for?'

'Freda's using my room.'

'Why?'

'She's nervous about David. I didn't want her down in the cottage alone.'

'This place is turning into a boarding house,' Heather said. She went to the sunroom door and stopped. 'I'm going in with him. I suppose you'll think that's wrong?'

'In with him?'

'In his bed. He likes it. You needn't look like that. Nothing happens. He just likes a woman in his bed.'

'All right,' Alan said.

She closed the door, the light went out, he heard the bed creak as she got in. The moment when it had seemed ugly was gone and he saw how pure it was – the woman giving her company to the old man. It would complicate itself, start him off in several directions, make him shiver, but for the moment he let himself be pleased. She put her body in beside Robert Macpherson's, and put herself in beside his self, and warmed him in two ways, and no one had the right to question or complain. She was strange and frightening, of another order, denser in her flesh, thicker in her bone, and emptied out of common perceptions. Perhaps she loved Robert Macpherson in a new way. Almost certainly she was a neuter.

He listened to the silence in their room, and the hissing and sighing, the agitation, in the orchard, and pictured the house like a boat on a sea, anchored, unmoving, while all around shiftings took place and pressures went on. Formless out there. A pattern inside, a grid like the ribs of a boat: different compacts, different needs. He felt the placements, points of consciousness in the house: Heather and Robert Macpherson in the sunroom, close together, Alan Macpherson in the lounge, and Freda in the bedroom, in his bed. Lying awake? He was sure of it. Saw himself move silently through the house and down the hall. He opened the door. Her eyes gleamed from the corner. She put the sheet aside, made room for him, held out her arms. He wanted her. She was a gift. He knew, even, that he would delight her; counted her happiness in the sum. But would not go. Tonight or any night. Would not go. His compact was with himself and God. He was on the point of throwing his blanket aside, putting his feet on the floor, putting out his hands for direction – but was unmoving. He would not go. The knowledge of it was like a stone.

If she came to him what would he do? If she came barefooted through the house, with naked arms? 'No,' he said, and heard the word, flat and ugly, slapping on the walls. I've got to stop this, he thought, I've got to go to sleep. Tried to convince himself that he was mistaken, that he had misread her messages and signs; they were friendliness, they were relaxation and ease with a man she felt safe with, her brother-in-law. Perhaps it was the practicalities of her trade, her care of his father – washing him, oiling him, which he had watched fascinated through the half open door – perhaps that; or sitting at lunch with her at the kitchen table, asking for the bread, the salt, sharing a teaspoon, and watching her sponge a spot of honey from her blouse, and hearing her soft, disgusted, 'Shit!' Two days in the house with her had moved it away from the mundane; and the very ordinariness of their exchanges had set up a tremor in the part of his mind signalling *woman*. So that, by this third night he had known . . . known what? That she would do? No, much more. Known that Freda had an identity, and that it might, if he took care and time, connect with his own.

That was at the centre of things. Lust was not the centre.

What had she known, or apprehended?

'You're so different from him,' she had said.

'How?'

'I thought, being a soldier, there'd be all this macho stuff, you know? But you're a cream puff.'

'I don't like the sound of that.'

'Oh, I think you're tough inside. I think what you say you'll do you'll do.'

There was nothing in that, and yet wasn't she saying, Say you'll come to me? There had been a boldness in her when she spoke, but insufficient time in her glance. It made her seem uncertain, and made him uncertain now. Had she drawn back? Had she made no invitation at all?

He was not sure that he even liked her. He was used to women with more charm. They used certain gestures, certain words, ritualised, that told him precisely how far things had progressed; and they had a delicacy that Freda lacked. It gave an exactness to things. He knew what they were saying and what they asked, and he could be sure that his reply was understood. Freda was like someone from the kitchen. She would blurt out what she wanted in the end. Had she felt their difference, is that what she meant . . .

'Oh I'm definitely not officer class.'

'Is that what you think I like?'

'Yes, I think you do. You like things formal.'

'No I don't.'

'Tell me then what sort of woman you like.'

He could not. She would be too different from Freda. But if he took another step . . .

This can't happen in three days, he thought.

What was the thing that told him he might love her? It was not the way she looked – the sharp prettiness, the rounded breasts and hips, too large it seemed for her light frame – or her voice that had a shifting timbre, up and down, in close connection somehow with her eyes. Not all that. Her sexiness, that he almost smelt, an emanation? No. He would, in time, prefer that toned down. He had become aware of – what? – a kind of morality in her, and things she would allow herself and things she would refuse?

But not that either, for a code was necessary, a code was heart and lungs – even though he would proceed differently himself.

It was a small thing she had done as they sat at the table in the cottage, with dinner finished and the wine bottle almost empty. He had reached out and poured the last of it into her glass, which she had smiled at and allowed. She put her fingers in her hair and took her earrings off.

'These things weigh me down,' she said, and laid them on the table.

With that she had invited him to love her. He said, yes, Freda, although not to her.

That would seem to mean that he might enter her bed. But he would not do that. Freda was his brother's wife. He pictured her again in his room, in the narrow bed, lying awake, waiting for him, although his own signal had been clear: he would not come. His neat unfolding of the sofa had made it plain. On this humid night she would sleep with only a sheet. Would she sleep naked? 'I'll use the sofa,' he had said. 'Of course,' she had replied, eyes and voice meek, and possibly amused. And here he lay, popping the springs, like a boy with a hard-on for a girl he could not have.

Think of something ugly, he ordered, but nothing came; he could think only of what she might allow. How had she managed to tell him that giving pleasure was the thing she most enjoyed, that her sense of right and wrong would not interfere? She had said, in so many words, that she was no longer David's wife. Said: 'I'm not married to him any more.' Repeated the lifting of her lip away from her teeth. 'That cancelled it.' He saw again where the tooth had chipped, like a chip from a plate.

'When was that?'

'The day I walked out. I went straight around to my lawyer and filed for a divorce. So I'm free. I don't have to wait until some fancy court says so, it's me that says.'

He did not agree. It was too easy. Time must pass. And the thing must be formalised and sealed. He would slide otherwise, lose his feet, and lose his sense of himself, he saw it plain – and saw, for a moment, Freda and Alan Macpherson, ugly and amorphous, locked together. He thought, I can love her but I can't love her yet. I've got to keep her from hurting herself. And at last he was able to lie still on the sofa bed and let his mind carry him somewhere else. Not into sleep: to his talk with David; to the place this man, his brother, had taken in his life. It was in the jungle, in Sarawak, that he had first known the unseen one who might kill. Then again in Vietnam. But not, in either of those times, in a closely personal way, even though bullets might come from the trees, or grenades explode and shells burst. The enemy had no darkness about him but would break out in noise when he came and bring a tearing sudden or agonising death. And that would be personal enough. A man's death belonged to him alone. But only when Phoebe came had he known the rest of it, fear of a different kind. And now, with David, was he taken back to face it again? Something was in the man, more than slaps and bluster and rage.

It was as if he touched me, Alan thought. It was as if he put his hand on me. The place itched now, although he could not say where it was; it moved about, sliding on him, sliding in his mind. Yet maybe David was only bloody-minded, and insult had moved him to this point, where he might be cunning and sudden at the same time. That was the feeling he gave – that he would move into place with care and explode from it. Ground skills. But who would he attack? Were snarls and punches all he had in mind? And what had alerted him, in the kitchen, sharpened him inside while blunting him in his words and the way he moved?

Then there was the car, the Silverado with dusty panels and bull bars shaped like a grin. One headlight was crossed with masking tape: St Andrew's cross. It had followed him not just home from Nelson but into it as well, part of the way. So David had set up some sort of game – more than a game – and invented rules, and had played out some of it already. I should be able to beat him at this, Alan thought. I've got to do an appreciation. But he did not know the enemy and that was a huge limiting factor. Who was David? What was he after? Alan had no way of measuring. Instinct told him Freda was in danger. But that might result from his own guilt – although he had nothing yet to be guilty about. His father and Heather were a more likely target. He felt that he was somehow chosen too, an enemy. David had reached out and folded him in – and had already folded himself in. Dangerous, Alan thought. He's dangerous.

Freda thought so too. She knew it from experience. But he thought it likely that David had moved on since that time and Freda would not know the true danger. Measuring courses, plotting options, Alan decided that he must get her out of the house not just tomorrow but permanently. Make her vanish. She had told him that she might go to Auckland or to Oz – telling him that if he wanted her he had to be quick. She had perhaps too much impatience; she needed more stillness, and a sense of proper movement, proper time. Don't think about her, he told himself. Just get her out. Think about her later. And stay around tomorrow. Watch David with Dad. It occurred to him too that he must try with his brother, help him somehow. He had not tried yet.

The Silverado followed him as he moved towards sleep. It mounted hills, appeared at far corners, entering each straight as he left. And sometimes it was close behind and day had turned to night. It glared from its crossed eye and towered, square, at the back of him. He slept, woke, dozed, woke, on the lumpy bed. There was threat in each fragment of dream. In the dawn he lay awake and went over everything again – Freda and himself, Freda and David, his father, Heather, May too, who must be told what was happening. He must get Freda out of the house today; and he must face David and find out what he was after.

Heather passed through the room back to her own bedroom. He heard her in the kitchen making her breakfast, making tea. Then he heard Freda, and the two of them talking – practicalities, no friendliness. Freda brought him a cup of tea. She wore short pyjamas, nothing else.

'Thanks,' he said. She looked her age – puffy round the eyes, dry-skinned, dry-haired – and he felt a movement in him of regret and tenderness for the life she had known: no quietness and no ease, and no love that had lasted. He would love her, he knew, but was not sure that she would love him.

'How did you sleep?'

'Off and on. How about you?'

'Lousy. This bed's got lumps.'

'I'm sorry.'

He had expected 'Poor you' or 'You should have got in with me.'

He smiled at her. 'It's not your fault.'

She went off to shower and he drank his tea, thinking how he would arrange the day. Design for battle, he thought. What we need is a political war: no one gets hurt.

He took his turn in the shower and sat down to breakfast opposite Freda. It's like being married, he thought, except that we haven't got anything to look back on. He wondered if she was thinking the same.

'Well,' she said, 'what do we do?'

'Today, you mean?'

'What did you think I meant?'

'Nothing.'

'I had a lousy night too, Alan.'

'Yes, I'm sorry. But I just want to talk about now. I want you to go up to Auckland. I'll give you my key. You can use my place. When I come we can work out all the rest of it.'

'The commanding officer speaks.'

'Freda, don't. He's coming today. That's what we've got to worry about.'

'Don't you think we're over-reacting? All he can do is slap me around some more.'

'You told me you'd never let that happen again.'

'No, I won't. I'll kill him first. Oh, I'm sorry, I'm being melodramatic. Bad nights do that to me. I'm not going to Auckland, though. I'll just go away for the day.'

'Where to?'

'I thought I might visit May. Then when he's gone I'll come back.'

'Freda, he'll come here all the time, with Dad sick. He wants his share of this place. You can't stay any longer.'

'I might stay with May.'

'He'll go there. He'll find you there. You don't see the danger, you know him too well. I met him for the first time yesterday and I could see it.'

She seemed to lose heart. She lost her sharpness too, and sighed. 'Auckland. All right. Not today though. Tomorrow.'

'I'll find a place for you until your divorce.'

'Yes?'

'Then we'll see.'

'Poor Alan.'

He did not know what that meant but saw that she did not mean to hurt him.

'You can take my car to May's place.'

'He might see it's missing. I'll get the bus.'

'Take Dad's then. Why not? It's sitting in the garage.'

'I'd have to ask Heather.'

'Ask her then. She can hardly say no.'

He cleared the table, rinsed the muesli bowls, while she went to talk to Heather in the shed.

'That's okay, it needs a run. As long as I put some petrol in, she says.' Freda grinned. 'I think she's coming over to read the gauge.'

'You should get going now.'

'I asked her if she had any message for her mother and she said, "What sort of message?" She really is something, that girl.'

'He's unpredictable. He could get here any time.'

'Don't be so anxious, Alan. Don't be so stern.'

'We'll have to get everything of yours into the cottage. And make sure it's locked.'

'All this to save me a black eye.'

'It's more than that. You know it's more.' He felt himself redden at the meaning she might take. 'I'll have to talk to Dad too. Make sure he doesn't blurt anything out.'

'Robert's not a blurter. I'd trust him with a secret. You'll have to get Heather down if he gets bad. You know about the pills?'

'I know.'

She took her pyjamas and sheet and toothbrush to the cottage while he warmed up the car.

'God, what's this?' Freda said, coming into the garage.

'It's an old Rover.'

'It looks like a tank. I bet it gobbles up the gas.'

'You'll have to fill up in Motueka. Get them to check the tyres and oil. The radiator's all right, I've looked at that, but I've put a bottle of water in the boot for the hill, just in case.'

'Do you always worry like this?'

'Have you got enough money?'

Freda laughed. Again she surprised him as she'd done the night before, on the patio, by rising on her toes and kissing his cheek. She got in the car and backed out of the garage.

'I'll phone from May's before I start back, see if he's gone.'

'Get May to phone. Goodbye.' Look after her, he thought. Take care of her.

The old black car trundled away. He closed the garage doors and went into the house. At nine o'clock he phoned a travel agency in Motueka and booked Freda a ticket on an early flight to Auckland. Later he sat with his father, who had his best times in the morning. David should see him now if he wanted to get some sense.

'You know David's coming?'

'That girl told me. What's he want?'

'Just to see you. He didn't know you were sick until yesterday.'

'He'll be coming to see what he can get.'

'If you say so. We don't want him knowing Freda's here.'

'Why not? She's his wife.'

'There'll be a fight. He beats her up. It's best if he doesn't know.'

'There's nothing wrong with a man wanting his wife back.' He made a sound Alan thought might be a laugh. 'He'll drag her out of here by her hair.'

'He might try.'

'Do you reckon you might stop him? You fancy her yourself? She's a nice little bundle of goods but you better watch out for her tongue.'

'Listen, Dad –'

'Where is she, anyway? Was that her taking my car?'

'Heather said she could. Heather's not going to say anything so there's no reason why you should. It'll only make trouble.'

The old man tired of it. 'I can keep my mouth shut. When's he coming, anyway? Why doesn't May come?'

'She will.'

'You did what I asked? You made sure?'

'She's your daughter, Dad. There's no doubt. And Heather's your granddaughter.' She deserves this place, he wanted to say, even if she's just someone who walked in off the street. 'Do you know where her mother is? Is she still alive?'

'That one? Fay's her name. She's dead.'

'How do you know?'

'Because some lawyer wrote me a letter. She put me down as next of kin.'

'How long ago?'

'It must be ten years. All my wives are dead. All my women. I've beat the lot.'

'Have you still got the letter?'

'No, I burned it. I wasn't having her call me next of kin. I kept the other one.'

'What one?'

'It's in the box. You can show her. That one's proof.'

'What of?'

'In there. Have a look. See for yourself.'

Alan went to a small wooden trunk against the wall. It was banded with brass and roughly painted grey on its carved lid. Inside was a concertina file bulging with papers. Not the will, Alan thought, that must be with the lawyer. He did not want to see it anyway.

'T for Taylor,' the old man said.

Alan took out a manila envelope with *Taylor, Fay* written on it in a big round hand. He slid a sheet of paper from inside and saw that the woman printed and even so could not keep her letters straight. *Dear Robert,* he read, *You will be surprized to hear from me. I am writing to ask you to help me in bad times for old time sake. I wish I hadn't run away but it is water under the bridge. This is not a begging letter it is just for old time sake. Whatever you think of me I tried my best. Anything you could send me would be much apreciated. I can't work any more and it is hard trying to live on my pension. If you remember my trouble with my legs, my legs are swelled, not so pretty now.*

Someone told me Clare turned out bad. I hope you do not blame me for Clare. I tried my best but I could always see that she was bad. Your old friend, Fay (Taylor)

Underneath, his father had scrawled: *Sent $20, 14/1/79. Cheque no. 2471.*

'Is Clare – is that May?'

'That's her. A bloody stupid name if you ask me.'

'And this is proof you sent her mother money?'

'If anyone came at me. It's like a receipt. I told her not to ask for any more.'

'Twenty dollars?'

'It's worth more than that today. That'd be worth a hundred dollars today.'

'And May hasn't seen this?'

'No reason to show her. You can show her if you like.'

'I'll keep it for a while.' He wanted to get out of the room and burn the letter quick. It made him think of Phoebe. He folded it and put it in his pocket, where it seemed to itch against his thigh. He must burn it so that May would never see.

Out on the patio, he watched the pickers at work. They thrust their sharp ladders like spears into the trees and appeared in the branches, snapping out long-armed, denuding the tops. Wasps spun sharply in the bottom spaces. A cider smell, the ferment of trodden apples, filled the air. He would enjoy this if it weren't for the letter in his pocket, and for his worry about Freda. He looked at the mountains and thought of her crossing them – a small woman in a big car, controlling it, he had no doubt, with ease, and smiling her derisive smile. In that square-built tank she might front up to David in his Silverado. It seemed to him that she would have the courage. Beyond a certain point, though, courage did not work. He had seen enough of it to know.

He was on the patio when David arrived. It was eleven o'clock. The Silverado came at no more than a walking pace past the cottage and down through the S-bend to the house. Alan went into his father's room. The old man was struggling back from sleep.

'He's here,' Alan said.

'Who?'

'David.'

'Who?'

'David. Your son.'

'Is it night?'

'No, it's still morning. You don't have to see him if you don't want to.'

'Where's that . . . where's Heather?'

'Shall I get her?'

'Yes. Get her.'

Alan went out. He heard Heather's voice. She must have run down from the shed. David said, 'It'll take more than you to stop me seeing my old man.'

'I'm not stopping you but I want to get him ready.'

They faced each other by the open door of the Silverado. David seemed easy. He was grinning. Heather, panting, head scarf in her hand, was like a schoolgirl.

'Heather, he's asking for you,' Alan said.

She ran up the steps and crossed the patio. 'Don't you let him in till I say.' She vanished inside.

David grinned at him. 'Gidday, chief.' He reached back into his car and brought out a paper bag. He came up the steps in a slowed-down walk. 'I brought a few grapes.'

'Grapes?'

'He's sick, isn't he?'

'You'll have to wait till Heather's got him ready.'

'Have to, eh? She's boss, eh? Well, I'm not in a hurry.' He was wearing a white T-shirt with a scorch mark shaped like an iron high on one shoulder. The red of his cheeks was like a disease.

'What are they picking?'

'Delicious.'

'Good crop?'

'I think so.'

David winked, heavy-lidded. 'We've got to know these things. I might ask to see the books.'

'You've got no chance. She's manager, on a salary. She's in charge.'

'You've given up, eh? Suit yourself.' He propped himself against the iron rail. 'Well, it's nice sitting here in the sun. Have a grape.'

Alan could not work out what was happening. David was acting a role, he was sure of it, yet he could not see what it was. He was cheerful, aggressive, insulting by turns, and none was real.

Heather appeared in the open door. 'All right,' she said. 'You can have a quarter of an hour.'

'You're the doctor. Why didn't you tell me he was sick? You told this joker.'

'Robert sent for him. It was Robert's choice.'

'Sent for him but not for me?'

'I'm not here to argue,' Heather said. 'Do you want to go in?'

'Sure I do. I brought some grapes.'

'He can't eat grapes.'

'Okay, give them to his nurse or something. Where do I go?'

'In there. He's had a pill so you'd better be quick. He's getting dopey.'

David winked at Alan again. 'He always was dopey. She wouldn't know.' He went inside.

'You watch him,' Heather said.

'He won't hurt Dad. It's Freda he's after.'

Heather looked around for a place to put the grapes, then

set the bag down by the rail. 'I've got to go back to work. If he isn't gone in half an hour let me know.'

'He's got a right to see him, you know.'

Heather, halfway down the steps, rounded on him. 'No one's got a right. Unless I say.' She went on, and in the yard broke into a heavy trot and vanished up the road.

Alan looked across the lounge at the sunroom door standing ajar. He wondered if David would take his chance to go through the trunk, and was glad he had taken Fay Taylor's letter. There was no sound from the room, but a part of David's back came into view as he sat down in the bedside chair. Alan moved across to the rail. After a moment he sat on the top step and watched the pickers filling their bags then loosing streams of apples into wooden bins for the tractor to pick up. He went down the steps and circled David's Silverado. It was dusty – months of dust. *Feelth* someone had written on the rear window. It was like a farm vehicle: fans drawn by the wipers in the windshield dust, tools in the back. It seemed made for some brutal purpose, some mounting or breaking. He stepped away from it and saw David on the patio, watching him. I've seen men like that, he thought, ready to kill.

'What are you sliming round for?' David said.

'Nothing.'

'Why don't you piss off, then? Do some fucking manoeuvres. Just don't push me.'

It's time I stopped him, Alan thought. But David grinned at him suddenly. 'Brother,' he said, and went inside.

Alan stood undecided. Okay, he thought, I'll give him ten minutes. Then I'll tell him to clear out. He went into the trees and walked towards the back of the orchard, wanting to keep away from Heather. He circled back through Cox's Orange trees. Tomorrow he was getting Freda out – tomorrow morning. But would she ever be free? David would always follow. What does that leave, he thought, Phoebe's way? It struck him like a blow in his chest, almost doubled him up. His heart made an alarmed beating. 'No,' he said, and turned towards the pines, walked in them, felt their crookedness and their green weight. The tractor roared far off, like a beast. A car door slammed with the sound of a gunshot. He stepped round trunks that blocked his way. Dead matches and cigarette butts made a little pyramid in the needles. He knew they were David's but the knowledge had no significance, everything was far away and thinned.

He reached the sunlight. Over the shed, in the trees, he saw David rise on to the patio and stand with his back to him, looking at the mountains. He stretched his arms above his head and worked his shoulders. Then he went into the house.

'God help me,' Alan said. 'Help me, please.'

He went down from the pine trees, passed the shed and struck out through the Golden Delicious to the yard. Everything was changed; it was as though a sound had been deleted, wind or sea, or a colour taken from the spectrum. He went up the steps and into the sitting room. David was sprawled in an armchair, smoking.

'Where'd you get to, bro? I been looking for you.'

'Why? What's happened?'

'He went to sleep. Hey, you think I put a pillow over his face?'

'Did you talk to him?'

'I asked him how he was. He said fine. Well –' he stood up – 'gotta go. I'll see you, colonel. Keep me posted, eh. I don't want to miss the funeral.'

Something's changed, Alan thought. He's taken a step. We've both taken one. He followed David out and watched him get in his car. David rolled the window down. 'You look worried, colonel. You got something you want to say?'

'Was that you smoking up there in the pines?'

David stubbed his cigarette out on the car door. He flicked the butt at the base of the steps. 'Not me, mate. You got the wrong man. Enjoy the grapes.' He winked at Alan and drove away.

He's in control, Alan thought. He knows something I don't know. Again it came to him that David was ready to kill. Cheerfulness was sometimes a part of it. He had the still excitement and the single gaze, even when he stood and lurched, slewing his eyes here and there. Men who were ready could not hide it. You used them then or you sent them back down the line. All I can do is watch and be ready too, he thought. He was close to something he could neither touch nor understand.

At lunchtime, when Heather came to the house, he drove to Motueka and put petrol in the car, checked the oil and water and the tyres. He wanted to be ready to take Freda to her plane in the morning. Then he went to the travel agency and picked up her ticket.

May did not ring until close to five o'clock. 'Alan, has he been? Has he gone?' He told her yes and she called Freda to the phone.

'Did he ask about me?'

'No, it's all right. He sat with Dad a while and went away. You can come home.' 'Home' was on the table now, for them to contemplate.

She said, 'Why don't we eat out? In Motueka? There's a restaurant called Pete's Place. It's not as bad as it sounds. Will you make a booking?'

He agreed. It was best that she spend as much time as she could away from the orchard. The smoker in the pine trees worried him, although he saw now that it could have been a picker sneaking off.

He told Heather he was going out and that Freda was leaving in the morning. 'You'll have to get a new day nurse. You should get a night nurse too.'

'Don't tell me what to do. How long are you staying?'

'As long as he wants me.'

He met Freda at the restaurant at seven thirty – and she had altered. She had turned her hardness round to show a softness on the back; and seemed to be saying that she liked him how he was. He wondered if it meant that she and May had talked about him. He showed her Fay Taylor's letter.

'You can't let May see this,' she said.

'No, I'm going to burn it.'

'Let's do it now.'

They moved to a table on the smokers' side and burned the letter in an ashtray. A waitress ran up with a jug and splashed the flames, sending wet ash across the cloth. They moved again, chastened by her scolding, and ate their meal quietly at a back table. Over coffee Freda said, 'May told me you were religious.'

'Yes. Does it bother you?'

'It's interesting. I've never known a man who was religious before. I mean, you go to church and drink the wine and all that?'

'Yes. I'll be going tomorrow after I put you on the plane.' He gave her the ticket and for a moment her sharpness came back.

'I'm paying you for this. I don't want to be kept.'

'I've never "kept" a woman in my life. Tell me how you met David. How did someone like you . . .'

'Do we have to talk about him?'

'I just want to fill him in a bit. There must be more . . .'

'There is. He can be charming. What a word! I mean' – she shrugged – 'he pays attention, does little things, like you with doors, but not that.' She looked at him sideways, made a deprecating face. 'Sexy things, you know, that point to bed and just, well, make you feel good. Made me feel good. I can be excited by a man. That's been my downfall. He doesn't have to have much up top.' She grinned. 'That's bad too. But David wasn't always a thug. It's just when things don't go his way that he gets like that.' She drank the last of her coffee and signalled with her cup to the waitress for more. 'That's enough about him. Tell me about you.'

'There's not much to tell.'

'I think maybe a woman did something bad to you.'

'Something bad happened.'

'A woman you loved?'

'Yes, I loved her. I still see her every time. With every woman I'm getting on all right with she comes and stands in the way.' He saw that he would tell her about Phoebe and that she would not wear Phoebe's face.

'Do you mean you can't love anyone else?'

He shook his head. 'She doesn't spoil it that way. I don't love her any more.'

'What is it, Alan?'

'I've never told anyone.'

'Tell me. Did it happen when you were in the army?'

'No, later. After the army. She was younger than me. I was forty-six. She was thirty.'

'And married to someone else, I'll bet.'

'Yes. She was married to a man who owned a chain of sports stores.'

He told her about Phoebe – how they met. The firm he had found work with kept her husband's books. He went sailing with them out of Westhaven, on their launch, and he and Phoebe became lovers after the second trip. Two or three evenings a week she came to his flat and they had the sort of non-stop sex he had only read about. He was as virile as a boy. He could not tell Freda this – could not say words to her he had used with Phoebe, although he knew Freda would not mind. Nor could he explain his love – could not separate the carnal from the non-carnal parts. He no longer knew whether Phoebe had loved him and he could only say to Freda that her excitement had seemed to match his own. It went on for a month in a kind of frenzy of tenderness and invention, and he began to wait for the next part of it, the settling down and calmness that would reveal what they must know of each other beyond this. He saw he would not have her until they moved there.

He told her that he wanted her to divorce her husband and marry him. It turned her silent. She was a woman who verbalised everything. It was for him, a quiet man, part of her fascination. She asked him not to talk about it yet, and in their next two meetings, though she spoke – loved to talk herself and him through their love-making – he heard a whisper in her, another voice, as she held a conversation with herself. He could not make out what she said, and wondered if he was being tried, assessed, for the role he had asked her to let him play. It disturbed him, and he told her that they must always be out in the open with each other.

They lay still, side by side, fingers twined after making love. She said, 'He's a rich man. I can't let all that money go.' 'Money,' he said. He picked the word up, handled it like a piece of machinery that would not fit. 'I've got enough. We won't be short.'

'Alan,' she said, 'you don't know money. I know it. I've

learned all about it.' She kissed his cheek. 'Be quiet, love.' He was quiet. 'I've been thinking,' she said. 'Yes?' 'You've been a soldier. You must be able to do it. You must know ways.' She looked at him quickly, but his stillness gave nothing away. He was stunned. His heart lay stunned like a fish. She said, 'It could happen out on the boat. He could fall over the side. Alan? Alan? It wouldn't be hard to hold him under.'

'She wanted you to kill him?' Freda said.

'Alan, listen. You could jump in and pretend to rescue him but what you'd do is hold him under and I'd turn the boat round and come back for you, but by that time he'd be dead. He's small, Alan. He's not big like you. We could do it.'

He knew that when he looked at her she would be ugly. He looked at her. His heart gave a flap and beat again. But now he was in a wrong element. He smelled their love-making, sour, corrupt, and smelled her breath. He looked into her eyes. His own eyes were wrung and squeezed and dry. She said, 'What's wrong?' He said, 'You want to murder him?' She put her hand on his chest and pushed herself up, away from him; looked at him sideways, said, 'I've done it wrong, haven't I?' Said, 'You're not the man I thought you would be, Alan.'

He told her to get up and get dressed. She fizzed and spat. He told her to go away and not come back; and said that if her husband met with any accident he would go to the police. She laughed at him. She broke things. She left the plug in the handbasin and flooded his bathroom. Then she went away. She did not become beautiful as she left but remained ugly. She was, for all that, the most beautiful woman he had known; and she had not stopped walking in, walking into his head, wearing both her faces, and striking him again so that he lay stunned.

'I got out of that flat,' Alan told Freda. 'And I changed my job as soon as I could. But I haven't been able to keep her out.'

'Do you think we're all like that?' she said.

'More or less. Not just women. People.'

'And that's why you're religious?'

'I suppose it is.'

'It makes me shiver.'

'It should.'

'No, you make me shiver. We're not like that.'

'Freda.' He took her hands over the table, held them a moment, let them go. 'When David came today I went out into the trees and I found myself thinking, I could kill him, that's what I'll do. I could keep him away from you by killing him.'

'But you won't, will you?'

'I just felt how easy it would be. Then you and me . . . That's what I thought.'

'But you won't. She would have. Phoebe. And for money.' She took his hand. 'Alan. You've had a hard time, I can see. I can see how you make sense of it all, with God and stuff. But to me you're just a man I like. I'll start from there. I'll take the rest of it as it comes.'

'I make you shiver. You said it.'

'Not when I hold your hand. You've seen things I haven't seen. But you've got, look, five fingers just like me.' She squeezed them. 'Now let's go.'

He followed the black car back to the orchard. She closed the garage and climbed to the patio. 'I'm sleeping in the cottage tonight. No, don't argue. I want to do it your way.'

'Freda –'

'If we're in the same house I'll climb into bed with you. I can't help myself.'

'I'll sleep in the cottage.'

'Ha. All right. I'll let you. Then we'll be safe.'

'Are you going to bed now?'

'We've got an early start. And I don't want to be with you any more today. I want to think.'

Heather was watching television in the lounge. She told them that she had rung round and hired a nurse. Alan fetched his toilet gear from the bathroom and found his pyjamas under a cushion on the sofa. Freda came outside with him. She did her trick of rising on her toes but this time kissed him on the mouth.

'There,' she said, 'that's a start.'

He turned in the drive and saw her standing in the lighted doorway. She raised her hand, then went inside. He walked to the cottage and made a bed on one of the bunks and lay in the dark. The mattress smelled of mouse, and gorse made glassy squeaks on the window pane. Phoebe approached with her dreadful step. He turned her away. Freda took her place. Safe, she had said. A start, she said. The empty wine bottle from their dinner the night before gleamed on the sill above the bench.

After a short time he went to sleep.

MAY

SHE MADE a dozen sketches for tile paintings and showed them to Evan. He liked those with flax bushes in the foreground and water behind but paused at the sketch of the woman in her dinghy. 'Are you sure about this one?'

'That was the first. That's what gave me the idea. I'm not going to stop because of the boat.'

'We'll get a new one. I want to give him time to calm down.'

'He never will,' May said.

'Junior and me go back a long way. He was the first bloke I knew in New Zealand. I was concreting paths with him a week after I got here. He taught me a lot.'

'Not how to pot, though. You taught yourself that.'

'Yeah. Poor old Junior and his pots. Hey, do some of the river. You and me in the river.'

'These are for family consumption.' Then she corrected herself: No they're not. I don't want to do just pretty pictures. Why not Evan rising from the water, with dripping beard and hairy belly and thick penis and thick legs? A river god. The Aorere seemed to ask for one and Evan was the perfect model, pre-Hellenic. He was ugly and close to primal things. Yet he was man too. He did all the man things so well.

She turned from him as she always did when surprised to excess in this way. But a hum of expectation had begun in her. She would paint him. It was time.

She spent the morning making further sketches, and kept him out, although he was an unseen presence behind the waterfall and in the waves and, always, standing in the river. How should I colour him? He would require a teaky red, and other times be pale, with a darkness where his organs would be. She coloured the sketches, bright colours, icon bright, then wondered if Evan was a shadow in the sea. She took a sheet of paper and sketched him deep down, half man half fish, swimming fast with arms at his sides and face out-thrust and his beard pointing ahead. She liked it and laughed at it, but tore it out and put it in the back of the pad: Evan as taniwha. She chose the best of the coloured sketches and took them to him in the pottery.

'I thought we'd start with these.'

'Let's see. These are good, May.'

'I know they're good.'

'These'll sell. You know how to get the colours right.'

'I'm good with colour. How should we mount them?'

'We'll put a frame around them. Elm. We'll go for quality. Leave that to me.' He grinned at her and hugged her, thick-armed, keeping his clay-stained hands away from her smock. 'It's going to be a good winter, May. Just you and me.'

'I want to do some painting too. My own stuff.'

'Sure. We can sell them to your brother.'

May smiled. She did not think Alan, or anyone else, would want to buy the paintings she would do.

Later, as she was making lunch, she saw an old Rover 90 drive into the yard and angle into a parking place by the trees: her father's car. Impossible, she thought, he's far too ill. Then Freda got out and waved to her, and even though May did not want outsiders today, she said, 'Thank God.' She went out and hugged and kissed her friend.

'What do you think of my car?' Freda cried.

'How did you get that out of him?'

'I went to Heather. It's marvellous to drive, May. It rolls, it goes like treacle. Do you think he'd leave it to me in his will?'

'You'd better ask. How is he?'

'The same. No, worse. He'll always get just a little bit worse, every day.'

'Until he dies?'

'Until he dies. He's not suffering. He's fairly peaceful. He's nicer now than he's ever been.'

'That wouldn't take much. Shouldn't you be back there nursing him?'

'Alan's looking after him today. David's coming. That's why I had to get out.' She went round the car and took some paper bags from the passenger seat. 'Stuff for lunch. From Takaka. It's lovely here, May. I'd forgotten. I could live here. I went and had a look at Wainui Inlet. And the Pupu Springs. All that clean water. I wanted to take my clothes off and dive in.'

'You'd freeze,' May said. She took Freda inside and began to be pleased even more. All the years of Freda, the kindnesses and arguments and chatter and deep talk, had built in her a feeling close to love, and she was never able to turn it aside for long. 'How are you?' she said. 'I worry about you.'

Before Freda could answer Evan came in. Their liking had never advanced far. In Evan's opinion Freda did not have a great deal to her, she had a mind that hopped like a flea, and he would not accept May's judgement that Freda did not have enough time, was driven by an urgency that made her quick and eager and impatient. Urgency, Evan said, what does that mean? May could not explain; her formulations stayed imprecise – that Freda had to know, and know closely, and enjoy, that she had a hunger interfering with good sense . . . and Evan replied that he agreed, she had a hunger all right, for men. He was coarser than she liked about Freda. As for Freda's feelings about him – again May could not formulate; all she could say was that Evan did not work for her friend. And there was something in Freda that was shallow: she asked for good looks in a man, a Hollywood face. Am I fair in that?, May wondered. It was not at the very top of Freda's list, but was surely close. David had first got her attention with his John Wayne assessing look. But hadn't there been some desperation too in her lunge at him?

She listened to Freda talking, bright and fast, covering her indifference to Evan, and thought, She's a clever woman and she tries. She's generous. If she hadn't picked me up I might have died. She observed Freda's false sparkle and became aware of something deep and quiet at the back of it, an excitement that lay still and put a weight in her that May had not felt before. I know what's happened, she told herself. She would not speak of it until Evan had gone. Then she said: 'How are you getting on with Alan?'

'Yes, your brother,' Freda said. 'He's nice isn't he?'

'Nice?'

'Well, interesting. He showed me the painting he bought from you.'

'I wanted to give it to him.'

'Why should you? Painting's your job.'

'Yes, but finding a new brother – I thought it should be marked with a gift. I'm going to do some tile paintings. I'll give him one of those.'

'He's happy with the Wharariki one. It's beautiful, May. He's wrapped it up again, though; he's saving it for Auckland. He's funny, don't you think? I mean, everything has got to be a little ceremony.' She took out a cigarette and put it in her mouth, then jerked it out. 'I forgot, I'm giving up. Throw these things away, will you? Put them in the rubbish.'

May took the packet. 'What does this make? Four times? Five?'

'I've lost count. But it's real this time. David was the one who got me started again. You couldn't live with him and not smoke.'

'So who are you stopping for?'

'Myself.'

'Why don't I believe that?'

Freda laughed. She reached into her bag. 'Damn, you've got them. I'm going to do it hard this time. Have you got any gum?'

'I've got some barley sugars.'

'No. I guess I'll survive.'

'Who is it, Freda? My other brother?'

Freda laughed again. 'You know me. I'm a pushover.' Underneath her bantering she waited to be serious.

'Stop joking,' May said. 'Tell me what happened.'

'Nothing happened. That's the funny part. All we've done is have a few talks and a meal. I gave him dinner in the cottage last night. But I can tell he likes me. God, I shouldn't talk like this, I'm superstitious.'

'Superstition is something new,' May said. 'You spilled it

all to me when you met David. You wouldn't stop.'

'This is different, May. It is different.'

'I'm not arguing. But how long have you had? Three days?'

'Four. But you know how it is when you meet a man; you get the feeling, This one will do. God, doesn't that sound awful, like buying a bottle of wine at the supermarket. What I mean, it hasn't really happened before. With David I had to close a part of myself down. I put it aside for the duration. Alan, though, it's . . .'

'A sense of rightness?'

'Yes.'

'It's recognition?'

'Yes.'

'And love?'

'You're laughing. I don't want to talk about it, May. What I want is get him into bed. But he won't. You don't know how different we are.'

'I think I do.' She had a sudden picture of Alan and Freda striding on different paths towards a corner, like two people in a cartoon; but they stopped and would not collide, each sensing the other out of sight; then he, then she, reached around and felt the other's face, and would explore – would they? – then take hands and pull each other into sight.

'You know he's religious?'

'I didn't know that. I know he doesn't like it when I swear.' She grinned nervously. 'Or smoke. You mean he goes to church and all that stuff? I should have guessed.'

'Does it make you like him less?'

'I don't think so. It makes him – interesting. God, I'll have to be careful.'

'For starters, Freda, do you believe in God?'

'I don't know. Yes, I do. I think I do.'

May laughed. 'It's going to be quite a romance.'

'You don't, do you?'

'No, I don't. I think it's loony. I was hoping Alan would grow out of it.'

Freda's cheeks mottled, red and white. 'That's a stupid thing to say.'

'Is it?'

'How do you know what his life's been like? How do you know he doesn't *know*?'

'Faith, you mean? Let's not argue, Freda. But I wouldn't go pretending anything.'

'I won't pretend. I've never pretended in my life.'

'Okay. Calm down. What happens next? What are you and Alan going to do?'

Freda reached again for a cigarette. 'Bugger,' she said.

'You'll have to stop saying that.'

'I might and I might not. Have you seen him? All this standing up when a woman comes in, and opening doors; that's got to stop.'

May laughed.

'Maybe it was the army,' Freda said.

'He certainly never got it from Dad. Don't you think it's nice?'

'It could get on your nerves.'

'So, the great romance is over.'

'Oh, shut up, May. Alan and I are just getting started. So keep quiet. And give me my smokes.'

May cleared away the lunch dishes. Later they walked up to the tank and sat on the grass looking over the inlet.

'I'm not sure it's really going to happen. But I'm going to give it my best shot,' Freda said.

'How does he feel about . . . his brother's wife?'

'Not very good. It has to go slow' – she sighed – 'so goddam slow. I suppose it might be good for me.'

'I don't think it will do you any harm. How many men have you been serious about?'

'In my life? A dozen. Two dozen.'

'And every time you've just jumped in?'

'And made a mess. Even poor old Prentiss was a mess. It might be good to take things slow. I shouldn't have talked about this, May. I made up my mind I wouldn't, driving over. I might have spoiled it.'

'No, you haven't.'

May lay back on the grass and closed her eyes. She was

happy. She believed Alan and Freda might have a chance. Chance, she thought, that's how it starts, accidentally. But hard work comes after that. Freda might be ready to do it for once: make concessions, even make some changes in herself. It was possible. You moulded a bit, taste or prejudice or preference, pushed in your thumb, and it was like rubber and sprang back into place when the pressure came off, but after a time, if you kept on, it turned to clay. It might work for Freda because she was good. Oh, selfish, excitable, demanding, quick-tempered, but good for all that, and intelligent too. She liked before she disliked. She liked herself – essential that. She understood weakness (especially, although later on, her own), and she was not frightened of loving. May did not know Alan well enough to decide whether he had virtues equalling those, but hadn't she sensed in him, in spite of his hang-ups, a preference for yes over no? That was promising. She was glad this thing had started. What a pity David prowled around the edges of it.

May sat up. She looked at Freda, who had lain down too. Her eyes were closed and she had a smile on her face – a cream-licking smile. May was reluctant to spoil her pleasure. She gazed over the inlet – glossy water, still tide – and the red roofs and the sea. Pieces of the spit showed, ill-defined. A barge, low in the water, moved along to Takaka behind a white launch. Overhead, almost beyond sight, a silver aeroplane drew a vapour trail from north to south. Was it true that jungle tribes, newly Christian, took these things for the finger of God? She did not think that God, if he existed, would point to places on the map. Up or down he'd point, in encouragement or warning. He'd point his finger into head or heart, the way he had, presumably, with Alan. She looked at Freda again and saw her frown.

'Where does David fit in?' May said.

'Yes,' Freda opened her eyes, 'I was thinking about him.'

'Has he caught on about you and Alan?'

'Shit, no. Do you think I'd still be in one piece?'

'And he still doesn't know where you are?'

'Not unless somebody's told him. He followed Alan home

yesterday, but that's because he'd just found out Robert was sick. He's worried about what he's going to get. His inheritance. That's why he's there today.'

'Why would he follow Alan?'

'I don't know. Because it's his style. He plays games. I don't want to be an expert on him. Anyway . . .'

'Yes? Anyway?'

'I'm going up to Auckland. To Alan's place.'

'When?'

'Tomorrow morning. It's all right, May, I'm not going to live with him. I'll shift out when he comes. And then we'll see.' She made a grin that had a sour edge. 'I've gone from Mister Quick to Mister Slow.'

'Don't put too much pressure on him, Freda.'

'Thanks, but I don't need advice.'

She was confused, and would joke and tough her way through. The danger lay in her impatience and in what she called her common sense. Hey, it would tell her, we like each other, okay? So why are we waiting? May wished that she could oversee this early part of their coming together, and rescue her, perhaps him, when things went wrong.

'Don't interfere, May.'

'I'm not.'

'And don't worry. I won't hurt him. Now let's stop talking, eh? Have you got a bed? I could do with a kip. I didn't get much sleep last night.'

May showed her to the room Alan had slept in, then relieved Evan, who worked in the pond clearing weed for the rest of the day. She woke Freda with a cup of tea; telephoned the orchard; put Freda on to Alan and went away as they talked. Just asking about David, whether he had gone, had given her a feeling of dread that made her slightly nauseous. She drank some water. Freda was in love, or putting herself in position to be in love; but David – David was obsessed. She wanted to get on the phone again and tell Alan to get out of there.

'We're having dinner,' Freda said.

'Where?'

'Pete's Place. I love dinners with a new man.'

'I hope he's going to be more than – whatever number you're up to.'

Freda laughed. 'May, don't worry. I really like him. I told you, it feels right.'

'You mean, inevitable?'

'Yes, inevitable.'

'Oh, good. That sets my mind at rest.' She too would joke her way through; and try to push David to one side.

She saw Freda off at half past five; put the *Closed* sign on the gate; called Evan in. He showered the smell of weed off and sat in the kitchen drinking beer while she cooked.

'So,' he said, 'tell me all the girl talk.'

'She's in love.'

'Who with?'

'Alan.'

'That's quick. Three days. That must be a record.'

'It's four days. He likes her too. I could see it when he came over.'

'That's one day. They're both quick. Has she got him going on the old in and out thing?'

'You're wrong about her, Evan, she's not that crude. Anyway, he's a moral man' – putting a cynical twist on the word to soften her rebuke.

'Freda must be doing that hard.'

'I think she's quite intrigued by the idea of waiting. I wouldn't be surprised if they end up in church. That's where he'll take her.'

'But is it legal? I'm not sure you can marry your brother's wife. Hey, May, what's David going to do? Have you thought about that?'

'Yes, I have.'

It kept her awake that night long after Evan was asleep. She could not think of any way for Alan and Freda to be safe. When she slept, her dreams were full of shuffling undefined things leached of colour. She ran from them on dead legs but found them at her back, touching her with parts she could not see. She woke and lay not daring to move, even though Evan was beside her. She wanted to silence his fluttery snores so that she might know that nothing else was in the room. Then her fear emptied out, a rush of dead water, and she drew a free breath and rolled to face Evan and take his warmth.

Glass broke. It was like a knife, a silver blade. Sheets fell, clanking, shivering. A dog barked close by in the yard.

'Evan, Evan, someone's in the showroom.' But he had come awake with the breaking glass; was running, trousers zipped; was out the door before she could move from the bed. She pulled on her dressing gown and slid her feet in sandals and ran outside. A black dog sprang at her and jagged its teeth in her dressing gown. Evan and Junior Mott wrestled in the showroom. She ran, dragging the dog. She shrugged free of the gown and ran naked to the edge of the broken glass. Her sandals slid on it. She leaned through the window as Junior Mott broke away from Evan. His eyes and teeth made a jagged flash in the dark. He squatted and came up with his axe and swept it through the standing vases. Evan sprang, collided; knocked him, arms like spokes, at the window. The axe fell in the broken pottery. Junior screamed with joy. He stepped out the window like a long-legged bird and ran away. May had jumped aside, and she crouched as Evan threw the jagged base of a vase at Junior. It struck him on the back and propelled him forward. The dog ran after him, with May's dressing gown snagged on its teeth. She heard them crashing in the bush path, Junior still making his weka call.

She ran to the house and fetched the key, pulled on her parka from the rack behind the door. When she entered the showroom she found Evan sitting in a corner. She turned on the light and saw his bleeding mouth and bleeding feet.

'Evan, Evan.' She tried to make him stand up and come with her to the house.

'Don't touch me.'

'Evan, you're hurt, your feet are cut.'

'Look at what he's done. The cunt. The cunt.'

She did not want to look. She only wanted to look at Evan. She tried to lift one of his feet but he pushed her with it, leaving a blood smear on her thigh.

'Evan? Love?'

'Call the police. I'm locking that bastard up.'

She ran back to the house and rang the Takaka constable and told him to bring a doctor too if he could. She half filled a bucket with warm water, found rags and bandages and antiseptic. Evan, still sitting in the corner, let her wash the blood from his feet. She had thought his soles would be shredded but a puncture wound in one heel was the most serious. Somehow he had stepped clear of the great knives of glass leaning in the window.

'You won't need any stitches,' she said.

He had his eyes closed. His tongue came out and licked blood from his mouth.

'Evan, talk to me.'

'I'll kill that bastard.'

'No. Leave him to the police. There's not much damage, Evan. Just a few plates and vases. We can make some more.'

He opened his eyes and groaned and closed them again.

'The insurance will pay,' she said. 'It'll pay for the window. Evan, let me put a bandage on.'

She smeared antiseptic cream on his cuts and was pleased to see him wince – he was coming back.

'I thought the dog was going to bite me,' she said. She fixed a plaster on the puncture wound. 'The doctor will have to see it. There might be a bit of glass in there.'

Evan bowed his head and sobbed. She wiped away his tears. He said, 'This is all I've got, May. I've got nothing if I haven't got this.'

'Don't cry. Come inside now, love. I'll help you walk.'

She wrapped him in a blanket, gave him a glass of whisky, then dressed herself and sat on the sofa with him, waiting for the constable. When he came they told him what had happened and where to find Junior Mott.

'You might need a doctor for him. I think he's hurt worse than me,' Evan said.

The constable looked at the showroom. He put Junior's axe in the boot of his car. They watched from the living room window as he drove into the settlement. His lights picked out the face of Junior's house.

'Let's go to bed, Evan. We don't need to watch.'

'I want to see.'

A light went on in Junior's house and then in other houses one by one. The constable opened the door and the dog rushed out. He calmed it and stroked it before going inside. 'Be careful,' May said softly, but he reappeared soon, propping Junior up.

'I got him,' Evan whispered. She could not tell whether he was pleased or upset.

'Let's go to bed.'

A neighbour – was it Christine? – got in the back of the car with Junior. It drove away and the lights went out. She poured Evan more whisky to help him sleep, and lay awake herself into the dawn, thinking about what he had told her. She could love him anywhere, in any conditions, but he could only love her here. It did not surprise her; it seemed natural. She felt her world shrink.

Evan slept. She watched his face: not ugly in sleep but almost beautiful. There was dry blood in his beard. 'I love you,' she whispered. 'We can still be all right.'

She got out of bed and made herself a cup of tea and drank it at the window, watching the sky lighten. She did not want to see the showroom yet. They would keep the closed sign on the gate today, keep customers out, and clean away Junior's mess in their own time. She went out the side door, walked down the bush track and found her dressing gown near the bottom. It had tears in the hem and it needed a wash – but perhaps the rubbish tin was the best place for it. She climbed back to the house, and at the door heard the telephone ringing. She hurried to it, not wanting Evan to wake.

'Mum, is that you?'

'Heather. What is it? Don't tell me it's Dad.'

'No, he's all right. It's something else.'

'Yes?'

'Something bad happened here last night.'

I don't want it, May thought. I've got enough to think about. 'Tell me,' she said.

DAVID

HE WAS AT Uneeda Hire when it opened and he rented a pick-axe and a spade.

'Don't get much call for a pick-axe,' the man said.

'I'm cutting back a bank,' David replied, and seemed with the lie to have damaged the shape of what he was about to do. Don't talk to anyone, he told himself. He would get through the day clean, not let anything break in from the world outside.

He drove south to Wakefield and along a dirt road into the hills. Going from farms into forest was like going from day into night. He enjoyed the darkening. Halfway through he turned into a forestry road; then a firebreak; then into trees, where fallen branches crackled like bones under the wheels. When he stopped he felt he had come to the place allotted to him. It was an exclusion zone. No one could get in except him and Freda and the soldier.

He chose a place midway between two trees, scraped the pine needles clear, and marked out the graves with the edge of his spade. The earth turned to clay almost at once and he attacked it with the pick. In one grave he struck a root and had to hack through it where it entered and left. It was moist and pink and as whippy as a penis. He grinned as he tossed it away. This one would be the soldier's grave.

He left them shallow. Going further down would satisfy him but they did not deserve deep graves. He would flatten the soil on top of them, spread pine needles over, drag a few branches into a heap, and they wouldn't be found until the trees were felled, which from the look of them was ten years away. And maybe never. Never would be good, lying here and only him knowing where they were.

He backed out to the firebreak, leaving the yellow graves scooped in the ground. The soldier's was longer than Freda's, but even so he might have to put him on his side and bend his knees. The soldier would be first. He wanted Freda to see him dead and know what was going to happen to her. He cut a blaze on a trunk to mark his place. Then he drove to Wakefield, where he washed his hands and face at the service station and changed his sweaty T-shirt for the spare one on the seat. He took the inland road to the orchard.

Sunday would have been better, when there were no pickers in the trees, but with luck they would not be close to the house. The hardest part was now, getting the soldier out for the ten minutes he needed. Friendly, he thought, that was the way. Even if Freda was there he would be friendly. Tell them to go for a drive. Drive up the forest, why don't you, good views there. It made him laugh.

He stopped in Ruby Bay and bought some grapes. The cottage door was closed when he drove past and it struck him that Freda might be hiding inside. It amused him – he hoped she was and had not cleared out for the day. Or she might be in the trees down the back of the orchard, lying on a blanket reading one of her dumb books, and maybe the soldier would be with her. That did not amuse him. He felt his throat thicken. What they didn't know was that last night had been their last fuck.

The fat girl, Heather, ran after him to the house. He waited for her by the wagon and grinned at the way her breasts jogged. She saw it but came on sharp: 'If you want to see Robert you should telephone first.'

'It'll take more than you to stop me seeing my old man,' David said.

The soldier appeared, looking down from the patio. He looks like he wants to be saluted, David thought, but did not let that trouble him. What he knew about this joker was that he was dead. He felt lazy and contented and felt that he could auto-pilot through this part of things.

Fat Heather went into the house. David got the grapes from

the car and walked up the steps. He liked coming level with the soldier and felt that he could keep on rising and look down on him and see him small. As they talked he almost yawned. Heather came out of the house. He ignored her hostility and gave her the grapes.

'He's had a pill,' she said, 'so you better be quick. He's getting dopey.'

David winked at Alan. 'He always was dopey. She wouldn't know.'

He walked through the sitting room, pushed back the sun-room door and saw his father lying in a bed. His eyes were closed and his face only half the size it had been. The old bastard really is dying, David thought. The pity of it was that he hadn't got it over with before fat Heather had arrived. He leaned over him and cupped the palm of his hand half an inch away from his mouth to see if he was breathing. I don't want you dead right now, old man. He sat in the chair.

'Hey,' he said.

His father opened his eyes.

'It's me. David.'

'What do you want?' Slurred speech: David had to lean close to hear what came next. 'You've run out of money, I suppose.'

'Don't you worry about me. I'm doing all right.'

'Good.' A whisper.

'I didn't know you were sick. No one bothered to tell me.'

'Now you know.'

'Yeah. So what have you got? Does it hurt?'

'It's – cancer.' Then he went to sleep, the old bugger, just like that. A deep snore, unbelievable. David watched and grinned: I should have dug three. But went back, cancelled it; his father was another thing, he was not part of today. I'll sort him and the fat girl out later on, David thought. He tapped his finger on his father's jaw, then his nose, but the old man did not wake. David stood up and went out to the patio. The soldier was prowling round the wagon. He stood and watched him – red ears and freckled forehead and that girly slope in his shoulders. Easy, he thought.

'What are you sliming round for?'

'Nothing.'

'Why don't you piss off, then? I don't need a keeper.' Like some dopey private, not a colonel. 'Take a walk. Do some fucking manoeuvres, I don't care. Just don't push me.' The words came easily, dead right. Everything ran his way today. 'Brother,' he grinned, and went inside.

The old man was still sleeping. His mouth was white inside but darkened in the hole going down his throat. Drop something in, he'd choke to death. Some of his pills. David mimed dropping them the way kids played eyedrops with glass marbles. He went back to the lounge, saw Alan head into the trees and turn towards the back of the orchard. He moved quickly then, feeling his steps light and the floor elastic: looked in the bedrooms, saw where Freda and the soldier had slept. Single bed. They must have spent the night stacked up. He thought of the graves in the forest, close but never touching, and wondered how they would like that.

He closed the door, went down the hall past the wash-house and opened the door into the garage. The car was gone. He bared his teeth at the emptiness and drew cool air into his lungs. So. She'd cleared out for the day in the old man's car. Everything was the way he would have planned. He turned on the light. The sea-chest was still in the corner, where he'd hauled it for the old man back in '83, after the garage was tacked on to the house. It looked as if it hadn't been shifted since. Black tin with iron bands; a tongue and loop with a padlock like a woman's brooch. The key was on a nail, waiting for him. He opened the lock, then had to pull the chest out from the wall to give the lid room to go up.

The gun was lying crosswise on the patchwork quilt that had covered his bed all the time he was growing up. It surprised him. The old man had wrapped it in a blanket in '83 and stored it halfway down among double sheets he wasn't going to need any more. That meant someone had used it. The ammunition too – it had been in a box but now it was in a plastic coin envelope fastened with a bulldog clip. David was stopped short. Then he went on easily: the gun was offered to him and he did not have to dig. The patchwork quilt was right too, his finding and his recognition right. He lifted the rifle and felt its weight. He put it to his shoulder and sighted it at head height at the garage door. It was a part of him at once. It pointed out from him like a limb. Wood and steel. Straight and absolute. It confirmed him in everything he planned.

He worked the bolt and felt it slick and true. So, the old man had oiled it and cleaned it. Maybe he had been shooting rats or possums. Maybe fat Heather had – magpies or mice. David laughed. He felt the weight of the ammunition: opened the envelope, tipped half the cartridges in his palm. They looked okay. Looked almost new. He would not have to test-fire now. And there was plenty; there was too much. He wanted to see if he could do it with one shot each.

He spread the quilt on the garage floor and laid the rifle on it; knelt and admired. The black barrel, sharp foresight, worn wooden stock – it was beautiful. Older than him. Lovely trigger. His finger curled in recognition of the shape. He gave the stock a tap. 'Gidday,' he said. He folded the quilt across the rifle carefully, three times, then turned the ends in like Christmas paper and rolled again, feeling the package thicken up. He put the ammunition in his pocket. Closed the chest, locked it, hung the key on the wall. He remembered to push the chest back into place. One day, before they had been missing for too long, he would return the rifle and the quilt and the ammunition, and everything would be the way it was before.

He took the rifle through the house and laid it on the back seat of his wagon. A picker was singing in the trees, something about lonely roads. The tractor roared, hauling itself up a slope. He slammed the door, locking the gun inside, inside himself. Everything was slow. It was as if his heart was working at half speed, or was beating only when it had to. He felt like resting. A part of it was done.

He reached through the window and took his cigarettes. Sat on the steps to light up, but found the bag of grapes by the rail and ate one instead. Then he rose and stretched his arms and went into the house. His father was still sleeping, his upper lip flapping like a valve. David put his finger out and held it still, then let it start up again. Did that several times, then ambled to the living room and lit a cigarette. The soldier came in stoop-headed, and like that word of Freda's – looking fraught.

'Where'd you get to, bro? I been missing you,' David said. Fucking useless, he thought. God help us if the Chinese come down. He saw him lying in his grave with his knees drawn up. One shot under the back of his skull. The ammunition pressed on the inside of his thigh, where Freda liked to slide her fingers as he drove. His cock made a quarter turn at the memory, and he shook himself and made it stop; talked with the soldier, whatever words came into his head. He got up and walked out and sat in the wagon. Grinned at Alan when he followed.

'You look worried, colonel. You got something you want to say?'

'Was that you smoking up there in the pines?'

David stubbed his cigarette out and flicked the butt away. His mouth opened, flapping like old Tugboat Charlie's in there. 'Not me, mate. You got the wrong man. Enjoy the grapes.'

He drove into Nelson and pulled up at the flat, finishing the first loop of his day. He peeled off his T-shirt and had a shower, put on clean clothes for the afternoon. Light trousers, a sports shirt, proper shoes. He would get back in the others – working clothes – when it was time.

At half past one he went out for a pub lunch and a beer. He left the rifle rolled up in the quilt in his car and the ammunition in the pocket of his jeans. He did not want to handle them again until he used them. Back from the pub, he turned on the TV and watched the first Super Ten match of the season, but grew angry at the kicking for position and the mauls that never went anywhere. There should have been running in the backs and driving play. It made him feel blunted, and suddenly he was tired. He turned the game off and lay on his bed and went to sleep; and woke as if the day had started again and everything was laid out for him to do.

He changed into his jeans and T-shirt and sneakers; used the toilet, washed his hands and brushed his teeth. He wet his hair with water and combed it left to right across his bald spot. In the car he put the ammunition in the glove box, keeping things neat, keeping clean. He put his reefer jacket on the seat. Fitted his baseball cap on his head. Then he drove out to Tahuna and bought himself a Coke and a box of fried chicken – from the Colonel: he laughed. Then stopped laughing. From now on he was serious.

He did not want food smells in the car so he ate sitting on a bench, looking across the park at the tennis courts, where girls ran and hit, ran and hit. He heard the distant pock of balls, and cries of children in the playground by the beach. He would have to cross a barrier to go where they were, where people were, and they to reach the place where he was. He could see a shimmering between, holding him single and pointed on his way.

He put the drink can and the chicken box in a rubbish tin. As he drove westwards he saw a sunset starting, pink and green, not messed with clouds. There was no danger of rain but he hoped that it would rain tomorrow and settle Freda and the soldier heavy in their graves.

The space where he had parked the night before was filled by a caravan. He did not like that. It made a little misstep in his progress. He fitted the Silverado under trees, then climbed on yesterday's path and reached the road. A piece of grit thrown by a car wheel stung his mouth. He tasted blood. That's okay, he thought, I'm different. He crossed the road and climbed in the crotches of the trees. Without the binoculars it was easy. He reached the slip and crossed it and crawled beneath the scrub. The darkness of the pine grove came down on his face. He passed through, conscious of Freda and the soldier on the other side. He could taste them, lumpy in his mouth. His anger became jagged and unsteady. Yet his base of calmness remained. He knew how to do it, where to go.

The pickers and the packers were gone. A truck loaded with cartons of apples went out past the cottage. Fat Heather clanged and racketed. She locked the shed and went to the house and straight into the sunroom, where she stooped over the bed. Kissing the old man? He could not see.

A little mound of cigarette butts shone at his feet. He knelt and covered them with pine needles, tramped them flat – taking control of the soldier, changing a part of his memory. He waited for him and Freda to appear. The cottage had a hollow look, a tinny emptiness. They were not in there. He sat down and watched the house.

They did not come. He felt a thickness growing in his chest; felt something in his mind wrench and hurt. He got up and walked to the house, approaching from the back where it was blind. He went silently along the wall and looked through the high window in the back of the garage. Waited while his eyes adjusted to the dark.

The car wasn't there. She was still gone.

He crept along the side of the garage and looked in the yard. Empty too; no Camry. He felt a cry rising in his throat, breaking past the rigid thickness there. But kept it down. Wait on. Wait on. They had to come back. She had to bring the old man's Rover back. They wouldn't have taken off for long in different cars.

He retreated to the apple trees and climbed to the pine grove, where he tried to pull things back in place. It had not occurred to him that they would not eat in the cottage – they had done it once, it was established. That was when he would go down the hill for his car. He would leave it in the trees beside the gate and wait for them with the rifle when they shifted to the house. March them to the wagon with the gun in Freda's back. Make the soldier drive to the forest.

It had been like something already done. Now the pieces lay in a heap and he could not fit them into place.

Get them when they drove up? What if they did not arrive together? He needed them side by side so he could hold the soldier still by keeping the gun on Freda. But if it happened in the yard the fat girl in the house would hear. Maybe he should take the fat girl too. But no, no, she was not in this.

He ground out a cigarette he did not remember lighting and raised his face to the sky. One thing was clear: he would do it. It would kill him to stop now. He felt the lumpy thing in his chest twist and almost fracture at the thought.

Shoot them all! Shoot everyone! It might have to be, have to be that. It would please him to shoot his father. But this was not for pleasure. This was to make things straight. So it had to be just the two. Keep it clean.

Gradually his easiness returned. When the time came he would know what to do. It would happen as simply as it had in the house when he found the gun; when just thinking seemed to make it follow. One by one, together, here or there, Freda and the soldier were delivered to him.

He watched the sunset fade. Darkness came down the curve of the sky. Fat Heather fed the old man. She half closed the curtains in the sunroom and turned out the light, then sat in the lounge watching TV. It was like watching TV himself – the slow part before the good part came.

The Rover cruised along the drive just before ten o'clock. It stopped in the yard and he heard Freda open the garage door. The soldier's car appeared. He had stopped to close the gate. Freda climbed to the patio as though swimming up from the trees. He saw an earring flash, saw her teeth gleam. Then everything dimmed as the Camry's lights went out. The soldier climbed the steps and stood facing her. She put her hand on his chest and seemed to push him away. What were they saying? I should be down there, David thought.

They went into the house but left the doors wide. Fat Heather zapped the TV and talked with them, then the soldier went out of sight. A moment later he stepped on to the patio. Freda followed. What was this? She kissed him, rising on her toes. For a moment David thought they would go down the steps together and sleep in the cottage to be out of fat Heather's way – and that would make it easy, he could get them with no trouble. But the soldier went alone and Freda waited in the door and waved. It blunted David again; another misstep. Then he adjusted. So they were having a night off. He would get Freda from the house, get her first, and use her to pull the soldier out of the cottage. It was easy, just as easy. A picture of it happening formed in his mind.

Freda walked through the lounge and vanished. Heather watched more television. She switched the set off and locked the doors, pulled the curtains tight and was gone too. David waited. If I was that dumb soldier, he thought, I'd come up here looking with a torch. He imagined it and was ready for it – sinking back in the trees while the soldier prowled. I could garotte him, he thought, and felt a wire in his hands, pulled tight. But the cottage was dark. And the house was dark. He stood up. Then he heard a cry or cough and thought it was a possum. It came again and he pinpointed it in the house. He went down from the pines and approached through the apple trees. The lounge light went on, shining pink through curtains, then the night-light in the sunroom. Close up now, he saw fat Heather at his father's bed. The noise must have been the old man calling. He could not see what was going on, just her back, but she was doing something to him – and he had it: helping him pee. David almost laughed. What a fucking comedy. Heather went away with the bottle held in a towel, and the toilet flushed at the bedroom end of the house. She turned the lounge light off as she came back, and closed the sunroom door – and what was happening now? She took off her dressing gown, and this time a grunt got out of him and only wind rising in the trees made it safe. She climbed into bed with his father. Her naked arm came up and turned out the light.

Jesus, David thought, what's going on? He was moved aside from his course and tried to move back – but she was all right, not fat at all but kind of thick, and nipples like jaffas and tits like a porno star. She could be useful in bed – and the old man was getting it. Ninety-one and he was getting it. He wondered if Heather had found a way of killing him.

Later, he thought, I'll sort it out later.

He retreated through the trees, made a wide circle of the house, saw Freda's window dark, and saw it would be easier getting her out now, with Heather at the other end of the house. He passed the cottage, padding in the grass, opened the gate and left it ready, and walked down the road, keeping near the bank so he could step into the scrub if traffic came.

A few lights were on in the camp. A quiet party was going by a fire on the beach. He drove out and turned up the hill; eased in at the orchard gate and backed between two trees. The wagon was almost silent, it whispered in the grass.

He reached back for the rifle and unwrapped it on his knee.

Took the ammunition from the glovebox, laid a round in the breech and pushed the bolt home. The old .22 was ready. Single shot, but he could reload in the time it took to move half a dozen steps. He threw the quilt into the back and climbed out; put his reefer jacket on; got the torch from the glovebox; left the car door open to avoid making noise. He slid the ammunition into his pocket and walked two bends on the drive until the cottage came into sight. Then he angled off into the trees. Freda first. March her to the cottage. Use her to get the soldier out.

He circled to the side of the house where the bedrooms were, stopping several times as apples broke under his feet. He smelt the sour-sweet smell he had grown up with. The house was still. Amazing how still a house could be, and how all together it was, when inside the rooms broke it down into bits. He tried to see the rooms – and saw them. Saw this side of the house cut off from the other. Freda sleeping.

His torch picked out the back steps. The green-painted door. The wash-house window open two notches, as he had seen it in the morning when he went by to the garage. He put the torch in his pocket. Lifted the catch and let it down; opened the window wide; shifted a cake of dried-out soap from the sill. He leaned in and used the torch again. The key was there, in the lock, where it had to be. He changed the torch to his other hand and turned the key at full stretch, fingers straining. It slipped a half turn with no noise – a click at the end. Good on you, fat girl, he thought. She kept things oiled.

He left the door open, setting it against the wall to keep it from slamming in the wind, which was stronger now. He relatched the window. The hall was dark. He used the torch again, left-handed, keeping the rifle in the crook of his arm. Passed an open door, flashed in the torch and saw an empty bed that must be Heather's. He arrived at Freda's door. It was like the passage into a cave. He opened it and drew his breath, smelling her. He stepped in and shut the door behind him. Heard her sit up in the bed. She spoke.

'Alan? I heard you. Are you sure?'

He grinned. He liked it. He loved it. 'It isn't Alan, Freddie. It's your husband here.'

He heard her squeak, and shone the torch on her, saw her hand go up to shield her eyes.

'David?'

'Yeah, it's me. I dropped in to have a talk with you.' Then he wanted to change his way again and keep talk out – just move her and make the parts happen as he had seen. 'Don't yell out,' he said, and moved the torch from her, ran the beam up and down his rifle. 'As sure as Christ I'll shoot you if you make any noise. Get out of bed.'

'David –'

'You and me are going outside. Get up. Move.'

Open-mouthed, gasping, she put her feet on the floor. He almost stepped up and clubbed her then – loathed her white skin, her nakedness.

'Put your dressing gown on.'

Standing, she obeyed.

'And your sandals.'

She slid them on without sitting down. She held herself upright with a hand on the wall. He saw her earrings on the bedside table and scooped them up and put them in his pocket. He opened the door and pushed her with the muzzle of the gun into the hall. Saw her decide to bolt and swept the arm with the torch hard around her waist. 'Don't, Freda. This is a gun. You run and you're dead.'

'Where . . .' she said, 'where . . .'

'Outside.' He wiped the arm that had touched her on his jacket. A smell of sex was on her as though she had been doing it to herself. He pushed her ahead of him through the wash-house and out the door. The wind hit his face and freshened him. He prodded her with the rifle into the trees.

'David,' she said.

'Shut up.'

'You can't do this. This isn't the way.'

She stepped fast ahead and turned to face him. He almost shot her then. The trigger moved. 'Silly bitch,' he said.

'David –'

'We're going where we can have a talk.' He said it without thinking. It was in the plan. Keep her from freaking out, keep the bitch hoping. She must have let some tears go with fright in the house because they had made tracks on her face. But now he saw her nerve coming back and saw that she would run at him and grab for the gun. He stepped at her, and jabbed the muzzle hard between her breasts. She gave a glassy cry and fell back; was held in the branches of a tree.

'I'll shoot you. By Christ I will.'

'David. Please. Let me go. I haven't done anything.' She moved at him again.

'Stay still.' He saw he had to change things. Both of them together would be too much. A new set of pictures slid into place: Freda in the car, in the forest, where he put the gun under the back of her skull and pulled the trigger. Then back for the soldier. The soldier looking at her in her grave. It was good. It was the way.

'We're going somewhere to have a talk,' he said.

'Put the gun away, David.' Her voice had a wobble. Her eyes were leaking again and her nose had started to run. A dark patch of blood showed where the muzzle had skinned her chest.

'Turn around. Go that way. I won't hurt you. You needn't be scared.'

He walked her through the trees to the Silverado and made her climb in on the passenger's side and scramble across to the driver's seat.

'Stop there. You go out that door and you're dead.' He liked every word he spoke. They came as if he had rehearsed them. He handed her the keys. 'You always wanted to drive. You can drive now.'

'Where are . . . where . . .'

'Just down the road a bit. Don't be scared, Freda. It's all right.'

'You're going to shoot me.'

'No I'm not. We're going to talk, that's all. We've got some things to sort out. Start the car.'

'I can't . . . can't reach.'

'Come on, Freda, adjust the seat.'

She reached down, found the knob, managed to slide

forward. She sat under the wheel like a child. He gave her a nudge with the gun.

'Now the keys. Don't go looking at the cottage. That feller's not going to help.'

She fumbled the key in and started the engine.

'Go out on the road. And keep it quiet. Okay. Close the door. Soft, don't slam it. Keep your hand away from the horn.'

He pulled his own door shut.

'Now the lights.'

They drove down the road and through Tasman.

'Faster,' he said. 'We're not going to a funeral.'

'Where are you taking me?'

'A place I've got, where we can talk. And shut up, Freda, don't talk now, I don't want to hear you.'

They drove down the Moutere. Once he said, 'Dip your lights.' That was all. He watched her. His back was to the door and the muzzle of the gun touched her hip. She took one hand off the wheel and wiped her arm across her face. It came away smeared with snot and tears. He felt a deep revulsion as it gleamed, and he reached out and jerked the arm of her dressing gown to cover it. He had loved her and she was nothing.

In the dirt road to the forest she started to moan.

'Shut up,' he said. The closer they got, the calmer he became. 'I'm not going to hurt you. ' One shot was all. 'Slow down. Turn here.'

She stopped the car with its nose in the forestry road. 'I'm not. I'm not going in there.'

'Yes you are.'

'David –'

'All we're going to do is talk. I don't want to hurt you, Freda.'

'No –'

'Just drive. Drive.'

She went in as far as the firebreak.

'In there.'

'No, David.'

He reached across and turned the engine off. 'Get out, then.'

'I'm staying here. I'm not getting out.'

He reached again and opened her door. 'Out,' he said.

'We can talk here.'

'Silly bitch.' He broke her fingers from the wheel and put his foot on her and heaved her out; walked round the bonnet of the wagon; watched her stumble to her feet. He pulled her into the car lights where he could see her better.

'Here we are, Freda.' He felt in his pocket and took the earrings out. 'Put these on.'

'What . . . What for?'

'Just do it, Freda,'

Fumbling, she put them on and dropped her hands to her sides.

'That's good, now you look nice.'

'Don't kill me, David.'

He smiled. 'You and the soldier, eh. My brother.'

'What? That's . . .'

'No one runs away from me, Freda. And does that.'

'Nothing . . . it . . . nothing. I swear, David.'

'Come on. We're going up here.'

'No, I'm not going. I'm going home.'

He pulled her along a dozen steps, then dropped her and she fell to the ground.

'Get up, Freda. You can walk.'

'No,' she moaned.

'I want you to see the graves. One for you and one for him. I'm going back for him after you.'

She spoke no more. She got to her feet and walked back unsteadily into the car lights. He shot her when she was halfway there, aiming just below the bottom reach of her hair; and lost her for a moment as she fell; then saw her on her hands and knees in the light. Her arms collapsed. She rolled on her side. He ejected the spent shell, reloaded, and walked to her. She was making little grunts and staring on ground level straight ahead. Her fingers opened and closed.

He shifted her hair with the muzzle of the gun and shot her again, in the head. Her legs jerked out, her body spasmed. Then she lay still. The ease of killing her amazed him. He would have liked more to do.

His legs grew weak then and he sat down. He breathed

deeply, then heard someone laughing and was shocked. It was him. Next one, he thought, can't stop yet. He got up from the ground and put the rifle in the car. Began to see pictures again. No need for the spade, he would cover her later. And the soldier had to see. He would not shoot the soldier until he had shown him Freda in her grave.

He picked up one of her arms and dragged her along the firebreak. Using his torch he found the blaze on the tree. He dragged her over pine needles and broken branches to the graves. Stepped down into hers and walked along it and felt her flop in as he stepped out. He knelt and turned her on her back, then smoothed her dressing gown on her thighs. He pushed her hair back to show the earrings. When he shone the torch he was pleased with her. Her eyes were open, she still looked afraid.

'You deserved it, Freddie. Doing that to me.'

He turned and left her. Driving back to the orchard, seeing the next part open up, he tried to stop his killing of her from breaking in, but could not. He hummed with pleasure, felt it vibrate in him. He had done it easily, like a killer, like a man. Now it was the soldier's turn. Pictures of his death took turns with Freda's death.

He reached the coast road and turned towards Ruby Bay. Remembered to look at his watch. It was twelve minutes to one. He kept his lights dipped to show a short length of road and stay in a capsule, insulated, warm, and feel it move like coming out of space towards the soldier at the end of it. He saw himself at the cottage door and the soldier waking from his bunk; then the ride to the forest, and looking down at Freda in her grave. He heard the shot, smelled powder, and saw the soldier shrink in size. A second shot for him too: make it even. He and Freda lay like dolls in the hollowed ground. He covered them with clay, with earth, with needles, with branches, and left them there and went home.

David drove down the long hill towards Mapua and turned towards Ruby Bay. The store was dark. The party had finished on the beach. In the camp the tents and caravans and camper vans showed here and there a luminous panel, a yellow door.

He passed the entrance with a kind of affection. The place was inside the boundaries of his world, it had served him well. He was tempted to blow his horn as he went by.

He drove up the hill at an easy speed, no hurry, came round the corner, and saw at one side the sign reading *Ben Alder Orchard* – and ahead, on the open road, a cop car moving away from him, with its roof light flashing. He had started his turn into the drive and did not know whether to carry on or brake. He could not understand where the car had come from. It had not been ahead of him on the road. He stopped halfway through the gate. Then, over the rise, in the trees, he saw a glow of light where darkness should have been. The cops had been at the house. Their car made a U-turn and started back. He felt headlights burn his face.

Everything turned over. He was hanging head down in space. Then he righted himself and understood what he must do. Plunged the Silverado along the white dust drive. He went through the S-bend and saw the patio wall spring at him. All of them, he thought. All three. I'll do a clean sweep. He grabbed the rifle and jumped out of the wagon. Reloaded. The soldier appeared in the door. Light from the room reddened his ears.

David raised the rifle and aimed at his face, then lowered it to go underneath the patio rail. He shot the soldier and saw him step backwards into the room. He ran up the steps. The blue light of the cop car was speeding through the trees. He ejected the spent shell, put another cartridge in and closed the bolt. Went into the house. Find them quick.

The soldier was sitting on the floor with his back resting on the sofa. His hands lay palm up on the carpet, his head turned slowly, and his eyes were dark and enlarged. David saw where the bullet had struck him in the chest – a red splash, black in the centre. Bullseye, he thought. He raised the rifle to give him the finishing shot, but was aware of his father in the sunroom door. Tugboat first, he thought, and swung the rifle there.

Something struck him, hard and heavy. The gun went off. He slammed against the wall with the fat girl fastened on him. He tried to hit her with the barrel but she held on. He saw her face blazing. It flashed like strobe lights as they spun. Her hands dragged him to the floor and he was rolling with her and trying to pull free and club her with the stock but she was glued on him, he felt all the hard bones in her fat. Then other people had him, he felt their weight and the woodenness of their hands. His shoulders tore and made him scream as they forced his arms back. He lay still. It was over then.

Voices. The fat girl panting.

'Easy, lady. Stand over there. Look after him.'

He saw his father holding the door jamb. The fat girl came from one side and put her arms around him. David twisted. He saw the red wound, the upturned hands, the soldier's empty eyes looking through him. Nowhere eyes.

David laughed, with his chin resting on the carpet.

'Gotcha, bro. You're dead,' he said.

Epilogue

MAY AND ALAN AT WHARARIKI BEACH

In April the weather turned bad and it stayed that way, showery and windy and colder than was usual, until the end of the month. May called for Alan at the hospital and drove him over the hill to Golden Bay. They stopped at the orchard on the way and picked up a case of tree-ripened Granny Smiths. The nurse, a young woman from Southland (they could tell from what May called her Presbyterian r's), let them in singly to see Robert.

Heather came down from the shed as they were leaving. She was working alone there, sorting late apples for the local market.

'Did he recognise you?'

'He was sleeping,' Alan said.

'He opened his eyes but I don't think he saw me,' May said.

'They still want to come and get his statement. I'm not letting them past the door.'

'They don't need his statement,' May said. She kissed Heather, accepting with amusement her turned cheek, and got in the car. 'Are they letting you take enough money from the account?'

'I've got enough.'

They stopped in Riwaka to rest, and again in Takaka, and reached Woods Inlet early in the afternoon. May wanted Alan to go straight to bed but he sat for a while in the sitting room, looking across the inlet, where the tide was running out.

'A fine day at last,' May said.

'Have you bought a new dinghy?'

'Yes. I'll take you for a row tomorrow.'

The settlement shone like a toytown and the sea was silver-white, aluminium foil, with cloud shadows swallowing fishing boats. Alan felt like breathing deeply for the first time since he had been shot. Evan came in and shook his hand. Talking with this broad man, Alan felt his own lightness: all his bones porous, feather-light. If you dropped me in the sea I'd float like a bit of pumice, he thought. Evan would live there like a fish. Yet he felt natural, felt himself returning to life, and he drew air into his lungs, where at last it stayed without making him cough.

'May tells me Corporal Smith has gone.'

'Yes, with Sally. She said there was too much gossip here.'

'That's my fault, telling you who she was.'

'How old she was. That's what she was getting at. Don't worry about it.'

'We're taking an apprentice,' May said. 'We were getting rid of Sally anyway.' She remembered that Freda had once offered herself as an apprentice. There had been a bit of joke in most things Freda had proposed. 'Lie down now,' she said to Alan.

He took off his jacket and shoes and lay on the bed, and when he woke late in the afternoon took a moment to recognise May standing by the window.

'I'm like Dad,' he said.

'You look a bit like him. I suppose I must be like my mother.'

'You've got Dad's forehead. And his jaw.'

May crossed the room and sat on the bed. 'I looked in his box and found an envelope with her name written on it. It was empty.'

'He sent her twenty dollars. But she's not alive now,' Alan said.

'I know. I asked him. Why didn't you tell me?'

'I would have, but there was too much going on.'

'Yes. Well, I was never going to go hunting for her. He said there was another letter saying I'd gone bad.'

'Yes. I took it,' Alan said. 'I burned it, with Freda. In the restaurant.' He told her what the letter had said.

'The poor old lady,' May said. She smiled at Alan. 'Don't worry. My life has gone on way past that.'

She went back to the kitchen and her preparations for tea and saw Evan busy too, in the pottery. He would work until he was called. He's the one who gave me back my past, she thought. Not Alan really. And my mother could never have done it. He doesn't take the pain away but he makes it manageable. I'd have been like a huhu grub in a rotten log.

She looked at the showroom, the plates and the vases and the paintings on the walls. It was like a cave filled with treasure, and the new glass made a sheet of water closing the entrance. She could not forget Junior Mott, knobby as a starved man in his joints, dancing among the broken vases. Sometimes he seemed bad and sometimes sad, but he was never tragic or evil. She had got by Junior Mott all right; and Evan was finding his way past. They would not be shifted from this place. But she thought that she might go up one day and paint a magpie on the water tank.

The next morning she and Alan climbed the steps and sat in the sun with the tank at their backs. The pond was noisy with ducks that had taken refuge from the shooting season.

'They loved all the rain,' May said.

'I can see your dinghy shining.'

'Yes. I'm doing a tile painting of me crossing the inlet. Tile painting is my new thing.'

'Your beach one is still in the boot of my car. I showed Freda.'

'She told me.'

'She liked it.'

'So she should. Look, Alan. See the land agent's sign on the Otways' lawn. They're moving too. Remember George Otway? The man with the wife who beat him up? She's happy now. She's radiant.'

'Where are they going?'

'Khandallah. In Wellington. He told me she'd die here but he wouldn't die there.'

'Is he sure?'

'No, he's not. But he said she's his wife and he made a promise to look after her.' She believed some part of George

Otway would die, but wondered too if some part of him would come to life. He had seemed, last time they spoke, inexpressive, shrunken, but alive in some darkly contented way, as if he had contracted on to an unknown core. She wondered if he had found a way of loving. He would not express it so. And looking at Alan, she thought he had a way of loving too, strange to her, inexplicable.

She pointed out the spit, almost black in the washed air. 'Would you like to go there?'

'No. I'd like to go to Wharariki beach.'

'That's a bit of a walk. I'll have to get you fatter.'

She fed him and cared for him and drove him to Takaka for check-ups with the doctor. Several times they rowed on the inlet in her new dinghy. He took the oars in the still water and managed without straining the wound in his chest.

'Is Evan all right?' he said. 'He seems quieter.'

'He's ashamed of himself for calling the police when Junior Mott smashed our showroom up. I didn't tell you.' She described it. 'Evan had to call them. It was right at the time. Now, he's not sure. He wouldn't do it now.'

She saw Alan turn that over – 'right at the time' – and disagree. It was shifting, perhaps shifty, and he needed absolutes, while she would be unhappy without invention. Yet they could look at each other face to face. The dinghy was very good for that.

They stopped beside the jetty and he took a turn at the oars. He rowed with short strokes, keeping close to the shore, and brought them to the mudflats, where she tied the dinghy to its waratah. As they walked up to the house she asked him when he would be going back to Auckland.

'Next week sometime. I'll ring and make a booking.'

'And leave your car?'

'I'll have to come down for the hearing. I'll drive back after that.'

'What will you do in Auckland?'

'My old job for a while. Then' – he smiled at her – 'something you won't approve of. I'm going to see if I can train for the ministry.'

'Be a priest?'

'Yes.'

'But aren't you . . .'

'Too old? No. They like getting people like me.'

'So they should. I don't disapprove.'

'But you don't understand?'

'No. I'll try. I'll still let you in the house.'

'It's nice to be welcome,' he said.

They went to Wharariki beach the day before he left. He had almost got his strength back. They walked across a paddock, where sheep jumped and skittered as they came up silently, and across the long dunes by the creek.

'We've got it to ourselves,' May said. 'Do you need a rest?'

'A little while.'

They sat on the sand. It was half tide and the inner island joined the beach. The two outer ones were locked together and would not separate till they walked south. A few black-backed gulls dipped and rose in the wind and oystercatchers stood at intervals, territorial. Metre-high waves thumped the sand; hissed up, rustled back, sliding into the sea with an undercutting motion that May felt echoed in herself, a gain, a loss. She lay back on her elbows. 'You need to go down there to see the arches,' she said.

'I've got them in your painting.'

'A cheap copy. Did Freda really like it?'

He looked at her sideways and smiled, not with any freedom but admiring the way she went ahead, her artlessness.

'Yes.'

'Were you going to be . . . would it have gone anywhere?'

He thought about that, making a shake and then a nod of his head. He picked up sand and trickled it away.

'I think I might have wanted to marry her. Perhaps not.'

'That's probably the way she felt about you.'

He grinned. 'Is that a bit of feminism?'

'A bit. She'd had enough of marriage. Look what it did to her.'

'That was personal. David killed her.'

She agreed. Strongly agreed. They would not argue.

'I go over that night,' he said. 'I did the wrong things. I heard his car go, it woke me up, and I knew straight away what it was.'

'Yes?'

'Desk soldier, that's what I am.'

'More than that.'

'I should have followed instead of going up to the house and calling the police and all that. If I'd got out there on the road I might have caught them.'

A fantasy, she thought, but with some reality in it. He had been confused and slow. He might have followed, saved her; or died. David had turned fantasy into reality that night, so why not Alan? He would, she thought, have been ready to die.

'Come on, let's walk. I'll show you the arches.'

The oystercatchers flew away screeching, and circled back and landed on their spot, each one. Her last visit to Wharariki had been made with Freda – Freda with a swollen mouth and a broken tooth – and how could it have been as recent as February? 'Drop dead,' Freda had said to the birds; and of the seals basking on the rocks above the kelp: 'They're like slugs.' She had come to tell May that her marriage was 'a write-off', and May had brought her here to – how had she thought of it, wash her clean and start her on a new way perhaps? For a while it had not seemed to work. Freda saw a monkey profile in one cliff and Muldoon, full faced, in the next. And when an archway opened up and legs of stone stood slanting in the sea, it was, she said, like a tired old elephant leaning on a wall. May had not seen monkey or Muldoon but saw the worn-out elephant and did not like having it imposed on her. She was sorry she had brought Freda here. Then Freda had pointed at the islands: 'I'd like to swim out there.'

'A German tourist tried last year. They had to rescue him in a helicopter.'

'I'm going for a short one anyway.' And she had stripped her clothes off and run into the waves and splashed and dived, and had come out bent and gasping but with a grin on her damaged mouth. She ran up the sand with her arms crossed on her chest and her skin as white as china clay.

'That's got rid of him. Shit, here's people, where's my clothes?'

May had been wearing a cotton scarf that day. She took it off and gave it to Freda to dry her hair.

'He went berserk when they told him you weren't going to die,' she said to Alan.

'Yes, I know.'

'Will you ever try to see him?'

'I don't think there's anything I can do. All the same . . .'

'Yes?'

'I might.'

'He's like that because of Dad. Like you and me.'

He looked at her patiently, not smiling. 'Not entirely.' He made a grimace, still no smile. 'Dad's another matter. I can't talk to him either.'

'Not a very good start for a minister.'

'No,' Alan said.

'There's an arch. It doesn't look possible, does it?'

Broken water made white splashes at the entrance. On the other side the horizon seemed lifted and the sky was featureless.

'It looks as if it's leading somewhere. Will you do a tile painting of this?'

'I'll try.'

They reached the southern headland and turned back. She saw his freckled forehead reddened by the wind.

'You should have worn a hat.'

He said, 'He looked at me and told me I was dead. It was like a command.'

'Heather was marvellous,' she said.

'Yes. I had some sort of special sight. It wasn't just because I had a bullet in me. I saw something in him – a thing. It was wet and grey and out of shape. I don't know what the shape should be.'

I might understand that if I can paint it, May thought.

'That's why I'll see him again. One day,' Alan said.

'All right,' May said.

They walked up the beach. The arches closed. The oystercatchers flew off flat and low, and circled back and settled again. May and Alan climbed into the dunes and walked through the farm to their car and drove home.

The next day he flew to Auckland. She made sketches for a tile painting of the Archway Rocks.